JANGAM

RELIVING DEBENDRANATH ACHARYA

JANGAM
A forgotten exodus in which thousands died

Translated by Amit R Baishya

Vitasta

Published by
Renu Kaul Verma
Vitasta Publishing Pvt Ltd
4348/4C, Ansari Road, Daryaganj,
New Delhi - 110 002
info@vitastapublishing.com

ISBN: 978-93-86473-17-2

First Edition 2018
Third Reprint 2024

MRP ₹ 495

Typeset & Cover Design by Vitasta Publishing Pvt Ltd
Printed by Thomson Press India Ltd.

Preface

The tempest that was the Second World War cut right through the heart of Assam nearly four decades ago. But hardly any signs of this massive calamity that faced humankind has registered in our literature.

This is the story of a group of ordinary people.

A group of extremely ordinary people who were dislocated by the devastation caused by the great war—they are universal symbols for suffering humanity. This novel is the poignant tale of people who embarked on a great, unknown journey with the fervent desire for survival burning in their hearts, but whose goals were thwarted as they succumbed, with their wishes unfulfilled, to the cold embrace of death.

All the characters in this book, albeit unacknowledged by history, are imaginary. Any resemblance to persons dead or alive is entirely unintentional.

—The Author

This preface was written by Debendranath Acharya in the late 1970s—Editor.

Dedicated to the cherished memory of
Sailajananda Baruah

—The Author

In Memoriam

Jangam is the third novel authored by my husband Debendranath Acharya (1937-1981). Debendranath had planned to write this novel for a long time. While he was pursuing his M Sc in Engineering from Imperial College, London, he would visit the British Museum Library in his free time, read various books and articles on World War II, cull information from them, and note these facts and stories in his diary. He also procured a few books on Burmese history and studied those carefully. He was very dedicated to any task that he undertook.

Debendranath began writing *Jangam* when he joined the Assam Gas Company in Duliajan. Whenever he finished a major section or chapter, he would request me to read it aloud. If he wasn't satisfied with a segment, he would mark and rework it later.

Debendranath had no set time for his writing. He wrote whenever he had time. When he had to travel to Guwahati, Delhi or Kolkata to represent the Assam Gas Company, he arranged his notes and materials in his handbag beforehand so that he could write whenever he was free. At that time, he was also associated with the Duliajan branch of the Xahitya Xabha. He was busy performing numerous tasks for the Xabha, besides working assiduously for his company. He was also frequently being invited to deliver public lectures. People from the rural areas adjoining Duliajan often paid him a visit and sought his advice. Our four daughters, my mother-in-law also lived with us at that time. Members of our extended family came and stayed with us occasionally. I still find it surprising that he had the energy to complete *Jangam* despite his numerous activities and obligations. The fact that he was composing the deeply-affecting, tragic story of *Jangam*, while performing his numerous duties in the private and public realms, and its relevance was something I couldn't quite fathom at that time.

I believe that *Jangam* has a universal appeal. Since it was written in a local language, this fact limited its readership. This is what inspired us to go ahead with the translation of this work, and when Amit Rahul

Baishya approached us we were more than happy to let him proceed with the English translation.

I extend my heartfelt thanks and wish Amit a bright future ahead.

Mahashweta Acharya
April 2018

Translator's Note

Although massive tomes on numerous events occurring during World War II (1940s) abound, the 'forgotten long march' is one of the least documented events of this period.[1] During this march an estimated 450,000-500,000 Burmese Indians walked to British India fleeing from the Japanese advance and also from escalating ethnic violence in Burma. The forgotten long march was a culmination of a series of anti-Indian riots that had been raging since the 1930s.[2&2a]

---

1 Hugh Tinker, 'A Forgotten Long March: the Indian Exodus from Burma, 1942.' *Journal of Southeast Asian Studies*, Vol.6, No.1 (Mar. 1975).

2 For an account of these conflicts, see Martin Smith, *Burma: Insurgency and the Politics of Ethnicity* (London: Zed Books, 1991), 43-44.

Burma was finally incorporated into the British Indian state in 1885 after a prolonged spell of wars between the British and the Burmese. Although contact between the Burmese kingdoms and the Indian subcontinent existed during the precolonial period, a lot of Indians migrated to Burma during the colonial era. The Indian migrants, some of whom went voluntarily and others coercively taken as indentured labourers, were of mixed socio-economic status. While the *Chettiar* moneylenders from Tamil Nadu were despised by the Burmese for gaining control of 'over 3 million acres of paddy fields in the lowlands of Irrawaddy delta',[3] a lot of Indian settlers were poor farmers, labourers or petty traders. However, 'Indian migrants and settlers were the most visible faces of the colonial domination of Burma'.[4] While many Indians stayed behind in Burma after the Japanese attack, the spectacular fall of the British colonial state impelled others to flee towards India in panic. An estimated 10,000-50,000 people died during the journey.

2a The exodus during the world war was not the only instance when people of Indian origin were expelled from Burma. Large number of people of Indian origin were also driven out after Ne Win's coup in 1962. For an account of these later expulsions, see RK Ranjan Singh. 'Status of Burmese Refugees in Northeast India.' *Dimensions of Displaced People in Northeast India.* Ed. C Joshua Thomas. (New Delhi: Regency Publications, 2002), 170-78. There is a substantial Tamil community in the border town of Moreh in Manipur.

3 Anand Pandian, *Ayya's Accounts: a Ledger of Hope in Modern India* (Bloomington: Indiana University Press 2014), 182.

4 Ibid, 182.

After a few refugees managed to escape via air and sea, the rest took three successive overland routes: via the Arakan to Chittagong, via the Chindwin valley into Manipur, and through the hilly passes of Hukawng valley into Ledo (Lekhapani) in Assam (this third route is represented in Debendranath Acharya's *Jangam*). While the long march was a comparable humanitarian crisis like the migrations of 1947, very few works, literary or otherwise, have dealt with it. Amitav Ghosh's observation in a 2000 interview that there is a great silence about this catastrophe from the Indian side still holds largely true.[5] Consideration of Indian voices will help initiate the 'perspectival shift' where: '... no longer are we looking at devastated humanity through the horrified yet fascinated eyes of the imperial traveler, bureaucrat or novelist...we are now inside the minds and bodies of the dying millions who were the subjects of British empire's palliative attention.'[6] Instead of witnessing from a distance, the accent shifts to representations of survival in conditions of extreme duress.

Since the publication of Amitav Ghosh's *The Glass Palace* (2000), which treats the march in a brief segment,

5 http://www.outlookindia.com/article/coming-under-burmese-fire-was-surreal/209696.

6 Upamanyu P Chatterjee, *Natural Disasters and Victorian Empire: Famines, Fevers and the Literary Cultures of South Asia* (London: Palgrave Macmillan 2013), 199-200.

there has been a slow but steady trickle of memoirs in English about this harrowing trek.[7] To be sure, films like the Hindi *Shabnam* (1949), the Tamil *Parasakthi* (1952) and the Assamese *Dhumuha* (1957) allude to the exodus of Indians from Burma, although they don't represent the contingencies faced by the refugees during the journey directly. To my knowledge, the 1984 Sahitya Academy award winning Assamese novel *Jangam* (The Movement) by the Assamese writer Debendranath Acharya is the only sustained fictional treatment of the long march, although brief allusions to the march are made in the embedded narrative of the troubled British soldier Jim, in Siddhartha Deb's *An Outline of the Republic* (2006), and more recently, in Charmaine Craig's novel *Miss Burma* (2017).

A Note on the Translation: I used the version of the novel in the *Debendranath Acharya Rasana Xomogro* instead of the stand alone version published by the Axom Prokaxon

---

7 For memoirs, see Yvonne Ezdani (ed.), *Songs of the Survivors* (Panjim: Goa 1556, 2007) and Bilal Raschid, *The Invisible Patriot: Reminiscences of Burma's Freedom Movement*, (Bethseda: Createspace Independent Publishing, 2015). *Ayya's Accounts*, Pandian's ethnography cum memoir of his grandfather, MP Mariappan, also discusses the march. Ghosh collects memoirs by survivors on his blog. There are memoirs in other Indian languages—in Assamese, see Purnakanta Buragohain, *Patkair Xipare Na Basar (*Dhemaji: Purbanchal Tai Xahitya Xabha, 1993).

Parixod.[8] Acharya's style can range from the highly poetic (especially in the 'Background' section) to the rigorously observational—I attempted to capture these shifts in stylistic register as much as I could. Since this is an Assamese novel, I kept words like *pithaguri, japi* etc. untranslated. The use of such words would definitely be odd in an actual Burmese context, but I retained these words keeping the original version in mind.

Acknowledgements: Aruni Kashyap first told me about *Jangam* during a conversation in 2011—without our conversations, this translation could not have materialised. I thank Auritro Majumder, Tanmoy Sharma, Purbasha Mazumdar, Rini Barman, Ankur Tamuliphukan and Kenneth Hodges for their comments on the manuscript. I owe special thanks to Vasavi Acharya for our conversations on Debendranath Acharya and her efforts in securing the copyright for the novel. I also thank Preeti Gill for being so generous with her time, encouragement and assistance. Papri Sri Raman edited the manuscript meticulously—I am very grateful for that. Sumana Roy helped me during a critical moment, and I am indebted to her for that. Amritjit Singh informed me about the memoir by Bilal Raschid. I thank Dr Singh,

---

8 Debendranath Acharya, *Jangam* (Guwahati: Axom Prokaxon Parixad, 2006).

Nalini Iyer and Rahul Gairola for inviting me to contribute my essay to their edited collection and Amrita Ghosh for asking me to present my paper on the novel at the panel she organised at the SALA (South Asian Literature Association) Conference in January 2015—researching the essay/presentation on *Jangam* was the conduit for this translation. Andreea Marculescu and Anirban Baishya have always been excellent sounding boards for ideas and doubts. Finally, I thank my trusted 'research assistant'—my father, Dwipen Baishya—for hunting down sources, people and materials in Guwahati. This translation is dedicated to him and my mother, Anima Baishya.

Background

MANKU

The mighty Irrawaddy encircled this little hamlet near Mandalay with love. Nearby were Ava and Amarpur, the two abandoned capitals of Burma. They were tragic pages of a lost history—desolate palaces and heaps from the eroded pinnacles of pagodas that once kissed the sky, remains of stone-carvings kept safe by the all-embracing carpet of moss, the spirits of thousands of sacrificed men and women haunting each fallen petal of that decayed past. Sitting in that terrifying cremation ground, history wiped away its tears after getting lost in recollections of its past. Hundreds of neglected marble-heaps of statues of the *Tathagatha* in these broken, weeping pagodas meditate with eyes shut in fixed *padmasanas*, counting the eras swept away by the merciless currents of time.

The expansive ranges of the Arakan Yoma were located in the western banks of the Irrawaddy: tall, rocky, lofty. The tuneful music of the confluence of the Irrawaddy and the Chindwin resonated loudly. These rivers were blessed with small, fleeting pleasures when their heads collided with the feet of the heartless mountain ranges. These collisions created an intimate union of an ethereal, wonder-struck, still condition of being, and a swelling, speedy crescendo. To the north was Mandalay, the emerging capital of Burma. This beloved new bride of the royal family was well-decorated, ornamented and brimming with youthfulness—an empire of self-indulgence and the fulfilment of pleasures. The calm and peaceful gilded Arakan pagoda very near Mandalay, which was surrounded by innumerable turrets and sky-kissing crests, smilingly disregarded the luster and pomp of royalty. Inside, the straining sinews of the tonsured, saffron-clad priests were brimming with emotion, along with the resonance of *Om Mani Padme Hum* produced by monks and devotees reverentially circumambulating around a massive meditating statue of the immortal Buddha. The serene, transcendental visage of the Buddha was calmly meditative and seemed void of attachments in the midst of the golden luster of his commemoration. It seemed as if the shame-inducing, destitute visage of the poorly-clad Buddha was ridiculing the abundance of resources and luxuries in that place with a smile. The echo of *Om Mani Padme Hum* in the intervals between the chants made the disgust and contempt experienced about these decadent eras bubble up to the surface, and strongly emphasised the meaninglessness of glamour and glitter, useless pleasures and drunken revelry.

The Irrawaddy! A tranquil, extensive body of water flowing slowly and seriously. Tumultuous gurgles in its bosom, tremendous anger in the flow of its subterranean currents, treacherous, violent eddies in each and every part. On both banks, twisted lines of mountains were visible against the backdrop of the limitless sky. The sharp spires of the pagodas glittered on the hilltops, the red soil of the *jhum* fields in the bosom of the hills shone.[1] The wedges on their boundaries seemed like staircases ascending to the skies. The sun set in the Arakan Yoma range lying towards the west. The silver currents of the Irrawaddy resembled a stream of blood when it was touched by the afternoon sun. During that period of the day, the glittering golden pagodas, glowing in the bosom of green towards the east, disappeared from view. An infinite number of gold-like flames encircled the pagodas. In such delirious moments, the solitary, tallest peak of the Arakan Yoma resembled a meditative stone-idol enraptured by the seductive play that

---

1 Both *jhum* and *tou-iya* are forms of swidden or shifting cultivation.

nature conducted before it. Mundane desires disappeared in those sky-kissing heights lying in between that limitless ocean of beauty. The entire being of the witness rose in revolt against everyday surroundings when faced with this immense natural backdrop. An uncontrollable desire arose to acknowledge one's insignificance, and to feel blessed by merging with the uncountable, miniscule drops circling incessantly in the whirlpools. A desire arose to swell with pride from the great fortune of mingling with the eternally beautiful, great soul of nature, and smashing the arrogance of science and civilisation into smithereens. The lustre of even a minute speck of dust in this awe-inspiring carnival of beauty was inappropriate. Perfection in its very being! The great joy stemming from such untouched independence—incomparable!

Ava and Amarpur: two forgotten chapters in Burmese history, two melancholic sighs mixed with the currents of flowing time. In a bygone era now erased from memory, an obscure oracle foretold the future to the Burmese monarch thus: 'According to divine commandments revealed in dreams, the bountiful blessings of incorporeal spirits have rained in and around the environs of Ava. For the welfare of the kingdom and the royal family, it would be advisable to establish the capital in this place where spirits roam around innumerable trees and uncountable formations of stone.' Such pronouncements shaped the royal decree. Groups of Burmese craftsmen were immediately summoned. The lords sacrificed numerous men and women and established the foundations of the capital. The capital was ornamented with a colourful, palatial pagoda and royal chambers that were constructed with great speed. Entrusting the welfare and safety of the kingdom to the spirits of the sacrificed men and women and the incantations engraved on stones, the Burmese king became engrossed in seeking pleasure in his newly-constructed royal palace. His subjects began to while away their time too in gambling, drinking jousts, and festivals of song and dance.

However, the wheels of time turned one day. A new group of oracles made their entry into the royal court. These new astrologers, suppliant at the monarch's feet, delivered news of impending ill-fortune: 'The period of the guardian spirits of the city now stands eclipsed. A supernatural light is radiating from one of the pagodas. A delirious child is articulating ill-omens; an astrologer witnessed an inauspicious dream. Tidings from the heavens were heard in certain hermitages, ill-omens were visible in the waves of the sea and in the stars seen during the night of the full moon…'

The royal decree to shift the capital followed almost instantaneously. Ava went, now arose Amarpur. Thousands of men and women were ceremonially sacrificed again, and the burden of protecting the city was transferred to their spirits. Young boys and youthful men, girls of tender age and older ladies, pregnant women and decrepit old men—none were spared! Once again, a group of Burmese craftsmen were engaged in endowing the new capital with renewed splendor. An uncountable number of peerless palaces and pagodas hewn out of bricks and wood were crafted by their expert hands. The old capital became a deserted cremation-ground, the palaces and pagodas crumbled and were reduced to rubble, crests that once kissed the sky slowly eroded and merged with the soil. Like a new bride, the current capital was showered with a lot of love and attention for a few days. After that, history again flipped its pages at the behest of the astrologers. Amarpur too was deserted like a withered harlot. Mandalay arose in its stead. These capitals, conceived by regressive traditions dependent on dreams and prophecies, eroded and were destroyed. Moss gathered on these stony foundations of human sacrifice and bestiality. Even though the Mindon monarch became extremely powerful after the spirits of the hundreds of pregnant women he had handpicked for sacrifice merged with the spirits of their unborn children, he was eventually unable to protect these cities that were washed away by an infinite number of curses, painful sighs and tears.

None of these curses, the poisoned breath of these sighs, however, could shift even a tiny particle of the

Arakan pagoda very near Mandalay that proudly raised its head with its lofty pinnacles kissing the skies. A gold-adorned statue of the Buddha sat under the bejeweled, white canopied platform in the inner chamber of the pagoda, focused on meditation, void of attachment, steadfast! According to local tradition, this statue was forged by the Hindu king Shakra with his own hands to welcome the Tathagatha after he converted to Buddhism.[2] It was said that the latter, in an ancient time, appeared via a skyway and alighted in the remote Arakan region. An exact likeness of Gautam Buddha's earthly form was captured in this statue; it was a life-like doll. Even the Buddha himself embraced this statue, enraptured by the likeness and mistaking it for his earthly self. Radiating the heavenly scent of the blue lotus, this statue then recited the teachings and maxims of Buddhism and discussed these with the Tathagatha.

For many centuries, this historically renowned, richly-adorned statue of the Buddha was carefully guarded in the Arakan kingdom. However, many powerful monarchs of the adjoining Burmese kingdom dreamt of whisking away the statue and establishing it in their own domain. The Burmese king Anawrahata conquered the Arakan with

---

2 Shakra is another name for the god Indra.

his large army with this precise intention.[3] The massive size and weight of the statue of the Buddha, however, thwarted his desires. The sole white elephant of the king, considered to be the best instrument chosen to drag the statue of the Buddha, was unable to move it. Thinking that it would be an insult to the Buddha if the statue were to be dragged by other ordinary elephants, Anawrahata, the conqueror of Arakan, returned home empty-handed. Like earlier, the Buddha remained rapt in meditation in this uninhabited forested region of Arakan. Thwarted in his desires, Anawrahata proclaimed that the Buddha's statue was haunted by spirits. It was not possible to move it unless these evil spirits and spectres were driven away with incantations.

Eventually King Bodawpaya relocated Buddha's statue from Arakan to Mandalay, and established it in the Arakan pagoda's massive courtyard.[4] Just prior to the attack on the Arakan, a group of exorcists, disguised as pilgrims, were sent to the place where the statue stood. This group exorcised the evil spirits residing in the statue. According to inscriptions, Bodawpaya was able to wrest this statue from remote Arakan to Mandalay, crossing innumerable hills and mountains on the way, solely through the help of

---

3 Anawrahata (1014-77) was the founder of the Pagan empire.

4 Bodawpaya (1745-1819) was one of the major rulers of the Konbaung dynasty.

great qualities like forgiveness, compassion, non-violence and so on. Actually, a group of thirty thousand soldiers, enduring tremendous hardships and suffering, dragged the statue to Mandalay.

A market where foodstuffs, leaves of gold, incense sticks and candles were being peddled was located on both sides of the long pathway lying between the Arakan pagoda's gateway which was ringed with stone lions and the courtyard. A crowd of people buying and selling goods was visible. During the full moon festival in the spring, a massive crowd gathered to cover the Buddha's statue with gold leaves. At this time, groups of Tibetans also gathered in Mandalay's streets with the purpose of selling valuable stones, medicines, snake tongues, the blood of bats and scented beans. The precinct of the massive courtyard was reached once the dirty, disorderly bazaar had been crossed. In the middle was a finely chiseled, massive turtle. Groves full of palmyra trees populated this vast grounds, along with innumerable artistic carvings strewn about sporadically and fragments of stone statues everywhere. Six pairs of men and elephants fashioned out of brass stood on the other side. These figures were the guardians of the courtyard. The Buddha was in the inner chamber of the courtyard. There were groves of creepers and bushes in the backyard—spaces for concentration, meditation and immersion. These solitary groves were sanctified by the meditative pursuits of the half-naked hermits and monks. Every speck of dust here was rendered pure and clean by centuries of sacrifice and self-abnegation. It was as if this were a different world altogether, a unique environment! This place did not dwell in the bosom of time.

I

Manku—a tiny hamlet surrounded by undulating hills of varying height. It looked very beautiful when viewed from the Arakan Yoma range, as if a green *riha* laid out in the mild morning sunshine and decorated with embroidered patterns of a red hue was playfully waving in the wind. Cultivated fields lay at the foot of the smaller hills; in between there was a level area filled with huts. A thin road wound through the village, merging with the paved highway in the neighbouring village of Mitukan, and finally ended in Mandalay weaving its way alongside the banks of the Irrawaddy.

A village of twenty families, Manku actually was equivalent to a small hamlet of poor farmers and labourers. It was an impoverished colony of Burmese and Indian peasants and labourers who expended the sweat of their brows toiling for half of the produce of the land that they cultivated for the rich landlords. They sated their hunger for six months of the year while enduring an acute shortage of food during the other six. The Indian peasants had been transported by the British monarch to increase the wealth of the Empire by cultivating the pure and verdant lands of Burma. They weren't loan sharks like the Chettiars, but peace-loving, hardworking peasants. At one time, the Burmese families were landowners, old custodians of these low-lying paddy fields. Desirous of increasing their fame and status by indulging in gambling, singing and dancing, drinking, musical soirees and massive, showy feasts open to the public, they were reduced to penury after pawning their paddy fields and harvests and mortgaging all their land to the high rates of interest charged by the Indian Chettiars from whom they had taken loans. They were now a group of hapless people cursing their fate, forced to sell their lands and foundations, surrender half a share of their harvest to others, and destined to have one meal only to skip two more—a consequence of transferring the burden of tending their fields and cultivating their lands to Indian labourers. They had immersed themselves in gambling and other pleasures, and consequently got buried neck-deep in debt. They were like a herd of beasts staying barely afloat. A group of unknown, unacknowledged, yet indispensable ordinary folk that, in the midst of the cornucopias in their dreams, woke up to the painful realisation that they were now destitute. They wiped away their tears and counted the number of days they would probably survive on their fingertips. Inhabitants of the lowest rung of society undiscernible to the collective gaze, they were a group of vanquished soldiers defeated in the battle of life, surviving in anonymity to hide the shame of being poverty-stricken.

A few scattered hovels of divergent shapes were visible in this village that was in the midst of green fields engulfed by innumerable hills, and on top of an elevation that the Irrawaddy's currents could not reach. There were forests with huge, green trees on the taller hills, and a proliferation of betel-nut trees and shrubs of various sizes in the smaller ones. The small hill in close proximity to the village was virtually denuded. Blotches of red earth were visible here. This red soil was very fertile. Its smell reminded one of the blood-red soil of Manaung.

Like Manaung, Manku too was full of betel-nut trees. In between there were plants of betel leaves creeping up the trunks of bamboo, and fields that yielded *fa-laung* rice. The posts in the houses here were covered with fresh thatch. The beams were made of wood, which was found in abundance in the forests. All they needed to do was to chop and use it. The walls were made with pounded bamboo. Their surfaces were plastered with clay. Numerous complex patterns emerged when twisting, winding cracks opened up on these surfaces in the scorching heat of summer. Most of the huts were elongated in structure, while some were square. Their roofs, supported by horizontal inclines, were frighteningly bent on both sides, as if they would collapse this very instant. Dense foliage was cleared to open up a level space on the sides of each dwelling; each household reared cows or pigs there. The Indian farmers had wide clearings before their huts which they plastered with earth. The Burmese households had bamboo groves on the side. Each Burmese household had a bamboo platform close by to collect the flesh of cows or pigs that were sacrificed during their *deo-pujas*[5].

Between the hills, there were tall platforms used to keep a watch on crops. During the harvesting season, the Chettiar-tormented villagers would stay put in these platforms to keep an eye on their fields. Hordes of *hooluk bandors*, hog deer, wild boar or bears would take advantage of nightfall to forage on the ripening grain. The birds and pests were there anyway. These enemies of the impoverished farmers would trample and waste ten times as much as they could eat. There was no other choice but to stay awake all night on these platforms in groups, and keep watch

5 worship of resident deities.

over the crops armed with bows and arrows, catapults and sharp weapons.

The milkmen from the village put their cattle to pasture in the thickets in the medium-sized hills. Every morning a procession of cattle, their frames glittering, would wind their way through the narrow embankments in between the rice fields. Moving alongside them were the skeletal herdsmen with their bamboo hats. All of them wore patched trousers whose original blue colour had long faded away. Their torn vests resembled fish-nets. They had betel-nut in their sickly pale mouths, a stick in their hands, a slow, indolent gait and walk, an empty, directionless gaze. The cattle and the herdsmen combined were a group of hungry, quiet souls, as if all their desire and will to survive had ceased a long time ago.

As soon as it was dawn, herds of hooluks began screeching. The *bulbuls*, doves and *mynahs* also began their cacophony. In the soft light of the morning, the smoke-hued clouds and the white *patoli* trees seemed to be suspended like clumps of cotton between the peaks of the glittering hills on the west side of the Irrawaddy. A wholesome kingdom of green lay below. In between, the forest floor was occasionally painted deep blue by scores of gentian flowers. A long row of red *seri* flowers, several columns of white flowers hanging in bunches on the branches of the *paniphals*, glistening red soil on the hills. Broken clouds of smoke wafted their way to the skies from spaces in the forests that had been cleared and burnt for the purpose of jhum cultivation, clambering up the footholds at the edges of the cultivable land. The verdant green cover came down layer by layer and merged with the Irrawaddy's pebble-filled bosom; after that, the silvery billow of the Irrawaddy's splashing waters. Occasionally, riverbanks populated with *jhau* trees and sandbanks layered with tiny pebbles came into view.

The hamlet was peaceful and tranquil. The prevailing agrarian conditions hadn't made the population angry or agitated as yet. They took slight and slow steps through life's journey. A lot of women were busy thrashing paddy in their yards, which would later be taken away by the loan sharks. Some of them tied their lower garments on their chests and were husking grain with their mortars and pestles. Others were arranging threads in their looms. The beams and the reeds of the looms were respectively on the laps or the hands of the younger maidens. Quite a few of the older women, sitting with their backs turned to the early morning sun, were checking their daughter's or granddaughter's hair for lice. Some of them were separating seeds from cotton plucked in the jungle; others were spinning thread in their spools. Everyone had something or the other, however small, to do. There was no hesitation or commotion anywhere. The desire and enthusiasm to accomplish something out of their work was conspicuous by its absence. The agony caused by poverty was evident in the midst of the chores and responsibilities that characterised everyday life. They were a group of people compelled to work incessantly for the sake of survival, like a group of wound up mechanical dolls, tiny ants working by force of habit. Indolence, mute and slow, measured footsteps, all stemming from the weight of life's rough road characterized them. The still environment allied with the lazy flow of the cold currents of the Irrawaddy close by seemed to have brought the ceaseless flow of time to a halt.

II

Having slept late into the morning, Ramgobinda shielded his eyes from the blazing light of the sun as he emerged from the darkened interior of his house. He stretched his body, rubbed his eyes, and then sat down in the space outside. He sighed as his gaze rested on his aged mother who was sitting and fanning herself with her back towards the sun on the other side of the courtyard. Another night had passed by when he could not sleep, assailed by worries. Black circles caused by insomnia and stress were visible around his nearly sixty-two-year-old mother's aged eyes. Lacchmi, his wife, had wrapped her sari tightly around her waist and was pounding grain in the mortar near the *meji* made of hay. Her healthy, plump body had a dancer-like gait; her sparkling youthfulness seemed to rise and fall regularly and rhythmically.

Spring had just set in; the monsoon season was still far away. The mornings tended to be cloudy. The sun rose very early these days. Although it wasn't cold, a chilly wind blew in the mornings. The black kitten had curled up into a ball and was sleeping comfortably near the meji. The warmth of the sun was above, that of the hay below. Although it wasn't too long ago that this kitten had joined their family, she had quickly become familiar and intimate with everyone. She wasn't afraid of anyone in the family. Ramgobinda's seven-year-old son, Thanu, named her Minoti—Mini, in short. He had his meals with her. Ignoring Lacchmi's objections, he wrapped a small portion of his tattered blanket around the kitten and let her sleep with him. He would gambol with her during daytime. He also tied a small rope around her neck and led her around the house and courtyard throughout the day. He would lead her to the river every morning and wash her while taking his bath. Mini would shake away the droplets of water in her wet fur and tremble. She would then unsheathe her claws, make low growling sounds and try to scare Thanu.

'These domesticated animals are very happy', Ramgobinda mused. 'They don't have any cares or worries, no pressing concerns about where they will live, no torments or sorrows, and no need to labour either.' The newly-constructed granary was infested with mice that greedily devoured the grain that the family had stocked up throughout the year. However, Mini kept sleeping comfortably. She would lazily flick her eyelids open when a tiny mouse would scurry before her and then go back to sleep again. Actually, she began behaving like this after a misadventure with a rat. Ramgobinda chuckled whenever he recalled the incident. These large, sharp-toothed, aggressive rats that looked like mice would squeal loudly and release a terrible stench from their bodies. Dogs and cats purposely avoided them. However, Mini chased and captured one of these specimens the other day. Not only was she unable to devour the rat, but the terrible stench released by the animal also made her turn away from milk for quite a few days. Disgust and hatred for the entire race of rodents set root in her mind after the botched experience of her first hunting expedition. Nowadays she didn't even entertain the thought of prowling for prey.

Grains of different varieties were stored in the granary near the meji. According to the terms of the mortgage, a large portion of the stored grain had to be delivered as soon as possible to the landlord. A few Chettiars sold the grain wholesale; the rest transported them to Rangoon. The Chettiars, who had amassed a lot of wealth and land by charging interest owned almost all of the low-lying rice fields. The Chettiars were aristocratic people of high status who recognised wealth easily, but did not pay any heed to the grain in the fields or the poor peasants who expended the sweat of their brows on their ploughshares. They hadn't seen any villages or fields. Their salaried agents would visit the villages twice a year to maintain contact with the rural public—once just prior to the planting, to revisit the terms of the mortgage; the other during the harvest, to collect the dues of the landlord. They never gave a plot of land to the farmers permanently, fearing that the serfs would lay a legal claim on the land. The farmers too didn't add any fertiliser or clear the weeds from the boundaries of the plot of land that they leased annually. The land, thus, grew barren and infertile over time. Production too decreased progressively. The stock of grain that the farmers accumulated after their back-breaking labour scarcely lasted them six months of the year. Therefore, many peasants had abandoned cultivation and preferred working as labourers. Some of them had also adopted the path of banditry.

Ramgobinda's granary had been fortified with a tin roof two years earlier. Before that, the roof was made of thatch. Buffeted by storms and winds, the thatched roof had almost fallen in. The seeds began sprouting in the granary itself. Noticing that his aged mother was very distressed by this deterioration of the family's only resource, Ramgobinda purchased a few tin sheets from the black market and replaced the roof of the granary. He had to sell at least two months' worth of grain from the family's stock to raise the money for the tin roofs. That particular year proved very difficult for them. The war had just begun. Although prices were already inflated, they hadn't yet skyrocketed. Now the war had assumed an all-consuming avatar. There was a shortage of food; prices in the black market had hit the roof. On top of that, the ordinary public was on edge—no one knew what might happen and where. The Japanese had already bombed Rangoon. The local shopkeeper, Ballabh, said that the entire country would pass into Japanese hands in the near future. British troops were retreating and the Burmese were hand-in-glove with the Japanese against the British. However, the military officer who came to purchase fowl for the troops said, 'Do the Japanese have the capability to eject the British? The British Empire is the one where the sun never sets. Those piddly Japanese are going to be smashed to pulp when they exert pressure'. Whose words could you believe? Rumours abounded that thousands of Indians had fled via sea to India, crossing Chittagong. Those were, of course, the rich people who escaped with their tails between their legs at the slightest sign of trouble. Ramgobinda would listen to stories from various sources and narrate them to his mother later. His old mother would stare at him with her aging eyes, shocked by his stories. Actually, the old woman didn't understand such complex matters and didn't feel like listening to the stories either; she would just pretend to listen fearing that her son would feel offended if she did not do so. Her stomach would churn when she heard stories of war and bombing, of guns and ammunition and of the deaths of thousands of people. Lacchmi barely found free time as she was busy with her household activities. Where did she have the opportunity to sit and listen to such stories? Thanu was busy all day cavorting with Mini. Furthermore, they were exempt from such worries. Bitter experiences hadn't stunted their vitality. Exempt from duties and responsibilities, their lives were colourful and full of fun.

Ramgobinda's twenty-eight-year-old wife Lacchmi was winnowing rice. Her green sari was tied around her waist like a sash. Her movements brought to mind the effortless vivacity of a hill maiden. Her lively, restless mannerisms, sparkling youthfulness and the regular and rhythmic rise and fall of her bosom resembled the seductive, unpredictable dance of the water agitated by the wind. The *sindoor* in the large *phoot* on her forehead was mixed with droplets of sweat and had become larger. Ramgobinda liked it when her phoot was large. She looked very enthusiastic and seemed redolent with the sense of fulfilment that arose when one lived for the welfare of others. A new guest would arrive in their household in about four months or so. Signs of this guest grew more and more visible day by day. According to her mother-in-law, a woman should not perform intense physical labour during this period. Her mind should be free and happy. It was also harmful to give way to indolence and sleep. To be sure, Lacchmi hardly found any free time in the day. Worries hardly entered her mind. Only Ramgobinda worried about war and destruction—the rest of the household were bound to their own responsibilities. It was difficult to guess what the old woman was thinking as she was busy making *bisonis*, fly-swatters and baskets. Mostly her thoughts were centered on god. Therefore, Ramgobinda emerged as the sole arbiter of profane, worldly affairs in the household.

Ramgobinda went inside, picked up a clod of coal from the fireplace, and brushing his teeth with it, stepped outside again. The tea in the kettle placed atop the fire burning outside was now gurgling. Lacchmi would offer him a mug of black tea in a while. She must have noticed that he was performing his morning ablutions; nothing inside the household escaped her keen vision. She would methodically perform all the necessary activities for the household, from drawing water from the nearby pond to small tasks within the house. Her mother-in-law didn't have to bother with those things nowadays. The old woman would expend all her energies either tying together strands of bamboo or making thread from cotton in her spool. The cotton came either from Meiktila or Pakkoku. Ballabh used to sell it in his shop. The old woman used to weave cloth in her loom earlier; all the clothes they needed for the household came from that loom. But her fading vision forced her to abandon weaving. Nowadays they bought *dhutis*, saris and American-made cloth from the landlord's depot. These rough pieces of clothing were woven in a mill and didn't last too long. Lacchmi would occasionally embroider a fabric or two. But she could hardly extricate herself from the daily, unending series of tasks in the household to find time to weave. Once she determined that she would weave a dhuti. But it took her more than two months to finish it. The cotton began to rot in the loom. Finally, her mother-in-law was able to salvage something from it. They managed to make money selling the threads made in the spool; however, the prices they got weren't equivalent to the labour expended on them.

'This old woman's life was spent making thread. Happiness hardly graced her existence', Ramgobinda thought. His middle-aged father had migrated to Burma, allured by the promise of a good life that could be earned through hard labour after spending a large portion of his life in extreme poverty and privation in a remote village in India. His father dreamt of returning permanently to his old village to take care of his ancestral property after he had amassed wealth and fortune in Burma. He had heard that he could strike gold in Burma's fertile lands. Great quantities of gold were strewn in the pathways in Burma; clusters of pearls apparently hung on the trees and bushes. The permanent inhabitants of the country were not very intelligent, lacked diligence and loathed labour. Therefore, if he was prepared to work hard, there was no end to the wealth he would be able to amass. Thus, putting his fingerprint in the record-book of some overseer and travelling with his wife on an obscure boat, Ramgobinda's father set foot in Burma.

Initially, they somehow managed to procure a few meals for themselves by cultivating a few fields and working as labourers in the islands near Rangoon. Subsequently, as droves of Indian labourers entered Burma, the possibilities for employment in those areas decreased substantially. They managed to mortgage a field from a Chettiar and survive on it for a few days. But the rate of interest for the mortgage began rising steadily. The crops too didn't produce the anticipated yields because the Irrawaddy hadn't flooded over for two consecutive years. After they gave away the promised portion to the Chettiars, there was nothing left for the farmers. They had to survive for a few months only on gruel. In the meantime, the British government had leveled many of the hills and opened up some low-lying lands. After drifting for a few years, Ramgobinda's father eventually settled down in Manku. The Burmese were initially the owners of these newly opened low-lying lands. However, these soon passed into the Chettiar's hands by means of mortgage, interest and rent. Once again, the old situation repeated itself: infertile lands that hardly yielded any produce rented at high rates. The Chettiar would take away a majority of what they produced. A few months later, Ramgobinda's father was once again neck-deep in debt. His dream of returning to India never materialised. This hard-working peasant's life ended in Burma. The bodily traces of Ramgobinda's father disappeared after his corpse was burnt on a pyre in a nondescript hill near Manku.

Ramgobinda was born in Burma. From his childhood, he had accompanied his father to the fields. He had never seen his father's ancestral village in India. Occasionally, there was talk of returning while his father was still alive—he recollected such chatter vaguely. However, shortage of money meant that these wishes remained pipedreams. Ramgobinda's entire perception of his ancestral village was formed from the occasional titbits provided by his mother.

It was a village somewhere in central India surrounded by a green, peaceful natural backdrop. The inhabitants were poor and did not have the means to procure two full meals a day. But they were hardworking, simple and happy people. They constituted the dregs of society whose existence had been sucked dry by the communities around them. They were a group of ignorant, simple folk operating purely on the necessities of the present moment and out of a sense of duty. Their poverty-stricken lives were still colourfully vibrant and filled with good health which was a product of hard labour.

Almost all of them were tenants of the landlords. No one managed to keep behind produce that would last them for the entire year. These people who otherwise survived on greens picked from the forest and fruits, used to treat illnesses with medicines prepared from herbs. Even in the midst of all that poverty, they managed to celebrate after the harvest was over. Young men and women would dance wearing the colourful clothes they made in their homes. The entire community would feast together. The village would vibrantly resonate with the sounds of the cymbals and drums played in the fields in those nights. After the festivities which would last for three days, the villagers would go out in groups to seek employment in the nearby towns so that they could get enough money to buy salt, cooking oil and other provisions. During the period of cultivation, groups of tiny tots would head towards the fields squelching in the mud. They wore only a slip of cloth and carried bowls of rice gruel or stale bread with them for their fathers or elder brothers who were tending the fields. They would gambol without a care, abandon their slips of cloth on the banks, dive into the pond, spend a lot of time frolicking in the water, and then face the wrath of their mothers when they returned home in the latter half of the day. They would secretly pick up the fruit that fell in the backyards of other's houses, fish in the pond, and look for live grasshoppers and crickets in the grassy fields. They would imitate cowherds carrying a stick in their hands, and sit in the hollows of the trunks of banana stems as others dragged these around. The younger women would take care of the homestead and prepare meals for the cultivators. They winnowed the grains during the harvesting season. In the afternoon, they would all proceed to draw water with vessels on their heads from the only well at the center of the village and spend a long time talking and exchanging news with the others. They would often pair up a young woman with an accomplished young man from the village and tease her. They would all congregate once a week in the temple to offer prayers. No one seemed to have any fears or wicked intentions in their minds. These lives endowed by nature were taken back by it in old age. No one killed or destroyed one another with the weapons created by humankind. Despite the harsh demands of their many responsibilities, the lives of these poor peasants passed by floating merrily on the currents of laughter and happiness. Likewise, this world habitually shifted its position while slumbering peacefully....

The sun fell on the blue-hued trees full of gentian in the distant hill and rendered it purple. Clattering sounds indicating that Lacchmi had begun serving tea emanated from the kitchen. His mother, who was making a bisoni, looked up at him. 'The days of bisonis have arrived again.

It will become very hot soon' he thought. It was as if the sun was already clinging to the surface of the earth this February morning. The heat was unbearable! The eye could not focus on the hot winds tremblingly rising upwards like a scorching fire. Dust storms came along with the howling, twisty and fiery wind. It seemed like the sky, wind and the earth were all cruel and life-sapping. There were dust storms in the Irrawaddy's slender bosom. The heat seemed to have assumed the guise of the dust and was spreading itself throughout the land.

Cracks had begun appearing in the courtyard that had been constructed out of earth and cowdung. The geckos hung like lifeless beings on the walls and the ceilings, affected by the heat inside the house. They had to keep the tiny windows of their house open in the hope that some breeze would waft in. Besides the dust, hordes of sparrows entered through those open windows. The geckos would scatter in terror at the sound of the fluttering of their wings. 'The sole task of these tiny beings is to save themselves from predators and to ceaselessly try to amass food with the aim of survival' Ramgobinda thought and sighed. 'Actually people are like that too.' Along with the sparrows, a few butterflies would also enter the house fluttering their wings. These were colourful butterflies of varying sizes. After fluttering around the household for a while, they settled on the roof or the walls and became absolutely still in an instant. They would exhibit a riot of colours fluttering their two wings. After that, when they noticed the geckos lying still with their eyelids shut, they would flutter their wings and once again fly out into the open spaces outside.

Ramgobinda sat near the fireplace which was dark even in daylight and poured some water on the *pitha* in his bowl with the intention of softening it. Sprouts would appear in the rice once the grain had been winnowed. They couldn't do anything else with that other than make pithaguri—otherwise they would have to throw that excess away. Therefore, they ate boiled pithas in the mornings and the evenings. There was no milk. Their cow produced around half a *xer* of milk for about six months. That milk was not sufficient for Thanu and the kitten; hardly anything remained for Ramgobinda's mother. The pithas were slightly fermented because they boiled them in molasses made from dates. Of course, they had these meals during the season when they didn't have to tend to the fields. Once he went out to plough the fields, boiled pithas weren't enough; they were digested very quickly.

During the season of cultivation, they needed food that wouldn't be digested quickly such as chapatis and parched or cooked rice. It was difficult to make rotis as the price of flour was high. Wheat and jowar didn't grow in these places. The Chettiars and the big officers would fall like vultures on whatever little stock arrived from North India and finish those at the source. To have rotis was a stroke of fortune. Occasionally, a farmer would exchange three or four *xers* of rice for half a xer of whole wheat. But even that amount had to be ground in the pestles at Jayanao or Nu-yin's places. They would preserve the chaff as feed for their cows or their chickens. But they faced losses even at that juncture. Ballabh had a huge pestle in his shop. He prepared flour in his own house. But the pestle was very heavy and couldn't be operated by a single person. The whole wheat hardly transformed into flour; most of it remained stuck in the wedges of the pestle. Still, it was good if they could head to the fields after having rotis and a cup of salted black tea during the cultivating season. Then they were able to plough the fields for a while without being assaulted by pangs of hunger.

The black tea in the bowl seemed to separate as Ramgobinda blew into it to cool it down. Black tea tasted horrible if it was too strong. As he was trying to cool his tea and pithaguri, he heard Gusenpung's voice and stepped outside.

III

During the fallow season, Gusenpung paid a visit to Ramgobinda almost every afternoon. He would wake up late, drink his cup of tea, and then go out for his rounds with the intention of whiling his time away with idle chatter. On that day as well, Gusenpung removed the bar on the gateway and entered the courtyard. The old woman, who was making her bisonis, raised her head, gave him a welcoming smile and once again got busy with what she was doing. The old lady had no time to talk to lazy wastrels like Gusenpung.

'Apparently light is streaming out of the Suley pagoda', Gusenpung sat on the wooden *murha* at the edge of the courtyard folding his green cotton *lungi* up to his knees. 'It seems like the reign of Prince Talai is probably over. It is also rumored that Rangoon will survive only if Alaungpaya's defenses hold. Yesterday night I saw a dream where the sea spilled over and swept Mandalay away.'

Gusenpung belonged to the Kanung tribe from the north. Actually, his family was an old inhabitant of the Sumpra Bum region on the banks of the Irrawaddy in Upper Burma. Since it was difficult to cultivate anything or to make a living in that region, a wise ancestor of Gusenpung relocated the family to the fertile regions of lower Burma and settled permanently in Manku. They soon became owners of sufficient land and property. Nawapung, Gusenpung's son, had mortgaged all his ancestral property to the landlords and had been reduced to a penurious state. However, they still managed to get by the entire year with their produce. They were relatively prosperous by Manku's standards. The villagers would often seek succour from families like Gusenpung's during times of acute need. If someone was unable to sell their grain, Gusenpung's family would procure that unsold stock at half the price. They still owned a plot or two of low-lying land. The rest of their plots were cultivated paying rent. They still had enough to help others even after they had two full meals per day—wasn't that very fortunate? If the villagers were forced to go hungry for several days, they would borrow a small amount of rice from Gusenpung to satiate themselves partially. If the little children in the village wouldn't get anything to eat in their own houses, they would make a beeline to

Gusenpung's abode and get at least a bowl of gruel or a handful of dry food to munch.

Everyone knew about Gusenpung's dreams and visions in the village. No one gave any importance to them, however. When he didn't have any work, he would feel giddy after munching a lot of betel nuts and then visit a number of houses in the village describing his visions. He outshone the astrologers in his descriptions of visions and ill-omens. On any other day, Ramgobinda would have avoided him with a polite smile saying, 'Is that so?' and focus on his work. However, the mindset of the people had changed ever since this demonic war had begun. People paid excessive heed to minor matters and would get scared easily nowadays. Superstitions and irrational practices had taken root in their minds and the imaginations of people were terrorised by war. Nowadays, people went in droves to the astrologers and consulted their almanacs. They would pay careful attention to prognostications about their futures. Serious discussions centered on those same dreams and portents which were dismissed easily as irrelevancies earlier. The petrified minds of the people focused seriously on these meaningless visions and these allayed their fears and terrors for a while.

'What are you alluding to?' Like a little child excited to listen to a story, Ramgobinda eagerly approached Gusenpung and sat down on the floor near the murha.

'These are evil omens', Gusenpung said gravely. 'The country is facing great danger. The people will be struck by terror. These are bad portents; early warnings of impending destruction.'

'Can you please elaborate what will happen?' Ramgobinda quizzed him in a puzzled tone. Gusenpung always spoke in a cryptic fashion. It was difficult to follow what or who he was alluding to.

'The fire emanating from the mouth of the sea dragon will engulf the entire country. There is no way to keep death and destruction at bay now that the guardian spirits have abandoned the Suley pagoda.'

His words seemed like the denouement to some tragic drama. The old lady looked up from her work at Gusenpung leading to an error in her embroidery.

'The Japanese have already reached Rangoon, haven't they?' Ramgobinda said skeptically. He didn't have any interest in the finer points of Burmese theology. He was a practical man who firmly believed in the reality he saw in front of him.

'You can say that they have almost occupied Rangoon. They dropped a slew of bombs and drove away the British.'

'They must have found it impossible to hold fort', Ramgobinda sighed. The pandemonium created by war hadn't touched their tiny hamlet as yet. The first attacks were on the larger cities. But if Burma drowned, it would take

Manku with it. Slivers of bad news reached Manku bit by bit in the meanwhile. These fragmentary reports contained terrifying stories of murder, torture and rioting. The all-encompassing fire of war was engulfing all of Burma. The shards of news they received were about people and places that had been reduced to ashes in that blazing inferno.

'We should talk to Ba-Mao once about how things stand. We may come across a newspaper at his place as well', Ramgobinda said. Sometimes they would come across something new during their discussions at his place. These discussions helped in allaying their fears a bit. It was difficult to fathom what the people of the nation were thinking nowadays.

'How will Ba-Mao know anything new? He hasn't seen the face of any newspaper in the previous week. He will only narrate fifteen-day old news engagingly. The Japanese had just begun marching towards Rangoon at that time. Things have changed drastically now,' Gusenpung said. 'It's better to believe in dreams and visions than listen to such recycled news. If we can understand the meaning of those visions when we wake up, then that's it! That becomes fresh news.'

Earlier the peasants used to travel to Mandalay in the fallow season to work as labourers and earn some money. This damned war had put a stop to that as well. People were running helter-skelter. Folks from the urban areas were escaping to the villages. Who was going to employ them as labourers now? A few opportunities for supplying bamboo, hay and cane had arisen in far-flung places where the military had set up their bases; but, it wasn't possible for everyone to leave their families and homesteads behind and travel afar to procure wealth. While that was a good way to make money, their minds would find no peace and be full of consternation. Besides that, there was the obvious risk to life. Monitoring this situation, most of the people in the village decided to stay put after their last crops had been harvested. They didn't know how long they would have to stay like this.

'According to our prophetic almanacs, the hundred-year reign of the British over Burma is about to end. Once the British leave, the king will once again rule this land', stubbing a pattern on the ground with his eyes shut, Gusenpung spoke almost as if he were an astrologer calculating the signs on an alamanac. 'The British devastated this country tremendously during their reign. Burma became infested with foreign traders, landlords, office bearers and workers. The autochthonous population had to suffer grievous losses. The foreigners became rich sucking the fat off the land. Now, when the king's reign will begin again, not a single foreigner will be allowed to spit on this hallowed land. Tomorrow, there is a nationalist meeting conducted by young men in the school grounds at Mitukan. They are secretly conspiring to overthrow the British.'

'The idea of overthrowing the British must have taken deep roots then?' Ramgobinda asked. Internally he was feeling very apprehensive. The future of lakhs of Indians like him would lurch precariously once the British left.

'Is there any need to throw them out? They will be ejected anyway when the opportune time arises' Gusenpung replied. 'Can the British do anything else but flee when the Japanese arrive? Spectres reside in the Japanese bombs. Sacrificial blood is smeared on their bodies. The Burmese too have begun rebelling against the British. The youth have determined that they will ally with the Japanese. They are ready to do anything to drive the British away.'

'What will be the upshot of this? The alien British will leave; the alien Japanese will come in. What is the benefit in this for all of us?'

'No, no! Once the British flee, the other alien foxes too will have to escape clinging on to the tail of the British lion', Gusenpung said agitatedly. 'If we can remove these hordes of bloodsucking vampires now, it won't be difficult to get rid of the Japanese later.'

'Oh! So, now you are making arrangements to drive us away from here?' Ramgobinda said gravely. It hadn't even occurred to him in his wildest fantasies that the poor Indian farmers of Manku may appear as aggressors and interlopers for others. His peaceful fantasy being shattered to pieces, Ramgobinda looked at Gusenpung with a mute gaze, trying to fathom this cruel reality helplessly.

'No, not at all! I was only referring to those landlords and merchants who charge high interests,' Gusenpung hastily replied, embarrassed by both his impulsiveness and the fact that he had caused injury to the simple, uncomplicated mind of a person like Ramgobinda. 'There aren't a lot of you in Manku. Who is concerned about poor Indians like you all? You haven't oppressed anyone. You haven't cheated anyone. You haven't robbed the Burmese of their lands by mortgaging them at high rates of interest. You too are part of the oppressed. You too have lost everything.'

'But what are the consequences of this? Once a foreigner, always a foreigner', Ramgobinda said.

'Actually people like you cannot be considered aliens anywhere in this world, my friend. You will stay behind. There is no paucity of space for the likes of you in the bosom of this massive country of Burma. Instead, when the rich landlords flee along with the British, then arrangements will have to be made to redistribute manageable plots of land amongst people like you from the property that will rightfully revert back to the king. Apparently, according to the Tathagatha, sorrows will afflict everyone if property is not distributed evenly among the propertyless.'

'Oh-ho! You seem to already have prepared a scheme

secretly in advance.' Ramgobinda laughed drily, feeling slightly reassured and looked in the direction of his storehouse. 'Actually, the fears of people who settle in a foreign land is always greater in magnitude. They imagine seeing tigers even in shadows. On top of that, if a war ensues and creates chaos and disorder, then their trepidation increases because the threat of displacement grows.'

'I didn't realise that you were such a revolutionary in secret. You seem like a staunch *komunist*', Ramgobinda continued, putting a lot of stress on the last word. According to him, komunist meant any revolutionary dispensation fighting against the existing government.

'I am not komunist. They don't have a king' Gusenpung replied seriously like a wise man. 'We will have a king in our country. The king will govern with a council of ministers. Peace and prosperity will once again reign in this land like in the earlier days.'

'Whether its the komunists or the king…what will happen to us?'

'We will make you permanent residents here. We have to give you Burmese names as well', Gusenpung said. 'Otherwise our descendants may one day consider you foreigners. Actually, these British upset the orders of caste and community here. They converted people to Christianity and gave people funny names. I feel like laughing at these names: Sunny Jim Thantmint, Abraham Ba Nunt, Edwin

Saungsin, Stephen Miawmin—ha ha! Like fashionable crows, some of them deck themselves in suits and ties, go to church for one hour every Sunday, and swelling their chests, identify themselves as Anglo-Burmese.' Sensing that the mood had lightened somewhat, Gusenpung laughed loudly.

'The situation in the country is changing rapidly day by day', Ramgobinda placed his head in the cleft between his bent knees and stared at the courtyard. 'No one knows when a bomb may smash all of us to smithereens. If the Japanese flood in here like a tidal wave, then there is a lot of trouble ahead. Even if a handful of Burmese try to save us from the Japanese who will advance like a horde of tiny ants, will they be able to prevent anything?'

Pressing his weight against his crooked cane staff, Jayanao *maru* was seen hobbling down the path in front of the house. He halted for a bit in front of Ramgobinda's doorway, spat out a red gob of betel-juice and cleared his throat loudly. Jayanao was the *gaonburha* of Manku; an aged man who had knowledge of the ways of the administration. He was respected by everyone in the village. He would tender advice during times of need and help people as well. Sometimes he would hobble with the help of his staff, visit someone in the village, and check how they were doing. He would be presented with ground betel-nut or a bowl of black tea during those visits. He was the oldest man in the village. The others consumed tobacco or puffed *bidi*s. Therefore, when Jayanao visited someone, he would give advance warning about his presence by clearing his throat loudly. He would enter the household only after that; otherwise, the younger folk would get embarrassed because they didn't get enough time to extinguish their bidis.

The ancient, wizened Jayanao was probably even older than the village. His hair was completely white and wrinkles and creases adorned his shapely, ruddy face. Thin streams of red betel juice constantly flowed out from the two corners of his mouth. The old man, dressed in a silk *pa-so*, an upper body garment made out of bright blue fabric and with a large maroon turban on his head, commanded respect and love as he walked through the village alleyways leaning on his staff. People were comforted and strengthened by a single utterance from him during periods of crisis or illness.

There were only three households that owned their own plots of land in Manku—Jayanao's, Ba-Mao's and Gusenpung's. Amongst them, Jayanao owned the maximum amount of land. Since he was the gaonburha, the administration did not impose any tax on his properties and holdings. To be sure, Ballabh also owned a few small plots of land. But he was a businessman, not a farmer. He wouldn't till the soil with his own hands; instead, he would rent out the plots and take a portion of the produce. The two youthful sons of Jayanao worked on seven-eight *pura*s of land that he owned. He leased out the remaining three puras of land to tenant farmers.

His youngest son, Nungnao, did not want to continue in the family's ancestral occupation of cultivation and went off to Mandalay in search of a job. He worked as a clerk in some company there. Although he was attracted to all the trappings of the good life, according to Jayanao he was always in dire straits. Occasionally he would visit home in need of money as his salary was not enough. Jayanao would give him a portion of the money procured from selling grain, and bid farewell to him every time with the advice that he should leave his job and get back to farming. But, a person who had developed a taste for the bright lights and colourful clothes of the city, always found it difficult to get back to the slow pace and agrarian life of the village. Therefore, Nungnao never paid heed to his father's advice. To state the obvious, the boy wasn't very diligent. He wasn't as sturdy as the other two sons either. On the other hand, since he was very hirsute, he received a lot of affection from his mother during childhood and grew up very spoilt. Jayanao had also become very old by the time he had grown up and was ready to learn the arts of cultivation. Therefore, he couldn't accompany him to the fields either. Following his mother's wishes, he was enrolled in the primary school in Mitukan and also studied for a few grades in the English medium school there. 'Now even the mother is dead, while the son grew up in a garbage pit following the wrong path', Jayanao would occasionally muse in sorrow. 'I am the one who is drowning in the middle of this.'

Noticing that Jayanao was entering Ramgobinda's dwelling, Gusenpung vacated his murha and stood by the side with his head bowed. Jayanao smiled at him, left his staff leaning on the wall and sat down on the vacated murha. This time, Ramgobinda's mother stopped framing bisonis, adjusted her *uroni* over her head and sat down near Jayanao with a container of betel nuts.

'Nungnao returned home at midnight yesterday', Jayanao cleared his throat and said very gravely. 'After Marang, Margui and Bakpin, the Japanese have now begun marching towards Mandalay. One of Nungnao's friends, a Japanese doctor, said that bombs may begin raining on Mandalay any day now.'

'What happened to Rangoon?' Gusenpung, sprawled out on the floor, asked.

'The British fled from Rangoon a week ago. They escaped leaving the gates of the prisons and the asylums open. Now, bandits and ruffians prowl the streets of Rangoon. Government officials fled earlier. The few that remained behind are dead. Besides bandits, lunatics and soldiers, Rangoon is now deserted.'

'If Mandalay falls now…' Ramgobinda said worriedly.

'People are already fleeing Mandalay in panic. Some are

fleeing towards the villages. The foreigners are leaving for their countries of origin', Jayanao said. 'Taking advantage of this lawless situation, the Burmese are attacking Indians in droves. Scores of Indians are fleeing helter-skelter leaving their houses and property behind. Cruel acts of butchery and looting are taking place in the forests.' Jayanao halted for a while and then began again, 'All of you should be prepared to do something. Danger has already arrived at our doorstep. You will be beset with great danger if you remain inactive like this.' Jayanao turned his head and looked at the doorway.

Scared beyond his wits, Ramgobinda looked once at his mother and then at Jayanao. A look of sheer terror was evident on the old woman's wrinkled face. She wanted to say something, but her parched lips began trembling and she fell silent once again.

'Are you telling us to flee? You are asking us to escape by any means possible, aren't you?' Ramgobinda suddenly began screaming like a madman. 'The country is on fire. What other options do we have?'

Jayanao hung his head.

'But where will we go?' Ramgobinda asked again, his tone calmer and more composed than earlier. 'We are citizens of Burma. We were born here, everything we possess is here. We belong here, just like you. Isn't there anyone in this country who can explain this simple fact to the Burmese rebels?' Hopelessness, frustration and disgust burned in his eyes. The blazing fires begun by this revolution were surrounding him on all sides much like the red corral flowers that bloomed at the mere touch of the fingers during *phagun*. These were like funeral fires for Burmese Indians; an all-consuming, all-destroying vermilion blaze.

'Whom will you explain these things to? What will you explain to the rebels? They are outside the pale of logic and reason' Jayanao responded in a calm and composed tone. 'These are wild beasts. The anger and disgust stored in some distant corner of their minds for all these years is blazing like an uncontrollable inferno of hatred now.'

'But what did the Indians do to them? And even if there are a few rotten fruits in the basket, does it mean that everyone is like that?' Ramgobinda said. 'Actually, the British brought the Indians here.'

'You cannot fathom the hatred and anger they bear towards the British regime', Jayanao said. 'But they are also determined to wreak vengeance on the Indian capitalists and the oppressive rule of the Chettiars.'

'That is something justifiable. But we are poor peasants...although we are Indians...we...'

'Their minds are blazing with thoughts of revenge. They cannot discriminate between right and wrong now. They will burn anyone who stands in their way. We are but mere wisps of straw on their path. What can we do? Therefore, escape while you still have time.'

'But the point is, where will they escape? And whose sins are they being punished for? Do they have the capacity to flee just like that in these difficult days? Do they have the resources to do so?' Gusenpung impatiently blurted out after staying silent for quite a while. 'They aren't millionaires like the Chettiars. They are as oppressed and poverty-stricken as the ordinary Burmese.'

'The rich Indian capitalists have already escaped. There are no Chettiars left in Rangoon now.'

'That's a different matter altogether. These hordes of rich people are attracted like flies to the smell of money, and also turn tail quickly at the slightest whiff of danger' Gusenpung said. 'But the poor peasants don't have the money to buy a plane ticket to reach India within an hour. They have to labour and subsist on Burmese soil till the last moment.'

'Then they will burn needlessly as sacrificial beasts for the sins of others', Jayanao slowly closed his eyes and said. 'Have you ever noticed how insects are drawn to a fire during winter? Such death is meaningless. No one can take any pride in it. That's a coward's death.'

'The ones who have a full meal have escaped, but the ones who scramble for the dregs are condemned', Gusenpung mused thoughtfully. 'They created both wealth and enemies through their business of charging interest. Now they have absconded with all their wealth seeing that danger is at their doorstep and you insignificant beings will have to face the brunt of the malicious enemy.'

'We haven't thought ill of anybody. We haven't harmed anybody either. Instead we sweated and bled in our fields only to be rewarded with one full meal a day', Ramgobinda lamented. 'Your rebels will be cursed if they create unnecessary enemies of helpless farmers like us. God will never forgive them.'

'From the Indian families here, Ballabh will be the first to escape, mark my words. He has wealth and Chettiar blood flows in his veins. It's only poverty-stricken farmers like you who will face trouble', Gusenpung said.

'Why don't you all get together and do something? Even the tiniest of ants will be safe if they stay together in a group', Jayanao said. 'In all probability, the Japanese will cut off the escape routes from here in a few days. Then you won't be able to escape.'

'I have spent almost half of my life holding on to Burmese soil with my teeth like a guard dog. Do you think it's easy to just leave everything behind and flee from here?' Ramgobinda responded quietly. 'We coexisted like older and younger brothers in a family for so many years. But now the Indians have to escape not because of the Japanese or the British, but for fear of the Burmese. Can there be anything more tragic than this?'

'I understand that. Everyone in Manku understands that. But the entire country is aflame' Jayanao replied.

'Then please do something. Don't expel us with women and children in tow, converting us into food for beasts and vultures in the forest', Ramgobinda said plaintively.

The veins in Jayanao's ruddy face began throbbing. He suddenly looked very grave, as if waves of sorrow crashing against his mind couldn't find a way out. The minds of these people were simple and compassionate. They didn't express grief with tears or wails, but with a stern, hard demeanor. Although a tempest could be raging internally, the observer wouldn't get an inkling of it from their calm, composed facades.

'I should take leave. Let me inform a couple of others as well', Jayanao got up from the wooden murha, walked slowly towards the wall, and took his staff in his hands. He tapped his staff a few times on the cracked floor of the courtyard and thought about something. Then he once again spoke in that calm, composed voice of his, 'I have to discuss this issue with Nungnao as well. I will talk to him. However, he isn't a general, but a mere foot soldier. I don't know what he can do. It's best that you all be ready to leave'. Jayanao walked a few steps without looking at anyone and then whirled around and looked at Gusenpung, 'We are aliens here as well. We scrambled here from the highlands, searching for cultivable land. One day, we too will have to taste the poisoned fruit of division that the rebels have begun sowing now. After you leave, their gaze may fall on us'. Tapping his staff with a worried mien, Jayanao left the same way he had arrived.

Gusenpung once again seated himself on the murha. 'There is substance in what the old man said', he hung his head and said. 'This fire will have no consideration for anyone. Those who make a run for it will survive; the rest will all be reduced to ashes. You can probably abjure your love for the land, but can you leave your lust for life behind?'

'I understand that. But can't you…I mean, can't all the villagers band together and explain the situation to them?'

'Whom will you provide the explanation to? What will you explain? The poor Burmese in Manku will also be doomed if you try to reason with these insane rebels. Besides their lives, they have nothing else to sacrifice for your benefit. The main thing is that we have to consider his proposal seriously now.'

'I don't understand such highfalutin chatter. We are poor peasants, sons of the soil, the earth is everything for us. We spent our entire lives tilling the soil. Now we have lost our way floating helplessly in this flood', Ramgobinda said in an agitated voice. 'This is my own country, you are my countrymen. We will stay here on this assurance. We don't know anyone else. Who will give us refuge? Who will embrace us as their own?'

'We will have to meet Nungnao and discuss these precise things with him', Gusenpung responded. 'If he is willing, he may be able to do something. He has secret contacts with the rebel groups.'

Gusenpung took a betel-nut from the bowl and left munching it.

'What am I hearing, my son?' Ramgobinda's mother looked at his worried face with a helpless gaze.

'The country is burning. We will have to flee', Ramgobinda stared at the sky melancholically. 'The fault isn't theirs.'

'Oh my god, I have to dislocate myself in this evening of my existence. What will happen to you and your family? Lacchmi is pregnant, Thanu is just a baby. How will you cross those hills and forests?'

'And you? You are sixty-two years old. How will you travel?'

'Don't think about me. My life and expectations are all coming to an end. Just bury me somewhere here. I want to be close to your father. If you can, take some of my ashes with you. You can immerse them in the holy river', Ramgobinda's mother looked at him with tear-filled eyes and sighed.

Ramgobinda wasn't prepared to listen to such notes of

helplessness from the mother who had been such a source of inspiration for him.

'Just let that be. You don't have to worry about that. Do what you have to do. You don't have to worry about such matters while I am still alive', he said firmly. 'If we have to go, everyone leaves together. Otherwise we all die here. No one can stop us if we want to die here.'

'No, no…I was just being silly. What is stored in our fates will happen—who can avoid that?', the old woman said, wiping her tears with the edge of her *aasol.* Once again, she got back to making bisonis.

Ramgobinda looked at the curved plough hanging on the bamboo slats of the granary. The work in the fields hadn't begun yet. If everything went well, they would have to start in a few days. The fields with rice saplings would have to be ploughed at least once before the monsoon. He felt somewhat calm thinking about this. To create was his responsibility. If he fled at the mere sight of the demonic visage of war, then who would cultivate the fields? Just because it was wartime, could people survive without eating? An image of the luxuriantly fresh and peaceful appearance of rice fields wafted before his eyes. The green trees were moving in waves in tune with the rhythm of the wind. How generously those small, colourless stubs of rice grew once they were planted in the ground. After that, the seductive swaying of the ripened grain in the harvesting season—his mind was suffused with the pleasure arising from the ancient instinct for creation! For a brief moment, the horror and terror of war and violence was completely erased. Just a few more days and he would be immersed in his familiar routine of work. Once the work in the fields began, it was as if the outside world didn't exist for him. The tremendous sounds of explosions, the grating sounds of airplanes would all be reduced to nothing by the swaying green ricefields.

'Why did people get involved in this unnecessary war?', he thought. These people still hadn't realised the value of being swept away by the pure joy of losing oneself in nature's bosom assisted by the great peace that emerged after backbreaking labour. What benefits did humankind reap from the death, devastation and injuries caused by the pursuit of war? On the one hand, a society of sick, disabled people; on the other, a group of people that survived by gnawing away at the flesh and bone of their foundations and relationships much like those disgusting species of large rats with sharp teeth. Why was humanity unable to take even a single step forward to ensure peace and happiness for all?

Ramgobinda's depression increased when he noticed Lacchmi sifting grain in the other side of the courtyard. An image of a potentially new person emerging in the coming days with the expectation of being enfolded in a welcoming embrace wafted before his eyes when he gazed at Lacchmi's full, pregnant body. A being enraptured by the dreams and promises of the future! 'What will we leave behind for them?' he mused. 'They will mark their appearance on this earth shadowed by the pitiless curses of war. They will judge us guilty after confusedly losing their way in the hell that we created for them. What doom are we calling on our heads after murdering their futures in such a barbaric fashion!'

Ramgobinda spat a gob of betel-juice on the floor with great disgust and irritation and entered the darkened interior of his hut. Emerging with a red cloth draped around his body, he went out.

IV

Ramgobinda felt tired walking through the long alley that led to Ba-Mao's courtyard. Ba-Mao's small dog came out barking from the space below the floor of the granary. Once she came near Ramgobinda, she stopped barking and sat down on the floor wagging her tail. 'Who is it?', Ba-Mao opened the creaking bamboo door and emerged from inside the darkened room. Seeing Ramgobinda, he took two *pirha* from the place where they were resting against the wall, laid them on the ground, sat on one of them himself and indicated with one of his fingers that Ramgobinda should sit on the other. After that, he looked at Ramgobinda with a questioning look.

'Did someone come here?' Ramgobinda said, looking around him.

'Ballabh and Budhu were here. They just left. What

made you come here?'

'I came to ask whether you heard anything about the war', Ramgobinda replied.

'What new news will we get?', Ba-Mao said. 'It's rumored that Rangoon is facing a dire crisis and has fallen to the Japanese. It seems like the entire country will be conquered by the Japanese soon. It doesn't seem like Mandalay will hold out for very long either. On the other hand…', Ba-Mao suddenly stopped in the middle of his sentence.

Ramgobinda threw an interrogative gaze in Ba-Mao's direction. Ba-Mao was sitting and staring at the granary with a melancholic look. His face was agitated, as if he was hesitating to say something. Suddenly, the situation became very uncomfortable.

'I heard a few things about Rangoon' Ramgobinda said, looking at the dog that was now lying stretched out on the ground wagging her tail. 'I heard that Nungnao has come home tonight.'

'I am sure you met him', Ba-Mao almost jumped as he said this. 'Hasn't he said anything about the crisis that has befallen the Indians?'

'I haven't met him, but have heard a few things', Ramgobinda felt relieved now that this sudden awkwardness in their conversation had dissipated. 'I've heard that there will be no place for us in this nation, that we Indians have to pack all our belongings and bid farewell to this country forever like dogs that belong to another master. This is what the situation is in brief, isn't it?'

Ba-Mao nodded his head and putting some pounded betel-leaf from the cloth bag tied to his waist in his mouth, said, 'Can you call a single country in this world your own? When you or I will die tomorrow, we won't even need four feet of land. Will we take our riches or property with us? However, all our hatreds, fights and differences are centered on such petty things when we are alive.'

Ba-Mao's ruddy face had become as red as the morning sun in the strong sunlight of the afternoon. His straight white hair covered his head like a white cap. Shutting the small eyes beneath his fat eyelids, Ba-Mao said, 'My dear, hopes and expectations begin to diminish in the declining years of a man's life. I amassed a lot of property with these two hands. I lost two thirds of it to drinking and public feasts, and the other third to gambling. I mortgaged my land and property to the *mahajan*. He charges interest on my produce. Now I somehow scrape the bottom of the barrel to provide for the family. But look! I don't have the slightest resentment or anger in me. When it was the time to enjoy, I lived it to the fullest. I earned what I have through hard labour; but I also blew it away. Now my situation is precarious. Whatever was preordained by fate happened.'

'That is true; but do the rest of the folk understand that?'

'Who will understand? If fate dictates, good days are going to arrive themselves. Who understands that? The river floods during the monsoons, it dries exposing its bed in the winter. This is the law of nature. But these young boys don't understand this.'

'They think that Burma's situation wouldn't have been like this if droves of Indians hadn't rooted themselves here' Ramgobinda replied.

'But are the foreigners really responsible for our pathetic situation?'

'But isn't that so?,' Ramgobinda said. 'These Chettiars are the owners of the country's wealth, land and crops. Did they bring this wealth with them? No, they cheated others and amassed it.'

'Let's leave that aside! There are different types of people in this world. If some of them are poor, the others will be rich. Were there no poor people in Burma before the Chettiars came?' Ba-Mao shut his eyes again. 'There was unlimited land in this country in those days; no boundaries, no deeds, no taxes. One marked out one's territory by where the bullocks and the plough chose to stop. Of course, we still had people who couldn't manage two meals a day in those days. Earlier, the rich class was constituted of the Burmese, now it has been taken over by the Chettiars.

But the situation of the poor farmers remained the same. Scarcity and want dogged them. However, all these violent, evil and manipulative thoughts have rooted themselves in people's minds only recently.'

'We have enough evidence of that', Ramgobinda said. 'However, danger affects all Indians now. There is no discrimination between rich and poor, landlords and peasants. We too will be singed by the fire that threatens the Chettiars.'

'Young men rule the country now…some sort of mishap is bound to happen. They are angry with the Chettiars and also with the British for removing every obstacle and bringing them here. The helpless Indian peasants are also doomed along with them', Ba-Mao said. He looked everywhere warily and whispered in Ramgobinda's ears, 'I heard that this bunch of degenerates have also allied surreptitiously with the Japanese to overthrow the British. A group of untrustworthy traitors! Do you think the country will be free by chasing the British away only to welcome the Japanese with a red carpet? It is tantamount to inviting the ravenous crocodile inside your hearth.'

'Why? I am sure they made some arrangements with the Japanese beforehand', Ramgobinda replied.

'Huh! The British will leave and the Japanese will rush in to loot this nation. These Japanese lived like kings even during the time of the British. Just go to Mandalay and check—from doctors to barbers, tea shopowners, cloth merchants, watchmakers…all of them Japanese. They are quite intimate with the local population and know all the news about the country. I am sure they pass on that information to the Japanese government. Otherwise, how can a handful of people from that tiny island shake the powerful British Empire to its very foundations? It's already like this now. Once the Japanese set up camp in our country in the future, our poor Burmese will be faced with a great calamity', Ba-Mao said. 'Of course, the first victims of their retribution will be you folks.'

'Now what should we do? You've seen what's happening in the country…what would you advise us to do?' Ramgobinda asked.

'The others came with the same question…Ballabh and the rest', Ba-Mao said. 'What can I say?'

'Jayanao dropped by in the morning. He said we should flee. But escaping is no easy matter. The roads are hilly and covered with dense forests; on top of that, where will we go with our families and all our belongings? What can we do?' Ramgobinda put his head on his hands and fell silent.

The afternoon sun was steadily growing unbearable. The bluish veins on Ba-Mao's red face were throbbing. He turned the pirha around, sat with his back to the sun and said, 'The poor, ordinary folk of this country will provide you refuge. However, even the British government is quaking at the sight of the hot-blooded young Burmese rebels. Who are we then? Have you tried talking to the young men in the village?' Ba-Mao halted briefly. 'Nungnao came last night. He knows the whereabouts and activities of the group. He secretly maintains contact with the Kempeitais.[6] It will be helpful to follow his counsel. We old men have no say in this.'

'Gusenpung said that there is no need for poor farmers like us to flee. The anger of the rebels is apparently against the Chettiars' Ramgobinda said.

'Gusenpung is a fool; don't place too much trust on his words' Ba-Mao said. 'These times are evil. Since the fires have already started, it's going to consume everything in its path, from tall banyan trees to small grasslands. The Burmese households in Manku are probably going to provide you refuge for now, but no one knows what they will do once the Japanese or the Burmese nationalists arrive here. Our lives will be on line as we will be dubbed enemies of the nation. The entire country is a nest of rebels…who will stand up to save these few families? The Kempeitais will come, the Japanese will come, the band of rebels will arrive. We will be left high and dry. How do you avoid stepping on such unwanted territory?'

---

6 The Kempeitais were the secret military police of the Imperial Japanese Army. Their role is comparable to the Gestapo.

'What do the Kempeitais do?'

'Don't even ask. They are the secret police assisting the rebel group. The Burmese who haven't joined the rebels quake in fear at the mere mention of their name. They have spread sheer terror across the country through their inhuman acts of torture. Although many ordinary Burmese may want to provide refuge to the Indians, they fear to do anything openly and go against the Japanese or the rebels because of this group. These people have unlimited power and ability to create a situation of chaos and disorder. Ordinary people close their eyes and ears and are forced to give way to them because of fear of the beastly torture that they can unleash. Therefore, there isn't even a smidgeon of hope that an Indian will get refuge in the house of a Burmese.'

'Think about what I said', Ba-Mao said after an interval of silence. 'Leave Burma while you still have time...for the well-being of yourself and others. Maybe you can hide in the forests for a while and return once all these troubles have settled down. But it's extremely doubtful that you will find the promise of safety and security here in the future', Ba-Mao pressed his chest with his hands after speaking for a long time without a break.

'We will die in the jungle as food for tigers and leopards, we will die here as prey for Japanese bullets and bayonets. Is there any difference between escaping and staying put for us?'

'Maybe there is no difference. But the fact is that if you escape, there is a greater chance for survival. You won't have that assurance here. People like us survive almost exclusively on this sliver of hope; otherwise, we would have been swallowed by the flow of time a long while ago' Ba-Mao said. 'Actually, we cannot stop death when it arrives. However, we struggle on with the hope that somehow we can straggle and survive for a few more days. There is no end to pain and suffering in our lives, but do we ever agree to embrace death out of our own volition?'

'Hmm…there seems to be no other alternative', Ramgobinda said. 'Since trouble has already arrived at the doorstep, either we have to stave it by escaping or jump and immolate ourselves in the raging fire.'

Nungnao had just made his entrance through the long alley. The young, healthy-looking Nungnao was dressed in long trousers and a Hawaiian shirt, much like a sahib. He had a thin mustache and was smiling. The eyes beneath the thin eyebrows were alert and shining. His smooth, long hair was brushed backwards and beads of sweat were visible on his brow. Wiping the sweat with his handkerchief, Nungnao reached the courtyard.

Ramgobinda and Ba-Mao silently welcomed Nungnao with warm smiles. Nungnao bowed his head respectfully in Ba-Mao's direction, then turned to Ramgobinda and said, 'I've just come from your place. Father said that you wanted to meet me?'

V

Rangobinda was about to say something when Ba-Mao raised his hand and stopped him and began addressing Nungnao.

'What sort of agitation is this that you young men have begun?' Ba-Mao asked. 'You have sowed the seeds of division between elder and younger brothers by allying with the Japanese. The country will go to the dogs if you summon danger inside your house like this. Will the Japanese be the saviours of this fractured country that lacks a backbone?'

Nungnao's demeanor suddenly became grave. His smile disappeared. Placing his hands in the pockets of his trousers with contempt and disgust writ large on his face, he stood up straight with a defiant gaze and said, 'It's not true that we didn't have a backbone; we had one. It was smashed into smithereens in your day. We are simply trying to suture it again. It will take another hundred years to drive the British from Burmese soil if we don't take the help of a stronger power.'

'Hundred years is nothing in the history of a race', Ba-Mao smiled in a conciliatory fashion to lighten the atmosphere. 'People have been struggling for thousands of years. We lost our freedom because of our own faults. But, the same faults for which we lost our freedom still inhabit the pores of our being. If we don't get rid of those faults first…'

'But, this is a golden opportunity to drive out the British, my dear uncle. Such an opportunity may not come our way for the next hundred years' Nungnao said. 'They are being pressured from all sides by this world war. If we can drive them out now, either by force or by stratagem, then it won't take a lot of time for us to tackle the danger that we invited into our households. The whole of Burma is rising. We will never give any leeway to the Japanese to pitch their tents here like you did with the British…be assured of this.'

'You are educated boys with employment. You will certainly understand such complex affairs better. For us impoverished farmers, the problem of somehow procuring one square meal and surviving is paramount. I am simply repeating what I understand with my limited intelligence',

Ba-Mao said, tousling his white hair with his fingers. 'However, these hairs haven't whitened without a reason. Don't disregard them. A domestic quarrel had also broken out in Assam in the older days. The Barphukan enlisted the help of our Shan emperor with the intention of installing a new king. The nation split into fragments as a result.[7] Sensing an opportunity, the British pitched their tents there and have been occupying the royal seat up to this day. Keep these lessons that history belches out in mind… otherwise we will be neither here nor there.'

'There is no point discussing those things', Nungnao looked at Ramgobinda and said. 'Just tell me why you summoned me here?'

'Why do you think we called you?' Ba-Mao said, simultaneously making a clicking sound with his mouth. 'There is talk of uprooting these people from here; please find some means to protect them. The British troops have already begun withdrawing. At the rate at which they are withdrawing, these people will have nowhere to go in a very few days.'

'Is there anything that I can do? I am asking you—the nationalist Burmese have woken up anew; who is going

---

7 Ba-Mao is referring to the actions of Badan Chandra Barphukan, the chief of the Ahom army in Lower Assam, who helped the Burmese during their invasions of Assam. The name of Badan Barphukan is often synonymous with betrayal and treachery in popular narratives in Assam.

to stem this flow?' Nungnao said. 'These are very difficult, intricate affairs. Can a movement against centuries-old injustice and repression be squandered just to protect a few helpless people? Would it be correct to let thousands of guilty people go scot free just to save one innocent person, my dear uncle?' Nungnao's tone was calm and serious. An unknown terror arose in Ramgobinda's mind as he listened to this voice that communicated a steadfast intention.

'Whatever the justification, it behoves you all to consider this matter carefully', Ramgobinda said. 'We have lived together like this from the day we were born. Can you push us into the jaws of certain death in this fashion now?'

'You aren't the only ones assailed by trouble, my friend! We are beset with much more. Just consider this...if every Burmese household in every village provides refuge to the Indians, wouldn't it thwart our great revolution? Won't the dream of driving out the foreign invaders that inspires each and every nationalist Burmese person be shattered if individual Burmese businessmen provide shelter to the employees of the British companies that they conduct business with? While our goal is a noble one, the road to it is difficult and harsh. We cannot differentiate between self and other, guilty or innocent and rich or poor. If we give even a bit of leeway to compassion, then there is the danger of slipping and losing our way at every step. We...'

'Come on now!' Ba-Mao became impatient, listening to Nungnao's extended oration. This young man may have a small, innocent face, but his pronouncements were so pompous! 'You can only set up your ideal kingdom by throwing out these poor Indian farmers?'

'That isn't the crucial aspect, my dear uncle. The important thing is whom should we keep and whom should we throw out? It will be tantamount to going against the rules and the ideals of the revolution if we provide refuge to a single person, a single family', Nungnao said.

'Why? Those rich Chettiars have already fled. The big officers, the employees of the companies and groups of those greedy businessmen escaped early on and have already reached India. The only ones who remain are these very poor peasants who subsist on the soil. There are lots of gaping holes in the fishing-net of your revolution, my dear boy', Ba-Mao grimaced. 'The big fish have all escaped, the smaller ones are entangled in the net.'

'That is the primary matter', Nungnao argued forcefully. 'We aren't going to stand in the way of anyone who wants to escape. Whoever escapes will be able to preserve their lives. Our goal is to drive foreigners away from Burma. Our struggle doesn't intend to threaten their lives. All they have to do is to get away from here, dead or alive', Nungnao was very agitated now. 'You don't understand, my dear uncle…I am but a tiny spark in this massive revolution.

I don't have any significance, ideals or thoughts that exist independently of the movement. Where does a small, insignificant droplet like me summon the strength or the audacity to withstand the flow of this mad, directionless deluge that has only recently broken through all barriers?'

'Okay, if Jayanao and I provide refuge to the Indian peasants of Manku, how will your band of rebels react?' Ba-Mao asked, peering intently at Nungnao.

'The tremendous surge of the revolution will sweep you away, my dear uncle. These inexorable processes have no compassion or rationality.'

'Can you? Can you do that?' Ba-Mao stood up, trembling with agitation, and then sat down again. 'Will you be able to hack down your old father and me and then throw these poor peasants out?'

'Of course, we can.' There was no sign or agitation or emotion in Nungnao's voice. 'If I won't be able to do it, the others or the Kempeitai will do it.'

'You all are demons, bloodsuckers! You aren't humans!', Ba-Mao said, somehow leaning against the wooden pillar in his verandah. 'You all are bloodsucking vampires misleading people in the name of the revolution. Rules, ideals…these are just empty words! You want to drink fresh blood and create chaos in the name of freedom. Looting and torture are your goals. You are villains wearing the mask of high ideals. You are disgusting beasts that want to create terror in league with the Keimpeitai. It is a sin to even behold your faces. Call it your luck that you aren't my son. If you were, I would have inflicted numerous welts on your body with a knife and applied salt on them. Ugh, your own father…!'

'You misunderstand me, uncle. The older generation is very emotional', Nungnao said in a very calm and composed tone. 'It is Burma's sheer misfortune that every family has ignorant people with no sense of judgement like you all. It is our misfortune that soft, simple people like you who don't listen to any reasoning nurtured us young people like meek, domesticated beasts. You buried our hopes and desires with your faulty education. Because of people like you, every Burmese family is distressed by the agony of oppression and the insulting conditions of poverty.'

'But who are you doing this for? Will you suck the marrow from the bones and enjoy the remains of this country that you will reduce to a graveyard with the help of the Japanese?' Ba-Mao asked.

'We will forge a new Burma for the future. Not a poverty-stricken, emaciated country under someone else's yoke, but an independent, new nation. How long do you expect this race to survive, gasping for breath because of the curses wrought by your superstitions and lack of foresight? We have raised our voices against oppression and torture today. Each educated Burmese youth is like a spark in this raging fire. No one will survive if they stand in the way of this revolution. Old people like you should not misuse the respect, status and empathy that you have enjoyed all these years due to your advanced age', Nungnao was slowly getting more and more agitated. The glare created by great anger and pride seemed to shine brightly on his blood-red face in the harsh sunlight. His eyes were ablaze.

'Your path is still cruel, inhuman', Ba-Mao said after staying patient for a while. 'It's not enough to set goals alone. One has to forge the correct path for it too. You are searching for peace, but follow the path of violence; you want to reconstruct by traveling down the pathway of destruction. You are dragging this unfortunate nation to ruin in alliance with the Japanese.'

'Who is responsible for that? You are responsible for the unfortunate predicament of this nation…' Nungnao wagged his finger at Ba-Mao and said. 'You bunch of old men have endowed us only with superstitions and flabby customs. The lord of death gave you an invitation and then abandoned you on the way. Foreigners did not dare to cast eyes on this land before your generation took root. They were never able to run rampant earlier. Do you remember, my dear uncle, the punishment that your grandfathers meted out to that Portuguese gun-runner De Brito when he dared to attempt to set up a kingdom in the Bo Cho island near Rangoon?[8] He was impaled on a stake at the foot of the Syriam hill and died after three days squirming in pain all the while. While he screamed "water, water" in extreme agony after the spears had pierced his sides, the bystanders put a bowl of water just out of his reach and laughed mockingly at his futile attempts to reach it. Such was an example of the entertainment that Burma in the older days received from opportunistic foreigners. And today? All of you laid out the red carpet and welcomed the British. You plunged the country into darkness. You frittered away the legacy of the ages in just a day…All of you should be punished!' Nungnao was now trembling in anger.

Supporting himself against the pillar with both hands, Ba-Mao kept staring fixedly at the ground. Only for an instant did he look up with the mute, piteous gaze of an innocent prisoner who had just been condemned by the judgement of a partisan judge. Then he again lowered his gaze. There was no defiance in Ba-Mao's look. It wasn't an angry or censorious gaze either. His melancholic gaze was clouded by the accumulated strands of disgust and contempt. That gaze of Ba-Mao's destroyed Nungnao's excitement and bombast in an instant. It was as if wild

---

8 Felipe de Brito e Nicote was a Portuguese mercenary in Burma during 1599-1613. He was executed by the forces of King Anaukpetlun in 1613.

savagery withered under the glare of that contemptuous gaze of humanness.

Breaking himself away from that piercing gaze, Nungnao calmly addressed Ramgobinda who was waiting nearby like a beast that had been dragged to the slaughterhouse, 'You are like an intimate family member to me, almost like my elder brother. I am sure you came here expecting some help from me. But my hands are tied. I can't do anything for you. You have to escape. Escape to the hills and the forests while you still have time. Don't look back even once. Burma will not provide you any refuge. Only the future will decide who is guilty. Most probably none of us will be alive to see that day. But please flee now for the welfare of everyone. My heart breaks bidding you farewell from Manku. I would love to see you stay on in Manku peacefully and with security. But the revolutionary nation bids you farewell…so please leave.' Nungnao turned his head away towards the granary, wiped the few tears that appeared in his eyes, and without looking at anyone began to slowly walk down the long pathway that led towards Ba-Mao's house.

VI

The day was unbearably hot. It looked as if the sun wanted to gobble up the earth in these last days of April. The shimmering water playfully reflected the swirling winds moving up layer by layer in the harsh light of the scorching sun. The harsh howling sound of the dry, hot wind was heard everywhere. Swirling clouds of dust accompanied these howls. The sky in May, the wind, the earth—everything seemed cruel, lifeless. The sand from the banks were blown away by the spiraling winds and deposited in the heart of the feeble currents of the emaciated Irrawaddy. The heat spread through each and every nook and corner of the country much akin to those fine granules of dust that settled everywhere.

From the time the war began, the Indian farmers from Manku had gathered in the cramped verandah of Ballabh's shop at dusk and discussed various aspects of the current situation, and also about their troubled present and their uncertain future. Normally, the topics of conversation included the news and rumours about the war that was spreading like wildfire through all the villages nearby. Other than Chinti, Budhu and Haricharan the young, old and middle-aged farmers of the village did not have any extended period of contact with the wider world for all these years. However, this war had suddenly stoked their interest in the outside world. Of late, a couple of daily newspapers that carried frightening pictures of the war began circulating. Most of them were in English and some in Burmese. Reading and tying together some of these sections and attempting to guess what happened in the rest, the group seriously discussed some of these fantastic and semi-fictional scenarios. Occasionally, Nitu would come from Mandalay. He often had some fresh news to report. He inflated the numbers of refugees he saw on the way at least ten-fold. That's why the conversation would take an interesting turn when he arrived. For a few days in the beginning, the discussions were quite frivolous and gossipy. Everyone enjoyed listening to these tales of horror and terror with a smile on their faces. Soon, the events reported became increasingly more serious and critical. The native Burmese had begun to cast an evil eye on the Indians in Burma. The British army began retreating progressively.

The Japanese kept advancing and the daily exchange of ordinary stories and information among the peasants of the small village called Manku, who gathered in the verandah of the shop smoking their bidis at the end of the day, began to assume a darker and more serious hue. The smiles on the faces of the people rapidly disappeared and the veins on their foreheads began to throb. Dark thoughts entered their minds. For the past month, their conversations were coloured by anxiety and fear.

Occasionally Ramgobinda also ventured towards Ballabh's shop in the all-enveloping darkness, wrapping his red *gamocha* over his vest. A spirited and loud discussion was taking place today among the people seated on a long bench in the verandah of the shop illuminated by the flickering light of a cheerless hurricane lamp. Nitu was visiting the shop after quite an interval. Everyone was questioning him eagerly. In the midst of the heated discussion, Ramgobinda silently entered and, unnoticed by anyone, sat on the bench.

'Apparently Jagat Chettiar of Rangoon has fled', Ballabh said. Jagat Chettiar was the shining light of the Indian community in Burma, its virtual backbone. He was one of the richest landlords in the country. Ninety per cent of the farmlands in the islands near Rangoon were owned by him. Jagat Chettiar was the kingpin of the trade in rice imports from Burma.

'He left a long time ago; sometime at the beginning of March' Nitu said. 'What could he have done? Rangoon was infested with Japanese. It was impossible to escape to Chittagong or Calcutta by sea. The Japanese had also set up bases on the road leading towards Akyab. Somehow Jagat Chettiar reached Manaut island in a fishing boat and escaped on a ship from there.'

'What wealth he had! What a massive business empire he owned!...and what did he carry with him?' Haricharan asked.

'Nothing, nothing! He was forced to leave everything behind' Nitu said. 'As if he had earned all that money with the sweat of his brow!'

'He amassed all that wealth sucking the blood of poor people like us...', Budhu chimed in.

'Forget about all that wealth, business and property. We have to preserve our lives first and then think about all that' Nitu said. 'All the family members of the Chettiar have escaped. They didn't even have time to withdraw their money from the bank. They escaped carrying whatever they had at hand. They have entrusted the rest of the property to one of their adoptive nephews.'

'The curses of the people have finally taken effect. All the sins they accumulated from their practices of usury and charging interest caught up with them' the aged Haricharan said. 'They lost everything while they are still alive, what will they carry with them when they are dead?'

'I heard that there are a lot of people from our community in Rangoon. Did the Chettiars still have to escape?' Chinti asked.

'What else could they have done but escape? The British are about to leave. Once they vacate this territory, the simmering resentment of the Burmese will be unleashed and wreak havoc on the Indians.'

'They have such a lot of money and so many people with them. However, if they have to escape despite all that, then what will become of the others?' Kalu queried.

'Can we follow the coastline and get to Chittagong via Cox's Bazaar nowadays?' Ballabh asked. He was a businessman and was naturally very practical.

'That road closed a long while ago. A lot of poor people have already escaped via that route. On the other hand, we will have to walk a long way if we escape via Prome' Nitu said.

'Rich people don't take that route. Besides, there are military checkpoints at every step—they use force, check you repeatedly. Very inconvenient!'

'If we can somehow preserve our lives and cross the forbidding hills of the Arakan Yoma and reach Taungup, then maybe we can cross over to the other side?' Ballabh speculated.

'Maybe' Nitu thought for a moment and said. 'From

there, we can hire some fishing boats that can take us to Chittagong. But it's no joke crossing the Arakan hills. Almost a third of us will have to be abandoned on the way.'

'Have a lot of people escaped already?' Ramgobinda's question, posed after he followed the conversation silently for a while, made him appear like an idiot. Immediately, seven pairs of eyes glared at him.

'Where were you all this while?' Ballabh said mockingly. 'From what I've heard, there aren't any Indians in Burma other than a few in some scattered, remote villages like ours.'

'It seems the clock is ticking for us, judging by the way things are going. Ba-Mao said that just a while ago' Budhu said. 'I think it's advisable to begin gathering our odds and ends soon.'

'Okay, you want to leave, but which way do we go?', Nitu looked at Budhu and said. 'The railway line going towards Monywa is now controlled by the Japanese and the Hind Fauj. The trains are now full of their troops. It would have been easy to travel to Imphal via Tamu through that route.'

'It would probably be more advantageous to go towards Akyab' Ballabh said. He was a well-travelled man and was well aware of what was going on in the neighbouring areas. 'Apparently Graham sahib has set up a naval base there.'

'What base? Seems like that won't last very long. Before

the Japanese arrived, only a few motor launches from the Indus and Burma companies guarded the small islands in that region' Nitu replied. 'And even if they are still there, how do you plan to cross the Japanese bases and get to Akyab?'

'There is no road through Arakan?'

'Go there if you want to...you will be obliterated there entirely. The Burmese are lying in wait there. Not only will they loot you, but they will take your lives as well.'

'But, apparently Brown sahib...'

'You must have culled it from those newspapers...don't believe them. Poor Brown sahib does not have any troops with him. He is just a leader in name' Nitu said. 'How can a handful of soldiers who escaped from a Japanese prison guard the road towards Arakan? Those are hilly roads with trouble stalking you in every ridge and gorge. But I have also heard that a lot of refugees escaped through that route. However, it wouldn't be wise to travel through the Arakan, blindly placing all our trust on Brown sahib.'

'Wasn't there a road via Kalewa and Tamu into Manipur? Is that still open or not?'

'I heard that the British have also retreated from Kalewa. It must have fallen to the Japanese already' Nitu said. 'Besides that, how do you plan to ford the Irrawaddy? The Japanese have blown up the bridges. The Burmese and Japanese operate the one or two dinghies that cross the river.'

'What about the planes at Misina[9]...' someone blurted out and immediately bit his tongue.

'Eeh! He wants to fly! Who is the one who wants to fly? Show us your face please', Nitu made a face and said. 'Who has so much wealth in his coffers? Hey, pass me a bidi.'

'I heard that thousands of Indians have massed together in Misina', Ballabh said, passing on a bidi to Nitu. Since he was wealthy, Nitu could not simply ridicule him.

'What do you know? Apparently there is no place to be found in Misina because of the sheer number of rich businessmen, officers and reputed people who have gathered there. Although they have offered large sums of money, they still haven't been able to procure seats in the airplanes.'

'But aren't a number of Douglas planes plying from there?'

'Yes, they were running...they are still running. But those planes cannot carry more than thirty people' Nitu took a prolonged puff on his bidi. 'But I've heard that around seventy to eighty people are crammed into those aircrafts. Even then no one agrees to vacate.'

'Why won't they leave? It's better to die in a plane crash than to meet one's end at the hands of the Japanese or the Burmese.'

---

9 Acharya refers to Myitkyina as Misina throughout the novel. We retain Acharya's usage throughout.

'Furthermore there are only three planes that are operational. Sometimes a wife gets a seat only for the husband to be left behind. Others have to leave their children or their parents behind. The fact is that there is no safety anywhere. We are surrounded by a wildfire on all sides.'

'But why are such huge numbers of people escaping? Are they afraid that the Japanese will massacre them?' Kalu looked at Ballabh.

'You fool, the Japanese won't kill us, but the Burmese will. Have you seen how they sacrifice cows during their festivals? Have you noticed how they drag the living cows to the bamboo groves, chop them up bit by bit and gather and throw them in their wooden platforms? The cow dies slowly squirming in agony, pools of blood lie everywhere…', Ballabh shivered recalling the image. 'The same will happen here very soon as well, just you see.'

'The Indians are fleeing from the cities that are being bombed to the villages. They find no refuge though. The Burmese inflict cruel tortures on them there. People are being killed by the hundreds, their properties are looted indiscriminately.'

Nitu said slowly, 'People are being murdered and robbed on the highway to Rangoon in broad daylight. Adding salt to the wounds, they have also opened the gates of the prisons and the asylums. Lunatics, murderers, thieves and bandits freely roam the streets.'

'Haven't the houses of the Burmese been looted too?' Budhu asked.

'Yes! Many of them are now settling old scores. But the Indians are facing the brunt of the attacks.'

'The Indians came here riding on the tails of the British; now they will depart this land holding on to their tails again' Chinti said.

'What are you saying? We came here to till land. Our people cleared these lands for agriculture, removing the dense foliage from the fertile land and leveling the hilly regions', Ramgobinda said. 'The Burmese took those tracts of land away as well. We laboured day in and day out. What did they do? Did they even preserve it for themselves?'

'They are a worthless, lazy race of people. They pushed away the Lakshmi residing in their hands with their own feet', Ballabh chimed in. 'Once they got the wealth from the agricultural produce, just look at how they squandered it away on drinking and showy feasts. The worthless scum could not rest in peace till they spent all their money. Even after that, they would waste the loans they took after mortgaging their lands and their produce. How long can they consume the produce of a quarter year? That's why they are in a penurious state for the other nine to ten months in a year.'

'Who will till their lands once we leave?' Ramgobinda asked.

'Do they have any land left with them? Most of it is mortgaged anyway.'

'That's the rub—once the Chettiars leave, they will reclaim the lands once again. I mean, they will forcibly take over.'

'Then what's their benefit in chasing us away? We don't own any land' Ramgobinda said.

No one was ready or willing to answer this critical question. Anxiety and terror filled their minds. The terrifying form of a frightening reality danced before their eyes—there was no place for Indians in Burma. That was the cruel truth! Why, how?—discussing these questions was useless. Thousands of Indians had escaped already. If they wanted to preserve their lives, the rest would have to leave too. Although they could reason otherwise, there was nothing more important than this fact right now.

'What do we do now?' Ballabh looked at Nitu and said. 'From the looks of it, almost all the roads and pathways are blocked. On the other hand, we can't waste a lot of time either. What do we do?'

'There is no easy way. To be sure, there is a way into Assam through the triangular region in northern Burma if we manage to ford the Irrawaddy. It's dark even during daytime, a very difficult road going right through dense jungles in the hills that are populated by wild beasts. Maybe we can try to escape through that route although that would be akin to jumping into the fire alive. Somehow, I don't feel that we can get to Assam alive and in one piece' Nitu said.

'That depends on fate. Death is inevitable if we linger here. Whatever it may be, there is at least a miniscule chance that we may survive if we escape from here. From what I gather, it won't be wise to delay our departure further. I don't know what you are thinking, but I think it will be safer for all of us to get away from this place as soon as we can' Ballabh opined. 'And we should all move in a group.'

'Danger will follow us each step of our way. Our courage will increase if we band together. We'll be able to help each other—it's good in that way. But the chances of getting exposed and caught also increase if we move in a group. There is no saying what will happen to us if a Japanese unit camouflaged in the jungle or a Burmese village notice our group' Nitu said.

'We shouldn't carry a lot of stuff. We can hide in the jungle during day and move at night. That will reduce the risk' Chinti said. 'But, does anyone know the roads and pathways?'"

'I know the road up to Lesin. There are secret pathways used by opium smugglers. There are lots of small, nondescript roads there. We will have to walk north' Nitu said. 'I have been that way a couple of times. Only the Irrawaddy stands in the middle. Does anyone have an idea of how we are going to cross it?'

'That's the main problem. We shouldn't leave the village before making foolproof arrangements to cross the Irrawaddy' Haricharan said.

'We are surrounded by rebel encampments. There are lots of hidden Japanese camps along the banks of the Irrawaddy apparently' Nitu said. 'It will be difficult to ford the Irrawaddy if we cannot enlist the help of someone who is in league with the rebels.'

'Nungnao!' Budhu exclaimed. 'We'll have to take Nungnao's help. He is still here, I think…at least till the evening.'

'Will he help us?' Ramgobinda said skeptically. He had lost all his faith in Burmese young men.

'Most probably he won't if we approach him directly; but he might if we approach him through his father', Ballabh said. 'Let's go to Jayanao's house tonight itself. If we meet Nungnao, it's even better. I don't think it will be too difficult to make some arrangements now.'

'When should we start then?' Kalu asked. No one was confused by the drift or the import of this question.

'If we can determine some way of crossing the Irrawaddy, then we should begin our journey tomorrow night. It won't be safe to delay it further' Nitu said. 'I am sure you will all be ready to leave.'

'What options do we have? Who here is not afraid of death?'

'We can leave tomorrow. Let those who want to die remain behind.'

A consensus was reached. Although personal issues clouded everyone's minds, no one demurred. Not a single one of them displayed the courage to embrace certain death by voluntarily stepping away from this group that had determined to flee.

VII

Jayanao was sitting on a murha in one corner of the courtyard of his hut and contemplatively gazing at the sky. The previous night Ballabh, Nitu and four or five other people had come to earnestly request him to talk to Nungnao. They wanted Nungnao to talk to the rebel group to arrange for safe passage across the Irrawaddy. This was a good task—could there be any bigger duty than helping desperate people in times of need? However, the task was also laced with peril. On the other hand, Nungnao was just a young boy and would not be able to explain the situation and clarify all the doubts of the rebel group properly. Riddled with indecision after considering such eventualities, Jayanao tried to stave the group off. However, Nungnao suddenly appeared from somewhere and jettisoned all his plans. He was just a young chap, but he had volunteered to perform such a dangerous task without a moment's hesitation. Of course, Jayanao felt that it was very necessary to perform something like this. But he wished that it weren't Nungnao, but someone else in the line of fire. Conversely, there was no other person in the village who maintained contact with the rebels or understood their patterns of thought. What could they have done even if there was somebody? Who would have the courage to do something like this when the surveillance by the Kempeitai was so stringent? Jayanao's hairs stood on end when the thought of the Kempeitai crossed his mind. He creased his forehead, shielded his eyes and looked at the sun. The sun was high up in the sky, but there was still no sign of the astrologer.

Sick with worry, Jayanao had sent his eldest son to Mandalay during the waning hours of the night to summon the astrologer. He wanted to consult the astrological chart of his younger son, Nungnao, and perform necessary sacrifices or religious ceremonies for his welfare. Although the astrologer said that he would be there before noon, he hadn't arrived as yet, and this made Jayanao anxious. 'Maybe he saw something inauspicious on the way' he comforted himself. These astrologers saw evil omens and ominous signs at all times. They emerged from the peaceful sanctuary of their hermitages to the dangerous environs of the outside world only after they were certain of the calculations predicated on their observations of the activities of the clouds, the change in direction in the winds, and the storms and tempests in the seas. Jayanao once again felt deeply worried.

The only reason for Jayanao's worry was Nungnao. Although he was a farmer's son, he was educated and had left for the town with a job in tow. That was the source of all the troubles. They owned some land, a few heads of cattle and a decent house. It was enough for them. They could labour in the fields and were guaranteed two good meals a day. Instead of doing that, what was the need to leave for the town and live in a dark, dust-infested room? In any case, the earnings from the job weren't enough. He came back to the village every month for money. Reflecting on Nungnao's way of life, Jayanao felt the youth of today were worthless sluggards. They wanted to earn a lot in a short span of time and were attracted to wealth that could be procured without expending a lot of effort. Pale, unhealthy-looking people wearing gaudy clothes and exercising their pens in their offices were the models they wanted to emulate. Hardworking, healthy farmers were objects of contempt for them. Jayanao's conservative mindset was affronted while contemplating this degenerated pattern of thinking common amongst the emerging generation of Burmese youth.

Of course, at this advanced age, Jayanao wasn't supportive of the way of life adopted by the ordinary. Burmese folk either. The wealth and mode of life squandered on alcohol, gambling and feasting were meaningless. A lot of wealth was necessary to organise showy drinking jousts and public feasts. For lazy and improvident people, gambling was the only way to amass such wealth. That's why the lives of the superstitious, fatalistic Burmese were akin to a game of roulette. There was no realistic solution to any of their problems. They left everything to fate and fortune and squandered their time and resources on gambling and other pleasures. They rushed to the gambling den as soon as some money fell into their hands. They would gamble away even the silk lungi they wore and then survive hand to mouth consuming cheap, plain *ahu* rice with servings of foul-smelling dried fish. After that, they would mortgage their lands and produce to the Chettiars and take loans from them. Then they would once again buy expensive and colourful silk lungis and wear flashy watches on their wrists and shiny rings on their fingers. Once again they would head to the gambling dens...During the prime of his youth Jayanao too partook of such pleasures. However, after he lost all his land and holdings, a deep sense of disgust against such a wasteful mode of existence took root in his mind. Jayanao was fortunate—he was able to extricate himself pretty early.

However, Jayanao didn't have to worry excessively about Nungnao during the early days of the latter's employment. At least he was occupied by something and was safe and secure in a way. But, Jayanao's sleep had been troubled for the last few months after he learned that Nungnao had left his job and joined a band of nationalist rebels. The rebellion meant going against the British by allying with the Japanese. That was no ordinary matter. Jayanao did not have even a smidgeon of identification or sympathy for this band of young men who raised slogans like 'Free Burma *Zindabad!*' against the all-conquering British and also assisted the cruel, inhuman Kempeitai. But still Nungnao was his own son—he couldn't simply abandon him. On the one hand, he was a young, innocent boy; on the other, he had jumped into a blazing fire driven by the hot-bloodedness of youth and misguided by the temptations offered by wicked men. There was no saying when he would fall into the jaws of terrible danger...that was the old man's primary worry. Muttering 'she forced him on the wrong path by educating him', he once again cursed his dead wife.

Someone appeared at the end of the long pathway when the sun was at its highest point in the sky. Although he couldn't discern who it was with his failing vision, Jayanao guessed that it must be the astrologer. His head was tonsured, his visage pale, his arms bare, and a yellow cloth was wrapped around his hands. The astrologer slowly approached the courtyard with a begging bowl in his hands, his almanacs safely ensconced under his armpits. Jayanao wiped a spot in the courtyard with the corner of his lungi, very courteously invited the astrologer to sit there, and cast a hopeful gaze on his face.

The pupils of the eyes of the lean and muscular astrologer were shining like stars. Looking up at the ravenous face of the sun right above him, he said, 'I understand your state of mind. But there are lots of obstacles in the distant future. Whatever may lie ahead, please give me your son's almanac. I need to check it carefully'.

Jayanao went inside and emerged with a thick, rectangular sheet of paper. There were a lot of circles, diagrams and scribblings in Burmese on that sheet. The astrologer peered at it carefully, plotted a few conical diagrams on the floor and remained silent for a while.

'Seems like the young man in question hasn't received any sustained training in a Buddhist religious institution for more than a year…' the astrologer suddenly shot a questioning glance in Jayanao's direction.

'No!' Jayanao was startled. 'His mother was alive at that time. He is our youngest child, hence, she showered a lot of affection on him. She created a huge ruckus when I planned to subject him to the harsh discipline, austere meditative practices and system of order in the monastery. There was a lot of tension in the household. I had to enroll him in a school as per her wishes. I wasn't very willing to do that. However, when she was alive, my opinions on such matters did not carry much weight.'

Jayanao's eldest daughter-in-law offered the astrologer some betel leaves on a plate. Removing the covering of one of the betel nuts, the astrologer said, 'It is a matter of great sorrow that the young man isn't well versed in traditional mores. His body and mind today are the fruits of his karma of his previous life; in other words, the baneful influence of all his faults, troubles, physical illnesses and his ten punishments persist in this life.'

'What options do we have now? What happened earlier is gone. Please tell me what sort of rituals or sacrifices you would prescribe to stave off these evil influences' Jayanao asked, secretly beginning to curse his wife again.

'The sins of people in close contact with foreigners have infiltrated the body of the young man' the astrologer creased his forehead and concentrated on a few signs drawn on the floor. 'Although these people have been reborn in human guise, the education and behavior they have imbibed from the foreigners have reduced them to the level of beasts.'

'But aren't these foreigners human as well?' Jayanao queried.

'Inhuman, inhuman! Although these people look human, they actually are vile creatures assuming the guise of human beings. Actually, only the residents of this vast, circular Burma of ours are truly human. The Arakan pagoda and the holy pilgrimage sites strewn across Burma are the nerve centers of this hallowed circle. Other than the inhabitants of this hallowed territory, no one else can claim to be fully human.' The astrologer paused a while, munched a betel nut and resumed again. 'All this is mentioned in our sacred texts—to the north of this hallowed circle are the all-sovereign Himalayas; the kingdom of the nymphs lie on the other side. Mount Meru and other magnificent peaks are located at the crest of this region. This locale is also the origin of the four great rivers: the Irrawaddy, the Chindwin, the Menam and the Mekong. Then there is the great ocean to the south with five hundred islands in it. A few beings lower in status than the human reside there. Therefore, we are the true human beings and our learning, manners and traditions are the true wonders of humankind. Of course, you aren't guaranteed the status of being human just because you are born in Burma. You have to follow the commandments of the Tathagatha, perform all the traditions enunciated in the holy books and spend a portion of one's life in the monasteries. A child is elevated to the status of a human being only by performing such consecrated activities.'

Jayanao was restless. 'Now please tell me what will happen to my boy. There is no end to my worries otherwise' he said.

'Baneful influences abound in this almanac. If these aren't staved off following the prescribed rules, great harm should be anticipated.' Jayanao's heart skipped a beat when he heard the astrologer's pronouncements. 'Harmful influences orbit and criss-cross his guiding stars....what is the young man doing now?'

'That is what I am really worried about. He completed his education and was employed as a clerk in a trading firm in Mandalay. He used to draw a monthly salary. Although his salary wasn't enough, he managed to get by somehow. He would occasionally ask me for money as well and stay in the city. Sometimes he would come home. That's how life went on. The demon entered his mind a few months ago. He left his job and joined the rebels. Young men have formed this group to eject the British. On the other hand, the war also began. There seemed to be no end to the chaos, uncertainty and troubles in this country. In this uncertain situation, this slip of a boy has caused me no end of trouble. Apparently they have allied with the Japanese. Please show me some way out of this.' Jayanao cradled his head in his hands and looked hopefully at the astrologer.

'These are dark days. The public has slipped away from the righteous path of religion and have instead turned their minds to violence, strife and war', the astrologer replied. 'No one seems to remember the Tathagata's teachings.' He kept looking at the almanac for a while and calculated something with the tips of his fingers, resembling an incorporeal statue in the blazing afternoon heat.

'Where is the boy?' the astrologer raised his head from

the almanac suddenly, startling Jayanao once again.

'He is here for the moment. Why? What happened?' Jayanao was discomfited. 'He just got home yesterday.'

'The signs are not very propitious. According to the almanac, the young man will be incapacitated by a terrible head wound that he will sustain in the coming days' the astrologer said. 'We have to take the proper measures to stave off this terrible eventuality without delay.'

Jayanao was stunned and kept staring at the astrologer.

'I will perform a ritual offering at the Arakan pagoda. You will also have to offer a gold flower weighing seven *ratis* to the idol of the *Mahamuni*. It will be a full moon night day after tomorrow...that will be an auspicious day. In the meantime, it wouldn't be advisable for the young man to step outside the house. Danger will shadow him everywhere.'

The astrologer suddenly stood up grasping the betel nuts and leaves arranged before him and said, 'Don't worry! Everything will go smoothly by the grace of the Lord Buddha'. He began to walk away slowly with measured, contemplative steps.

'Who was that?' Nungnao asked emerging from inside, looking at the retreating figure of the astrologer who had reached the doorway by now.

'The astrologer was here. He examined your almanac. These are evil days—we have to stave their baneful influence. You should stay here for a few days. Don't go outside at least till the ritual offering at the pagoda is done and over with', Jayanao said, looking at his motherless, hirsute son with a lot of affection.

'Forget about that! These are all superstitions and irrational practices. You and your band of old men can keep your faith in those. I have work to do and have to leave... today!' Nungnao retorted.

'You cannot leave. You can't go anywhere these next few days. Tell me, what is that great thing that you have to do now?' Jayanao asked.

'It is something big. I have to leave...right now...today!'

'Tell me, what do you intend to do?'

'There is a meeting at the school building in Mitukan. I want to try and save the Indian families' Nungnao said. 'Otherwise their death is inevitable. They won't be able to escape their fate.'

'You gave them your word suddenly last night without thinking of the consequences. But, will they agree? If they don't, what can you do alone?'

'I don't know if they will agree. But I can at least try.'

'What is the use?' A jolt passed through Jayanao's heart as he realised that his worst fears were coming true. He looked at Nungnao and continued, 'What is the point of setting sail against the current of an onrushing flood? Both the boat and the boatman will drown'. Jayanao's voice trailed away weakly.

'I have given them my word, father. Please don't stop me. I have a lot of responsibilities for the national cause. But these people, who have been belched out as undesirables by the nation, are also my own. I feel responsible for them too. They are facing great difficulty now. Can I just relax here now on the advice of your astrologer?' Nungnao said. 'Haven't I grown up in the laps and shoulders of these people? Why, when the Irrawaddy flooded, didn't the old Haricharan carry me daily on his shoulders to the school in Mitukan? Didn't Kalu box me in the ears and drag me before you when he caught me smoking a bidi at Ballabh's shop? I still remember mother repeating till her dying days that Ramgobinda delivered milk from his house to ours when I was an infant...This is the major limitation of you old men, father. You forget the past very easily.' Nungnao bent down, touched his father's feet and then looked up with tears brimming in his eyes. 'Please forgive me, father. I am going to perform a good deed. Please bless me so that I can perform my responsibilities well and set my conscience forever at ease. I am their only remaining hope. If I shatter their expectations, I will repent this action for the rest of my life.'

Jayanao was struck dumb with grief and pain and offered no reply. Nungnao departed. After staring for a long while in his direction with his aged eyes, Jayanao wiped away a couple of tears and stepped inside.

VIII

It wasn't easy to escape in a group with all their belongings in tow when they were in a place that was surrounded on all sides by hawk-eyed enemies. For fear of their enemies, the Indians could not approach any of the large cities or towns either. They also had to carefully keep away from the numerous Burmese villages strewn all across the road. No one could be trusted in this imploding country. Moreover, it was a group full of women, children and old people. The denizens of Manku were distressed and petrified by the prospect of traversing densely forested areas. But there was no other alternative and no time left either.

The Indian families from Manku were supposed to begin their unprecedented journey on foot that night. Since the morning, everyone was dejectedly occupied in arranging the few objects and trinkets that remained with them for the journey. There was no order in the arrangement—they took whatever they could. There was no certainty about what they would need on this unknown road. Even a tiny object could prove of immense value during the journey. On the other hand, carrying lots of objects with them would prove to be a difficult proposition during the journey on that endless, terrible road. They put their clothing and a few handful of rice in their bags and boxes. Everything had to go in a single box. It wasn't possible to take utensils with them. They sewed the few ornaments they had and a little bit of money to their clothes. It wasn't safe to travel with jewelry on their bodies. They packed rice in the remaining free spaces inside their boxes. Although this would increase the weight tremendously, rice was essential. In Ramgobinda's house, Thanu tried to sneak in a couple of his toys, but had to throw them away in the courtyard after he was scolded by his father. Ramgobinda's mother got some betel nuts and bamboo shoots in a small cloth bag and tied it around her waist. The old woman wanted to pack all her stuff from her granary and her kitchen. Ramgobinda was flabbergasted to see the empty cans, bottles and even pieces of tattered cloth that she had gathered in a pile before it was morning.

'Why have you collected all these? Who is going to shoulder their burden in the hills?', he asked.

'These are things of everyday use' his mother said,

casting a melancholic gaze on the pile of objects.

'I understand that; but how do you plan to take them?' Ramgobinda turned his head the other way after casting a glance at the pile of objects that his mother had painstakingly collected bit by bit over the years. 'We are supposed to escape through the forests like a band of thieves....' Sensing that his mother was deeply hurt, he kept quiet.

'Forget these unnecessarily heavy objects', he thundered again, noticing Lacchmi coming out with a brass vessel in her hands. 'Just pack a set of clothes, a few warm blankets and your earrings in the box. Take as much rice as you can manage. That will be our true saviour on the road.'

'This is the ritual vessel from our wedding', Lacchmi said, her eyes welling with tears.

'Dump it!' Ramgobinda looked at Lacchmi with irritation. 'What will happen? Something inauspicious? What could be more inauspicious than what is happening now?' He snatched the vessel from Lacchmi's hands and flung it away. Lacchmi wiped away her tears with her aasol, and went inside weeping.

Ramgobinda felt very bad. He had never spoken to Lacchmi in this fashion in the nine or ten years of their marriage. 'Even if we manage to survive, these things will be of no use for us, my darling.' He entered the room after her, held her by her shoulders and tried to console her. 'Burdens—heavy loads are nothing but impediments. We have endured nothing else in life', he sighed. Tears began streaming from his eyes.

'But that's the ritual vessel from our wedding. The same ritual vessel where we took our vows before the holy fire…'

'Don't be so stubborn, Lacchmi' Ramgobinda said, tenderly caressing her body. 'My real wealth is you, Thanu and the other one growing in your womb. All I want is to keep all of you safe and close to me. We will be able to get many vessels like this later.'

Lacchmi was sniffling. Her face was covered by her aasol and her entire being was trembling.

'A lot remains to be done. There is no time for crying now', Ramgobinda said in a tender, loving voice. 'Come… let's get going.'

In the meantime, Thanu arrived on the scene from somewhere dragging the kitten along with him.

'We will take Mini along' he demanded, and noticing Ramgobinda's swollen eyes began providing reasons. 'I mean, she will go by herself, side by side with us.' Ramgobinda looked at the kitten from the corner of his eye and went out without saying anything.

The old woman was tying up mounds of rice and other foodstuff in an old sari in the courtyard, muttering something and cursing continuously. Jayanao's elder son, Bunsanmao, was walking down the pathway and entered the house.

'The escape route is very treacherous and difficult' he said, surveying the pile of objects in the courtyard. 'Nungnao said that Japanese soldiers or Burmese bandits reign everywhere. Now that the bridge over the Irrawaddy has been destroyed, the nationalist rebels are crossing the river from the wharf at Ava' he sighed. 'Nungnao left for some meeting just a while ago. Father is very worried as well…who knows what will happen.'

Although he pretended he had heard nothing, disgust and anger filled Ramgobinda's mind. The parasites of murder and cruelty had lodged themselves in the blood of ordinary Burmese village folk after they had partaken of the taste of banditry. He was searching for a way out of this *sakrabehu*[10] of death. He needed to find some means whereby he could preserve the lives of his loved ones in exchange of all that he managed to save after a lifetime of expending sweat and hard labour.

'It must be good for all of you. This house and property, these farm animals, all this property will all turn over to your hands overnight', he looked at the pile of objects and said resentfully, as waves of sorrow pounded against his chest.

Bunsanmao understood the terror and pain these people were experiencing very well. He was a peasant

10 The reference obviously is to the *chakravyuha* from the *Mahabharata*.

himself. Peasants were symbols of peace and creation; they were used to hard labour and a mundane existence. It had occurred to him once that giving these poor, harried people a place of refuge and assuming responsibility for them was his sacred duty. But he was a simple, unsophisticated, illiterate peasant who did not understand the complexities of modern life. Such responsibilities were beyond his ken. Staring at Ramgobinda with a helpless, mute gaze, he slowly began making his way out. He couldn't articulate the words he had intended to say formed by the raging storms assailing his mind. A reality exceeding his limited experience and the poverty of his language combined together to bury those words in the recesses of his mind forever.

Tears began welling up in Ramgobinda's eyes again when he noticed the cows and the dry hay placed in the troughs in the shed during this peak period of the afternoon. 'You won't have any owners from now on', he whispered in the ears of the white bull and looked at the curved plough slung on the wall above. Expending a lot of energy, he had made the plough himself a few months earlier, geared towards this year's harvest. Short stalks of rice were hanging in some small containers. 'All my hopes died even before they sprouted…', he could not restrain himself any longer and began bawling loudly. All the fantasies of green, lush fields he would tend to in the future receded before his eyes. Everything that he saw in front of him had assumed a terrifying hue and seemed to be preparing to swallow him whole.

Lacchmi entered the kitchen and tied a substantial quantity of flattened rice in a bundle. She was primarily worried about Thanu. In an unsteady manner, the old woman packed a few shiny bottles that she had stored for a long time and a picture of Radha-Krishna along with a few old clothes. 'These will be very heavy', Ramgobinda said as he was passing by. 'This is the picture of the god of our clan. We have to take it with us' the old woman blurted. 'That's fine, it can come with me. You don't have to carry this burden.' The old woman took out the bottles from her bag and very lovingly arranged them in a corner of the verandah as if she would be able to take them back once she returned after a few days. She twirled the bisonis that she had made herself for the scorching summer heat around a few times, and then kept them back from where she had taken them. Her cloudy eyes moistened, hurt by some unspeakable pain.

'I leave you to your own fates from today', Ramgobinda fed the cows some dry hay and opened their binds. 'You are as unfortunate as us', he whispered in their ears. 'God will protect you.' Sorrow overtook Ramgobinda again when he noticed that the cows were standing in the same positions, gazing at him with blank stares that understood nothing of what he said. He drove them out from their sheds and kept looking at their direction for a while.

Jayanao and Ba-Mao visited the houses of everyone in the evening and bade them farewell. Neither of them expressed any sorrow nor shed a single tear. Keeping their raging emotions and inner pain in check with unnatural fortitude, they imparted some warnings and advice about the troubles they might encounter on the treacherous, forested pathway.

'This land and property belongs to you all from now on', Ramgobinda said in a mocking tone. 'We will never come back to claim our share from you.' Tears were welling in Jayanao and Ba-Mao's eyes. They hastily took a betel-nut laid out in the old woman's *bota* and left.

The sun was slowly beginning to set in the west which meant that there were only a few hours left. In the meantime, everyone in the neighbourhood seemed to be ready for the journey. Everyone had packed their very ordinary possessions and was waiting with an uneasy apprehension for the precise moment when their journey on an unknown road without a destination would begin. Nitu was the only guide, a veritable walking stick for the blind, for this group about to embark on a journey to their motherland, India, a place they did not know at all.

Evening set in. The appointed hour came and went. Nitu still hadn't arrived. The group of sixteen people with their boxes and belongings were waiting with bated breath behind Ballabh's shop in the steadily descending darkness. Thanu was sitting atop one of the boxes with the kitten in his lap. As soon as Ramgobinda glanced in his direction, he tightened his hold on the kitten, ran to the other side and waited in the darkness.

The people began discussing some random stuff to relieve the tension created by their doubts and apprehensions.

'Apparently, something very interesting happened the other day…on the day the refinery in Rangoon was set on fire', Chinti tried to spice up his narration of something he had heard about a month ago when he was working as a hired hand in Mandalay. 'It was around dusk. Suddenly the houses shook with something that sounded like the combination of a thousand thunderbolts. Immediately, the place lit up. People and animals began running helter-skelter thinking that some great apocalypse was at hand. The spires of two pagodas toppled over at the same time. After that, a lot of noise, a lot of fire! There was chaos everywhere. Some thieves and bandits, however, took advantage of this moment.'

'They must surely have looted the houses of the Indians', Budhu asked.

'For thieves and bandits, Indians and Burmese are the same', Chinti said. 'I heard that maximum looting occurred in the large shops owned by the Chinese.'

It was getting difficult to bide the time with such chatter. As the darkness steadily became denser, clouds of uncertainty and panic slowly enveloped their minds.

'Eeh! It is almost seven', Ballabh took out his wristwatch from his pocket and peered at it in the dim light of the lamp. 'It seems Nitu won't arrive today.'

Everyone turned pale and began fearing the worst, once the possibility that Nitu may not arrive was broached.

'Who knows where he is stuck in these evil times?' someone said.

'*Arre*, he has to leave with us too. How will he leave if he doesn't accompany us?' Chinti replied.

'Still, since he hasn't arrived yet, what do we do?', Ballabh said, as if talking to himself. Although everyone heard his query, no one was in any position to provide an answer.

'Since we are all ready to leave, we *have* to leave now', Kalu said.

'We have very little time', Ramgobinda interjected. He was a man of few words and spoke only when necessary.

'I think it would be best if we began our journey', the shopkeeper Ballabh said. 'Come, let's leave.' It seemed like he didn't quite grasp the implications of what he was saying. Thinking that decisions needed to be taken in moments of crisis, he spoke up as if he were the operator of a machine. Automatically, the rest of the group immediately lifted their boxes and belongings and stood up ready to leave. It was as if they were expectantly waiting precisely for such instructions for a while. Leaders emerge in this fashion during such moments of uncertainty.

At the last moment, Nitu arrived on the scene. 'The Japanese have broken through the lines and are advancing on Mandalay', he said. 'They will be there in a day or two at most. They bombed Mandalay in the afternoon.'

'Where did you go? Why were you so late?' although Ballabh heaved a sigh of relief when Nitu arrived, he showed no particular interest in the news about the Japanese advance. 'We felt like we have grown old waiting for you so long.'

'That's what I was saying. The bridge over the Irrawaddy has been destroyed by the bombing. Now the boats are being operated from the wharf by Burmese who are sympathetic to the Japanese.'

'We knew that from yesterday', Ballabh grimaced and said.

'How will we escape from here then?' Chinti asked.

'That's the big problem. The Japanese have set base in Misina. The eastern banks of the Irrawaddy are now under Japanese control. The route to Sagaing is blocked. Therefore, we have to cross the Irrawaddy at the nearest point as quickly as possible. After that, we have to keep moving upstream…'

'Are there no Japanese on the western banks?', Budhu asked.

'Yes, there are. They have a base in the banks of the Kalewa. Apparently the Tamu-Manipur road will get blocked soon as well', Nitu said. 'We have to head north after we get to the western banks—to Indawgyi via Shwebo and Unthaw', Nitu halted for a bit. 'Only if that road hasn't fallen to the Japanese by now…'

'Is there any chance that it will fall?' Gurcharan asked.

'That possibility is always there. However, I've heard that there is no Japanese patrol there, only tall hills and dense jungle on all sides. Therefore, they don't see the necessity of guarding that region.'

'So tell us which road you think is best for us now?', Ballabh asked.

'First we will go to Unthaw via Shwebo. We will reach an allied camp there. We will have to take some help from them. I don't know the road beyond Unthaw. I heard that we can get to Mogaung crossing Mansi and Indawgyi on the way. Apparently, that is the shortest route. However, that route is very difficult because of the hills and the dense forest.'

'Are there any roads there?' The faces of the people had become pale with fright.

'There are no roads for the most part, although there are a few secret pathways used by opium smugglers. We will have to advance hacking at the forest. Keep your machetes with you.'

'It's getting late. We should start our journey now. Let's talk about all these things on the road. We don't have time to keep chatting now', Ballabh said. According to him, what happened later could be dealt with later; the top priority was to get out of Manku quickly.

'Wait, wait! Don't be impatient. We should not hurry needlessly, but proceed with caution', Nitu said, and looked towards the end of the road expectantly. 'Before we begin this long and difficult journey, I want to discuss a couple of things with you.'

The crowd stopped murmuring. Raising his hand as if he was about to begin a public oration, Nitu said, 'My friends, the path ahead is extremely tough. Everyone will have to endure tremendous hardship. But ensure that all of you remain together as a group in all circumstances and times. Otherwise, we won't be able to tide through the innumerable difficulties we are bound to encounter on the road before we reach our destination…'

Jayanao entered the little path and approached them. Noticing him, Nitu stopped speaking and advanced towards him. Jayanao held Nitu by his shoulders and whispered something to him. He left immediately after, without turning around to look at the group.

'We shouldn't delay any longer', Nitu returned and

said. 'We have to cross the Irrawaddy before morning from the Ma-Ugong wharf near Iniwar. It's about twenty to twenty-five miles from here.'

Hope coursed through the veins of this silent, waiting group. They gathered their belongings and embarked on the journey together.

Thus began an uncertain journey of a group of destitute, helpless people whose names have been erased from the history of civilisation. The trees in Manku swaying in the gentle breeze bristled at this insult. The darkness of the night enveloping Burma too was bristling at this insult. Everyone had the same question on their minds—when would this journey end?

IX

When the group saw the Ma-Ugong wharf in the distance after advancing through the twenty-two-mile-long pebble-strewn road going towards Mitukan, the soft light of the steadily disappearing stars in the early morning still illuminated the long grass and the bamboo groves on the banks of the Irrawaddy. There was no water in Thayet Song which lay in between; only dry, sandy *char*s. The setting was calm and somber after they crossed this region. The silver currents of the slender-bodied Irrawaddy lay ahead, with sand banks proliferating extensively on both sides. The green hills in the distance replete with dense forests appeared blue because of the moonlight and merged with the horizon.

'We traversed this stretch of the road without incident and it did not take too much time either' Ballabh said.

'That's because this is only the beginning' Nitu said. 'We cannot proceed at the same pace in the jungle. People will tire easily.'

'Seems like the Japanese aren't here yet.'

'It's true that the Japanese aren't here, but this place is infested with their Burmese lackeys. The Japanese will probably be here in two or three days.'

'How far is it to the Hukawng valley?' Ramgobinda asked suddenly. He had heard that Hukawng valley was a literal manifestation of the gates of hell.

'If you walk quickly, you will probably reach it in a day', Nitu smiled and said. It was difficult to talk while they were walking.

'Right now, the problem of the Irrawaddy is paramount', Chinti said. 'Are you sure the boatman will help us cross over?'

'What's the guarantee? After all, it's a Burmese wharf. They are all allies of the Japanese', Kalu said.

'Nungnao said yesterday that he would try to do something if he could. However, what has he done so far?' Ballabh blurted.

'Who? Nungnao?' there was a note of doubt in Chinti's voice. 'Will he do anything to help us?'

'Why not? Nungnao is a decent boy', Nitu said.

'Say what? Do these degenerate Burmese have any decency? They are all the same. Bloody spies for the Kempeitai! Who knows what his intentions are?' Chinti said.

'Please don't talk like that. The poor boy has tried a lot. Apparently, he even argued our case at a meeting yesterday', Nitu said. 'No one listened to him, however.'

'What happened after that?'

'He said that he had made certain arrangements. Jayanao came to pass on that information yesterday just before we left. Nungnao will be at the wharf', Nitu replied.

In the meantime, the group was very close to the wharf. Two paddle-boats were tied there. In the dimming starlight, they saw a small lamp burning in one of these boats. Nungnao stepped out from the boat that had a canopy.

'You are very late', he said.

'We are late for our own funerals' Haricharan grimaced. 'What objection do you have for that?'

The group sat in the canopied boat following Nungnao's directions. Four Burmese boatmen wearing straw hats and with paddles in their hands were ready to steer the boat.

'My duty and responsibility for you ends right here' Nungnao told Nitu. 'Friends, I sincerely pray that your journey is successful and that I don't see you ever again on Burmese soil.'

Nungnao left hurriedly. The boatmen began rowing. In a while, the boat began weaving its way across the tiny islets and surrounding sandbanks that populated the heart of the mighty Irrawaddy. Droves of dolphins jumped and gamboled in the Irrawaddy at dawn. The exhausted people tried to keep sleep at bay. However, despite the putrid smell of the fishing boat and the assault of many mosquitoes, tiredness and sleep soon began overtaking the travellers.

'We had no way of getting across the Irrawaddy if Nungnao hadn't arranged this boat for us', Nitu said. 'On the other hand, all the other Burmese are apparently up at arms about this.'

'By the way, do the rebels know about us or not?' Ballabh asked.

'I can't say for sure. Probably they don't. However, since this issue was discussed at the meeting, everyone will know in a day or two.'

'If the rebels come to know about this, Nungnao is going to be in big trouble. Jayanao is very worried', Nitu said.

'Eh, I can't believe this…he is a rebel leader. Can't he save himself?' Ballabh responded.

'You don't understand…the rebel group is very bloodthirsty. Besides they have hit the jackpot allying with the Kempeitai. They won't listen to any leader', Nitu said, glancing at the direction where Nungnao had departed.

The boats docked on the sandbanks in the western side of the Irrawaddy in the morning. 'There are no Burmese villages around. You have to get down here', the head boatman said. 'It's dangerous to move further up north.'

They disembarked one by one, carrying their boxes and belongings on their heads or their shoulders. The Gengo range glittered green in the distance against the backdrop of the blue sky in the bright light of the morning. A sandbank extended right from the heart of the river for about a mile. They slipped and slided backwards with each step as they walked on the sand that resembled tiny pebbles. A sheet of water covered with thick and sharp aquatic grass lay ahead while bamboo groves were strewn in between. The Gengo hills began once they crossed that stretch of water. First there were rows of tamarind trees and a thinly forested region covered with spiky bushes. After that, the vegetation grew progressively denser. This was the beginning of the hill-infested Irrawaddy-Chindwin valley—an area of about two-hundred miles replete with virtually inaccessible hills and plateaus. According to Burmese legends, the gates of hell were located at the northernmost corner of this triangular valley. Before they were about to cross that valley of death, the group sat down and rested in that forest full of tamarind and palm trees. Soaking handfuls of flattened or puffed rice and some pithaguri in water, they managed to get some nutrition in the morning.

Once the sun reached the center of the valley with the Irrawaddy on the right and the Gengo hills on the east, the group once again began advancing. Yellowing hills of varying sizes appeared recurrently amidst the thorny bushes and cacti populating this forest. There was a pagoda on the top of each hill they came across. The group advanced hacking the plants and vegetation that had grown luxuriantly over the winding pathways.

'Do you know how long it will take us to get to Assam if we keep going like this?' Ramgobinda asked Nitu. He was silently panicking, thinking about the predicaments of Thanu, Lacchmi and his mother.

'It could be ten days; it may take up to a year. You may never reach your destination too', Nitu replied, shifting his bag from one shoulder to another. 'Everything depends on the will of Baba Hukawng.'

'And our fates…', Budhu added.

'It isn't easy to keep moving continuously like this', Ballabh said. He was used to a life of comfort and his body wasn't accustomed to hard labour. On top of that, it was excruciatingly hot. The travellers were getting very exhausted from the weight of the bags and boxes slung on their hands and shoulders.

'We have just reached the section with small elevations and scrubby forests. If you get tired now, what will you do during the tougher stretches ahead?' Nitu said. 'We will reach the really difficult stretch of forested and hilly lands two days from today. The dense vegetation shrouds those forests in a veil of darkness. You can hardly see the sun. Sometimes you can't even see the tree tops.'

Although everyone must have been struck with fear by these words, Nitu's words probably brooked no response because the group was extremely tired.

The group was dying with exhaustion by the evening. 'Let's spend the night somewhere here', Ramgobinda said. There were no indications that anyone objected to this. Nitu pointed towards a stretch of flat ground near the foothills underneath a grove of tamarind trees. The travellers went and sat there. Some of them stretched on the ground.

'We don't have a lot of time for relaxation', Nitu warned. 'We just crossed Toi-Indey and Sadang and are still a fair distance away from Shwebo.'

'We should receive a lot of help and assistance when we reach the base at Shwebo, no?' Ballabh said very hopefully.

'Hopefully', Nitu said. 'Everything depends on our luck.'

Chinti went up to the apex of the elevated ground. He noticed something and reported back to Nitu. After that, both of them climbed the elevation and scanned the area around them carefully.

'What happened?' Ballabh asked as soon as they came down. His suspicious gaze and fearful mind was fixated on them.

'There are a couple of sahibs wearing overcoats and two

of our own people on the other side of the hill', Nitu said. 'The sahibs are priests…possibly refugees like us.'

'It would probably be good to talk to those people', Chinti added.

'I don't think we should talk to unknown people like that', Gurcharan said. 'Who knows what people are up to in times like these?'

'If they are refugees, they must have reached this place bobbing and floating on the tide like us. If they agree to come with us, why should we demur?', Nitu said. 'The sahib might know the roads and can speak to the military in English as well. If the military notices them, they may be even more willing to help us out. It's good to have such people with us. They may be helpful in times of need.'

'I think I spied a village in the distance' Chinti said. 'There are about ten to twelve bamboo dwellings there. I didn't see any people around.'

'Leave those villages alone. You can't venture out there', Ballabh said. 'You will be dismembered into a thousand pieces if you fall into the hands of those rebels. We can't trust anyone.'

'We don't have a lot of provisions with us. Maybe we can get something there…that's what I am hinting at', said Chinti.

'That is Othawa village. You won't get anything there. Instead, they will kill us if they get a chance', Nitu said.

'And if you are planning to loot Burmese villages, do you have any bombs or guns with you?' Indicating that Chinti follow him, Nitu walked around the corner of the elevation to the other side.

The priests were initially terrified to see them. Their fears were allayed once they realised that they were refugees. They learned that the two priests used to work at the Mandalay mission hospital. The tall person wearing white overalls was a doctor; the short one wearing a black coat was his assistant. The other two, who seemed Indian, were patients who had been admitted to the hospital. Doctors and patients ran for their lives as soon as the first bombs fell on Mandalay. No one knew the whereabouts of other people. This quartet had crossed the Irrawaddy in the same fashion. Their goal was the same—Ledo. First they halted at Mandalay's railway station. However, since the railway lines had been bombed at several places, the trains had stopped running. They waited in the station for a day. Soon, that was bombed as well. There was no way to travel towards Misina. Therefore, they had no alternative but to escape through this route.

The two patients were leaning against a tree and dozing. 'You are a company of few. The road ahead is also very dangerous', Nitu began broaching what he had to say.

'We haven't been able to decide on the most advantageous route for us', the tall priest said. 'We escaped in a tearing hurry. We had no time to check the roads and the routes. We heard that it's almost impossible to cross the Hukawng valley. However, it seems like none of the other routes are available.'

'I suggest that all of us advance together as a group', Nitu said. 'If you don't have any objections, you can travel with us.'

It seemed as if the short priest was expectantly waiting for an invitation like this. He awoke the dozing patients and slung his bag on his shoulder.

'They probably don't have any food with them', Ballabh objected. 'It will be very difficult if they want our shares. We have very little food with us.'

'Now that you are talking about food, how long do you think the stuff that we have with us will last?' Nitu asked Ballabh. 'There are lots of advantages having sahibs with us. We can especially expect help from the military.'

'I can't believe it. If a military vehicle comes this way, they will decamp with the two whiteskins. Do you think they will even consider taking dark skinned people like us? Furthermore, these two dozing patients will also be strung like rocks around our neck', Ballabh said. 'There is no saying what will happen to us, and now he's asking us to assume the burden of others.'

'Okay, just forget about that. Now that they have come here, let them stay with us. They may prove useful in tough times', Nitu said, making a final declaration. No one felt the urge to go against his pronouncements.

Ramgobinda and Kalu managed to get a good bonfire going. They cooked rice in some covered bamboo vessels over the fire. A few of them munched some soaked pithaguri, puffed rice or flattened rice and stretched out in front of the fire. Once food reached their bellies, sleep began overtaking them. No one even mentioned anything about moving further ahead. Although everyone was exhausted, they took turns in keeping watch at night. It was important that they be careful since this was an unknown, uninhabited area infested with wild animals.

The night passed by in this fashion.

The new day dawned accompanied by an orchestra of myriad bird songs. No one made any allusions to food in the morning. Their provisions were running low. On the other hand, they would surely come across a lot of edible items throughout the day's journey across the forest. Wild bananas, *bel*s which had fallen on the ground and dates were abundantly available. Depending on nature's bounty for their future meals, the group set on their way. Once again that same path—twisting and winding, undulating and rising—and forests full of shoulder-length bushes strewn endlessly on both sides. Occasionally they saw the thatched huts of a few Burmese villages in the distance.

'We are getting close to Shwebo now', Nitu addressed

the tall priest. 'The newsapers report that there is a large allied base there. Apparently, some planes fly from there as well. On the other hand, I have also heard that these planes only transport soldiers wounded at the front.'

'We can't believe what they say about the war in the newspapers completely' the priest said. 'We will probably come across Kachin villages from Shwebo onwards.'

'Yes! I know the region up to Mingatha. I never traveled in the regions beyond that...we have to leave everything to God's will after that', Nitu said.

The tall priest clasped the cross dangling on his neck, probably experiencing the relevance of the almighty for the first time despite being an ardent believer his entire life.

'I heard that the Kachins aren't rebels', he replied. 'We may get some help if we enter their villages.'

'We should gather some information once we reach Shwebo. We can only be sure after that', Nitu said. 'Can we be certain that all Kachins aren't rebels?'

The jungle on both sides was progressively rising and growing thicker. The pathway wound upwards and then descended again. It was as if this wasn't a pathway, but a green tunnel covered by leaves and vines. A few places were totally dark even in the harsh glare of the afternoon sun. The forests were as quiet as funeral grounds. Occasionally hordes of monkeys would screech at the travellers. Bunches of raw and ripe bananas were visible on the wild banana trees with long leaves that grew in between the bamboo groves. The people would go and tear these bunches and consume them after carefully selecting the ripe ones from the lot. The bananas were tasteless and full of seeds. However, for these famished people, these bananas were like nectar from heaven. As soon as they saw a spring on the side of the road, they would cup their hands and drink their fill.

The scorching afternoon sun had heated up the heart of the forest like a furnace. Sweat streamed out of each and every pore of their bodies. It seemed like they lacked air to breathe. Round, fat leeches infested the long grass and plants that wound themselves around their legs. At the slightest provocation, hordes of chameleons would rush towards them speedily and steadfastly with long strides with their maws opened threateningly. These tiny creatures possessed such an indomitable desire to live on, were such an irrepressible inspiration for survival!

The group occasionally had to cross a few streams gushing out from spaces in between the hills. The streams were shallow; but their currents were very strong. Their beds were full of alluvial mud and small, multi-coloured pebbles. Once the clothes were pulled back to their knees, these streams could be crossed easily. The damp pathways in the forest were strewn with rotting vegetation and slippery mud.

The travellers felt very weak and exhausted as their nutrition for that day primarily consisted of wild bels, gooseberries, *ous* and bananas. The cheekbones had become prominent in the withered faces which were slowly getting covered with bristly beards. When it was evening, Ramgobinda's mother slumped on a stone on the roadside. The old woman's legs were giving way. In the meantime, Ramgobinda tied Thanu to his chest and carried him for part of the way. The little boy was fast asleep and his tiny head was constantly falling over and resting limply on Ramgobinda's shoulder.

'He slept the whole day. We should feed him something', Lacchmi said and sitting next to her mother-in-law began taking out some dried pithaguri from her bag. The pregnant Lacchmi too was extremely exhausted. Noticing that they were preparing to sit down, some of the others followed their lead and slumped on the floor massaging their aching joints and muscles.

'How will we proceed ahead if you succumb to tiredness now?' Nitu noticed what the others were doing and began shouting. 'A long road lies ahead of us.'

'Where to?', Haricharan shouted back and began massaging his legs. 'To the abode of the lord of death! Ha!' He started cackling, but fell silent once his eyes fell on the dejected, withered faces of the others.

Soon everyone sat down wherever they could. In the

meantime, Ballabh and Budhu had moved slightly ahead. Chinti shouted out and brought them back.

'That's fine. Let's spend the night here', Budhu said, noticing the state of his mother who kept dozing off as she was walking.

'It's just the early part of the evening and all of you have to stop already!' Nitu grimaced in frustration. 'From evening to midnight is the best and most advantageous time to walk along this route.'

'Not everyone here has the same youthful, energetic blood like you' Ramgobinda replied. 'We have people of all ages here, ranging from children to aged folk.'

'We have to go on like this for just another day', Nitu tried to argue. He felt guilty noticing that everyone was now sitting down. 'We can rest in the military camp if we can somehow keep moving towards Shwebo. They have food there. What's the point of having unnecessary delays on the road?'

'But can we just keep on going steadfastly like this without interruption? These bodies are made of flesh and blood, my dear', Ramgobinda's mother said. The skin had flayed off her legs and feet; her already dim eyes seemed to have sunk into the hollows of her head.

'That's fine! Let's rest somewhere here.' Noticing that Lacchmi had started distributing pithaguri to the people, Nitu said, 'But let's not stop here in the middle of the jungle. We will reach an open area if we advance a little further. The railway line isn't very far either. It will be convenient for us there.'

The group advanced a little further and reached a plain, open area. A small platform was attached to one of the big trees. It resembled a small tree house without walls and was constructed out of bamboo. At the very least, the platform provided shelter from the rain and also kept out leeches, other insects and wild animals.

'We don't have a lot of food left', Nitu said. 'We should scour the forest for some bamboo shoots and similar stuff', he looked at the other people.

No one made any sign of getting up, however. They blankly stared at the sky and in the darkness, heard the growls of leopards and hyenas coming from the nearby forest.

'Who wants to leave now?' Ballabh stretched out on the grass and said indolently.

'We have to make some arrangements though', Nitu said. 'What will we do when the rice and other edibles with us run out in a day or two?'

'Let us become robbers', Haricharan shouted out from where he lay. 'We should rob the Burmese villages. They made us suffer needlessly. Is it a crime to steal when we are hungry?'

Ballabh looked at the tall priest 'This seems to be the

only way. Do you have guns with you?'

'No' the tall priest looked at his shorter compatriot. 'He has two grenades with him.'

The priest wearing the black coat took out two grenades from his pocket.

'This is good' Nitu said, examining the two grenades in the firelight. He was the only person to recognise grenades in the group. 'That's why these priests wear long overcoats even in this heat', he thought. 'So that they can store everything, from Bibles to grenades, in them and walk around.'

'I hope we come across a Burmese village in a convenient location. We don't have to worry about rations any more then', Haricharan guffawed like a demon.

'This madman here just broached the subject of banditry and all of you are now up in arms with grenades', Ramgobinda spat on the ground in extreme disgust. 'Are we escaping to save our lives or are we here to increase our heroic stature by indulging in warfare and banditry?' He was secretly scared listening to the talk about guns and violence.

'We have to run to save our lives, we need strength in our bodies to run, we have to eat to gain that strength', Ballabh incanted, as if speaking to himself.

'Is there scarcity of food in this forest? There are bels, dates and bananas strewn all around', Ramgobinda's mother said.

'The palm trees don't bear fruits now.'

'We can also consume the sap of the palm tree. We can boil the stems of the *tal* tree and eat them. Bamboo shoots are to be found everywhere. God has given us so many things to eat', the old woman continued.

The ominous darkness of the forest was descending quickly. The songs of frogs and cicadas livened up about three quarters of the night. After munching a handful of boiled or puffed rice, the travellers settled down on the grass. A few wrapped blankets around them to stave off the bone-chilling cold. The people slept soundly with nary a care about the bites of mosquitoes, ticks and leeches in the forest. In fact, the fear of wild animals did not disrupt their sleep even slightly. Unlike the previous day, no one felt the need to stay awake and stand guard either. The whistling noises and mournful cries of the pine and casuarina trees were the only entities that were awake in this dark night in the thick forest. These people, who had grown in the lap of civilisation and had now been cursed by it, had become accustomed to this primeval, wild environment in just a day, and were now resting enveloped in nature's embrace without a care.

X

Dawn! The sun rose at a distance from the bosom of the Irrawaddy amidst the howls of the hooluk bandors and the combined music of the mynahs, cuckoos and *keteki*s.

Nitu's group once again began their journey without a destination as soon as it was morning. Once the sun rose up in the sky, the wild beauty of the surrounding forests glittered brightly. The hill streams, advancing foaming and frothing with a thousand currents, were separated from each other by moss-covered, slippery stones. Speedy currents amidst the peaceful, beautiful, calm visage of nature—ceaseless movement, *jangam*!

The shrubs gradually gave way to taller trees and thicker vegetation. Every step on that uneven pathway either went up or down. Sometimes, there was knee-deep red mud mingled with stones. At other times, the mud was black and had a rotten odour created by decaying leaves of teak that fell liberally on the ground. Thick groves of bamboo, numerous banana trees and rows of *toko* trees everywhere. The sharp, leafless twigs of bamboo flayed the skin and pierced the flesh. Tiny, thorny plants and sharp blades of grass that resembled the edges of a saw covered the forest floor. It was as if these twisting, winding pathways were a unique sakrabehu designed by nature to keep human beings, who prided themselves for their conquest of nature, at bay. The group almost seemed to be close to death after crossing the hills without taking a break, continuously assaulted by the red hot sun and the extreme heat.

By the evening they saw teak and eucalyptus trees on the slopes of the hills on both sides. Occasionally, clumps of multi-hued rhododendrons glittered in the waning light of the setting sun. From the top of one of the elevations, they noticed some platforms constructed out of toko trees and sporadic, green fields of rice.

'That's Dhonggup. The railway line and paved road lie on the other side', Nitu said. 'We'll get to the Shwebo military camp if we cross that.'

The faces of the travellers lit up like the rhododendrons at this sudden ray of hope.

There were uncountable welts and wounds caused by the bites of mosquitoes, ticks and leeches on the flayed, swollen limbs. Blood flowed freely from them. But at the mention of Shwebo, it was as if a boat had docked on the first sandbank of hope for these feeble, emaciated people who had become almost hunchbacked due to the terrible stresses of the exhausting journey and the sheer weight of the loads on their backs and shoulders. How much further… how much?

'And after Shwebo?' Ballabh asked. He was a businessman, and calculation came naturally to him.

'What comes later is for later', Nitu said. 'We cannot say anything for certain till we get to Shwebo.'

'We can avoid the Hukawng valley if the route via Kalewa is open', the tall priest muttered.

The military base at Shwebo was very busy and bustling even at seven in the evening. Nitu's group were able to get permission to meet the Major only after shuttling back and forth and asking people many questions.

From Major Paulwell's words they garnered that the situation wasn't good at all. Most of the people had moved to the camp at Shwebo after Mandalay had been bombed. Simultaneously, thousands of injured and sick soldiers had streamed into the hospital. Treating them was proving to be a big problem as there were hardly any doctors or medicines. They lacked vehicles to send people away to Calcutta; the roads were closed as well. To make matters worse, thousands of refugees had gathered in the camp trying to get to Manipur via Kalewa. The allied camp at Shwebo was the only refuge for this teeming mass of humanity.

'Why, what happened to Kalewa? Wasn't there a pathway into Manipur through Tamu there?' the tall priest asked.

'The British garrison at Kalewa had to move about a week ago. The British contingent retreating through Shwe-jin was also smashed into smithereens and is now on the run', Major Paulwell said. 'Kalewa is now completely in Japanese hands. I haven't seen a single plane for the last four or five days. However, sick and injured soldiers are streaming in daily. The camp is full and since there is no place to stay, people are resting in the open fields. There are no doctors or medicines. We are completely dependent on air-drops. Thousands of sick people have already died due to lack of care. Others are lying around in the fields and forests waiting for their turn to die. There is nothing we can do', the major stopped speaking, putting his hands on his head.

'We need to get to Assam. Would it be possible for you to make any arrangements for that?' the tall priest asked in English. 'Some assistance at the very least.'

'Impossible! Absolutely impossible! We don't even know what will happen to us. Our unit is trying desperately to gather whatever they can. I am worried like hell, thinking about what to do with these thousands of sick, hungry people if the order to retreat comes suddenly. I wouldn't know where to go or where to die…everything is so uncertain', the major said with frustration. 'The supply lines are being cut off one by one. There is no food left. You get nothing in such an accursed country either. Our people are surviving moment to moment barely subsisting on a few meagre rations. We are simply counting the hours to our deaths. What sort of battle can these people conduct? Thousands have already died, and it's difficult to bury each and every one. The last train left from here yesterday. However, what happens to it on the way is anyone's guess.'

'The only way to get to Assam is to Ledo via Mogaung', the major looked at the map and said after a pause. 'It's a difficult road full of hills and forests. In fact, even the Japanese didn't feel the need to keep that region under surveillance. Innumerable refugees went that way in the last two weeks. Of course, many tried to escape via Tamu. However, that road fell to the Japanese in the meanwhile. According to our reports, more than ten thousand people already died on that road. Corpses are strewn on that road like pieces of paper. There is cholera and malaria besides hunger and the struggles on the road. How much can a human body endure?'

'Please tell me what the best way to Mogaung is?' the tall priest asked. A sense of hopelessness and foreboding was evident in his voice.

'You will have to go directly north via Unthaw and Indawgyi. There is no other way', the major said. 'You'll reach the new road that General Stilwell has constructed from Kunming if you travel for a bit through Namkwin after crossing Indawgyi. This road going west touches Mogaung, goes right through the Hukawng valley and Pangsau pass and emerges in Ledo. The allies have set up a number of relief camps for refugees on the road from Shinbwiyang to Ledo. An uncountable number of refugees have streamed in from Misina too. Therefore, you can expect some help after you reach Mogaung.'

'I have heard about the Stilwell Road. However, from Mogaung onwards the route is…', the priest cast an interrogative look at the major. 'About two hundred and fifty miles', the major halted, noticing the extremely downcast look on the priest's face. 'I am not asking you to lose hope, but this stretch of the road is extremely difficult. Narrow paths traversed by bullock carts run for about forty to fifty miles. After that, you'll only get winding roads running through the forest. These are undulating, difficult roads covered with thick vegetation. You'll reach a river named Meja in the middle. It's a hilly river that twists and turns a lot. I don't know the number of times you'll need to cross it. There are tall hills and dense jungle on all sides and the region is the kingdom of wild beasts. After that…', the major closed his eyes and continued, '…it will possibly be easier to advance towards Namkwin, once you cross Moksau Sakhan, only if that region hasn't fallen to the Japanese as yet. We haven't received any news from that area in the last two-three days. There is a very tall peak on the way as well—Nawku. Wait…let me get a map for you all.' The major scrambled around the drawer of his table and produced a map printed on a piece of cloth. 'Keep this with you. At least a few important places and other peripherals are marked here.' Major Paulwell stood up, 'I am extremely sorry that I cannot help you further. I don't even have the resources to give you a full meal in this camp. We are simply surviving on some meager rations ourselves. Of course, you can share a little of what we still have left and rest in the field. You can leave in the morning.'

'Haven't the refugees from Misina come here?' the priest tried to prolong the conversation with the intention of garnering some more information about some related issues.

'Thousands! Thousands!' Major Paulwell again slumped on the chair with a thud. 'They have descended on us like locusts arriving from Sinbo. Many died on the road. The road to Tamu has also ceased functioning in the meanwhile.'

'I would appreciate it if you can tell us a little more about the road to Mogaung', the priest said. 'I guess you already noticed that we have very little idea about the road. We also have infants, women and old folk with us.'

'Actually there is nothing that resembles a road on that route. Most of them are secret pathways used by opium smugglers. You will have to clear the forest and walk occasionally. There are the mountainous routes. You'll find a few Burmese villages on the way…sometimes a few Kachin ones as well. The Kachins are favorably disposed towards the allies. You can recognise the Kachin villages if you notice a bamboo platform at the entrance gates…a bamboo platform atop four pillars. You'll find flowers and leaves on the platform and skeletons and skulls of dead animals hung on the pillars. The Kachins are very helpful and generally not as cruel as the Burmese. To be sure, if there is a Japanese base nearby, don't expect any help. Everyone in the village then will cower in fear.'

Major Paulwell looked at the map attached on the wall at his back. 'After you leave that place, you'll find an allied camp in Pantha. Maybe you'll get some assistance there. If you are lucky, you may also get a ride in a vehicle. Of course, finding means of conveyance for so many people is also difficult. You can get to Mansi from Pantha, and then Unthaw. The pathway is better there. Our 17th division escaped via that route. Most probably, the highway behind that is now in Japanese hands; therefore, you'll again have to take a route cutting through the forest. What can one say about that division! They don't have any food or ammunition. They left everything there after a hot pursuit by the Japanese. The naked soldiers somehow reached this place', Major Paulwell gave a dry laugh and once again turned towards the map. 'This is Indawgyi. Villages belonging to Kachin headhunters are strewn in and around this neighbourhood extending to the north. This is the kingdom of savages. Don't approach them...steer away from them carefully. There may be a good village or two, but it's difficult to recognise that. You don't have any weapons with you either. Occasionally, you will come across a few dwellings in the forest. Those are convenient places to spend the night...at least you will get some respite there.' The major looked at his watch, 'Anyway, I can't discuss anything else. You can rest here without any worries tonight.'

'How long have you been here? I mean...in Burma?' the priest couldn't suppress his amazement at the major's story.

'Around three years', understanding the priest's question, the major replied. 'We also received training and read documents about Burma at Sandhurst. That's how I know such a lot about this place. Actually, I haven't been able to visit a lot of places in this triangle' the major smiled wanly. 'I can harbour hopes to visit these places if this war continues for a few years.'

'Thank you very much. We will be forever indebted to you', the priest stood up and shook the major's hands.

'Huh! What are you saying? I couldn't help you in any way at all. I would feel better if I took you a short distance ahead in my jeep. I don't even have the means to do that. The attack on Seuni road could happen any time. Those

Jap fighters drop bombs even if they notice a lone vehicle of ours. I am very sorry—if only I could have kept the two of you behind…'

'Never mind', the priest said. 'We cannot remain behind leaving the others. Whatever happens, we received a lot of help from you. At least we have a clearer idea about the road ahead. Thank you, my friend! May fortune bestow her favours on you.'

'What fortune?', the major stared blankly at the wall. 'I don't know when we will have to retreat ourselves. Either the Japanese or the Burmese nearby are going to encircle us. Yesterday they burnt down several places on the Seuni road to Kalewa. They blew up two bridges as well. In a day or two, they might be here as well. Besides, we don't have any food.'

'That means the supply lines must have been cut entirely?' the priest never imagined that there would be such a paucity of food in a military camp.

'Where will they come from? The 22nd Division hasn't arrived as yet. The Chinese troops in Lesia are robbing the refugees because there is no food', the major said. 'Probably in a few days, they are going to eat the British troops and the refugees as well.'

'I pray that you will be able to get out of this place safely' the priest said, touching the cross on his neck. *Lead Kindly Light—*', he muttered and shaking the major's hand once again took his leave.

The rest of the group meanwhile made arrangements to sleep, finding an open spot in the grassy field. Most of them had already stretched out on the grass. They resembled corpses when the light from the jeeps travelling from the Shwebo military base fell on them.

Ramgobinda was very worried. Finding it difficult to sleep, he sat up and looked at the sky. His mother's feet were badly flayed. The old woman probably wouldn't be able to walk much further. Although Thanu hadn't walked for long, he was totally spent. He hadn't raised his head since the evening. Budhu's mother was an aged woman too, although she was younger than Ramgobinda's mother. She would probably be able to drag herself for a while. However, the terrifying Hukawng valley lay ahead. Who knew what would happen there? Lacchmi's predicament was also sending jitters up his spine. She was nine months pregnant and it seemed as if her legs wouldn't carry her any further.

'What's the point of worrying about all this?' he thought, after spending quite a long time in deep consternation. 'Everything depends on fate anyway!', his eyes were by now quite leaden with sleep.

Ramgobinda sighed, wrapped the red blanket around himself and fell asleep under the open sky. Thousands of stars illuminated the night sky at that time.

XI

The Shwebo garrison was up and buzzing with activity at the crack of dawn. The travellers were awakened in the early hours of the morning by the noise of the jeeps and the trucks that regularly plied the road to the camp. Of course, most of the people went back to sleep after that, burdened as they were by lassitude and exhaustion. As soon as it was light, they awoke and once again began getting ready for the journey ahead.

'There is no point delaying our departure any longer', Nitu said. 'We should leave as soon as we can.'

'Just leave me here and go, my darlings', Ramgobinda's mother said, looking at her flayed feet with a melancholic gaze. 'I finished all the rice in my box and my feet refuse to move any further.' Tears streamed down her cheeks.

'I will carry you on my shoulders', Ramgobinda said.

'Come, climb on my shoulder.'

'I heard that it's a very long road. How will you carry me on your shoulders?' the old woman argued.

'I asked you to climb my shoulders!' Ramgobinda retorted harshly, noticing that Nitu and the others were about to leave.

'Wait, it seems like the aches and pains in my legs have subsided a bit', the old woman massaged her legs and smiled appealingly at her son. 'Why don't you carry Thanu? I can walk by myself.' Ramgobinda could not fathom the meaning of that smile and looked at Thanu.

'I can walk', Thanu said, looking at the kitten curled up beside them. 'So can Mini.'

'It's getting late…let's go', Nitu said and the group began to move. 'If we can somehow make it to Unthaw, we can rest there for a while.'

'It's two days from here to Unthaw', the tall priest peered at the map. 'That is…only if we don't steer off course and keep following the correct path. It will be very easy to lose our way in these densely forested, winding pathways.'

By noon, the group left the plain area behind and began climbing the hilly routes once again. The sun above was like a scorching ball of fire, and looked as if it was about to fall on them. They were constantly short of breath. Their flayed legs found it very difficult to get a grip. There was no respite during that journey. The railway line emerged near the twisting pathway just as the afternoon had passed by. After that, a narrow, winding path covered with groves of cane and wild bamboo came into view. 'This should be the way to Khin-u', the priest looked at the map and said. 'We should follow this straight pathway.'

The condition of Ramgobinda's mother was growing steadily worse. The old woman found it very difficult to align one step with another. Ramgobinda carried Thanu on his shoulders and his box in his hand. Occasionally, he would put Thanu down from his shoulders and ask his mother to climb up instead, but the old woman steadfastly refused.

'I can do it...go, let's keep moving', she said. However, it was evident that her body was refusing to move any more. She dozed off as she was walking as if she were a sleepwalker. Sometimes she would stumble and fall on her face on a root or a branch on that undulating road. However, she soon arose almost mechanically and kept going. The travellers were moving...simply moving, as if movement was their only goal. Their bodies had become insentient like inanimate objects, but their stiff legs didn't stop moving even then. Mechanically driven by habit, the travellers proceeded ahead slowly at a funereal pace almost as if they were running on clockwork.

A narrow path ringed by thick bamboo on all sides; slippery and slithering like a snake. Khin-u wasn't far away.

'Watch out! She has fallen!' hearing the tall priest's holler suddenly, the group halted as if they were members of a trained army. After stumbling on a tree stump, Ramgobinda's mother fell face down on the ground. Her son sprinted to her side, clasped her in his arms and laid her on the ground. In an instant, the old woman was surrounded by the rest of the people. The priest held her left hand and tried to check her pulse.

'I can't get up any more. Please leave me here', the old woman wheezed and whispered. 'God will protect you.'

Blood streamed out from both sides of the old lady's temple. Lacchmi advanced forward and very carefully wiped the blood with the edge of her sari.

'My blessings will forever be with you.' The old woman managed a wan smile when she looked at Lacchmi. After scrambling through her bag with her feeble hands and producing a ring from therein, she kept holding Lacchmi's hands after failing to put the ring on her finger. The old woman's hands were trembling uncontrollably.

'What happened? Let's be quick about it', Ballabh shouted from the other side impatiently.

'Is there any point waiting here like this? What happened?' Nitu called out from the head of the line on the other side.

'You are getting delayed—please leave', the old woman's lips were quivering. She made a vain attempt to raise her head and look in all directions.

'The rest of you can leave. I am not going', Ramgobinda said in a faltering voice. He began to sob loudly, holding the two withered hands of his mother, which were once adept in making bisonis, very tightly.

'Does anyone have water?' the priest asked, only to be met with a stony silence from the group. In the meantime, Nitu and Ballabh too had arrived by the old woman's side. The old woman's lips quivered slightly as if she were trying to articulate something. Lacchmi brought Thanu over and placed his hands in those of his grandmother's. For an instant, it seemed as if the old woman's eyes lighted up while a wan smile played on her lips. Momentarily an expression of great tranquility appeared on the old woman's face. Her gaze fleetingly rested on each and every member of the group.

The tall priest, who was checking her pulse, suddenly froze like a statue. He released the old woman's hands that fell to the ground with a thud.

'She has passed away', the tall priest checked her heartbeat for a moment and then shut her eyelids. After that, he covered the old woman's face with the edge of her sari and made the sign of the cross on her chest.

Not a single person in the group could believe or fathom the cruel truth of this sudden tryst with death. All of them were thunderstruck and remained rooted to their spots.

'What should we do now?' the stunned Nitu said, backing off a little.

'We have to cremate her', Budhu said. 'The old woman was very orthodox.'

'Will it be possible to cremate her here?' Ballabh asked. His face had become as pale as a ghost.

'I could not even give my mother a sip of water at the hour of her death', Ramgobinda beat his chest and wailed.

'Wait, no point being so impatient now', Nitu said. 'We have to figure out a way to properly cremate the corpse—that's the moot issue now.'

'It's best that we bury her', the priest said, and clearing a space around the corpse began to remove the twigs, leaves and branches. 'It won't take a lot of time and we don't have to dig deep either.'

'Bury her?' Ramgobinda shouted incredulously. 'You will bury my mother?' He stood up and approached the priest. 'You intend to give a Christian burial to this orthodox Hindu woman who spent her entire life as a vegetarian devoted to the service of God?' he grasped the priest's overcoat tightly. 'That will not happen. That cannot happen while I am still alive. My mother will cast a terrible curse on me! Her spirit...'

'God is one, heaven is also the same place', the priest replied calmly. 'Come now, please move. Don't stand in the way of my responsibility.' He pushed Ramgobinda away slightly with one hand, cleared the rest of the twigs and branches from the designated spot, dug a small hole in the ground, and carefully placed the corpse in it. He covered the corpse with some dry leaves and grass, held the cross hanging on his chest over it and began praying under his breath.

'We can leave now.' The priest fashioned a cross out of two branches, placed it at the head of the grave, and laid two other twigs in the shape of a cross on the leafy covering. 'Please repeat after me—Amen!'

'Amen!' everyone spoke in one voice, even though they didn't understand the meaning of the word.

'Let's go', the priest shook Ramgobinda's shoulders. 'You have a long and difficult road ahead of you and an infinite ocean of responsibilities. We shouldn't delay any further.'

'Should I just leave my mother forever like this?' Ramgobinda blurted between his sobs.

'You have to go. You have your responsibilities—that's why you have to leave', the priest said. 'Your mother has ascended to heaven. You have to proceed ahead for the peace and satisfaction of her departed soul. Let's go, we have very little time left.'

Ramgobinda looked at both Thanu and Lacchmi and slowly got up from where he was kneeling. The dry leaves covering the deeply peaceful visage of his mother's corpse were rustling in the wind. There was a cross planted on the spot where his mother lay—that same holy cross which was despised by his mother during her lifetime as a symbol of the *mlecchas*. Ramgobinda advanced a couple of steps, suddenly remembered something, and turned back to where his mother's bag lay. He took out the picture of Radha and Krishna from her bag and carefully placed it on top of the cross lying horizontally on the ground. At that moment, it seemed as if all the different religions of the world mingled and transformed into the great religion of humanity! The petty differences of society were smashed by death's peaceful embrace. There was such a small distance between life and death, but what a tremendous difference nevertheless! Ramgobinda knelt down and prostrated himself before his mother's grave and then, with Lacchmi and Thanu in tow, followed the group that had already begun advancing in the meanwhile.

The undulations and curves on the pathway were progressively increasing. There were a number of small, sharp bends on the road. The walkers could not see the end of the line from the front. The slope occasionally was steep and slippery with dense jungle on both sides. On the one hand there were deep crevasses, on the other steep inclines. Sometimes they came across pole-bridges made of bamboo over the small streams. These bridges trembled and seemed like they would break under the weight of a single person. Only one or two people at most could cross those bridges at the same time. There were tall, sharp stones in the hollows below and the travellers felt dizzy if they looked at them. There were herds of black barking deer and droves of wild fowl in the forest. The black deer would retreat to the bamboo groves, stick out their short necks and observe the humans warily. A couple of them would bare their front teeth and release a few short barks. The herd had never come across human beings before and hadn't learned to fear them yet.

The travellers resembled statues immersed in deep contemplation, advancing forward in a stealthy manner. Scattered black clouds covered the sky in the evening and it began raining soon. First it drizzled, then some fat drops began falling, and finally bucketsful poured down. The primeval craving of nature found its manifestation in this massive downpour. The leaves and trees were dancing in joy, the smell of wet earth was everywhere. The sky deposited its bounty on the destitute earth to its heart's content. It was as if the sky, which wanted to keep its shame and poverty hidden, had nothing left to distribute to the thirsty earth. In a trice, the hilly streams which were reanimated by the rains began gushing. The agitated sheets of water that smashed against the tall grass and reeds suddenly evoked terror in those who saw it. This wasn't the familiar, life-renewing ecstasy of nature—it was akin instead to poisonous rain. The pointy peaks in the distance suddenly glittered cruelly against the background of the sky as if they were demons. A great sea of green and deep blue encircled the group completely.

'I think we have lost our way', the tall priest told Nitu. 'Otherwise we should have reached Khin-u by now.'

The path was extremely slippery. It was impossible to advance further. The group halted on a path in between the sky-kissing hills on one side and the bottomless caves on the other. Ramgobinda adjusted the sheet around Thanu who was sleeping soundly tied to his chest.

'Does anyone have a rope with them?' Nitu asked. 'I need a very thick rope. Everyone has to tie this rope around their waists tightly. There is a steep incline ahead. And please search for a walking stick for yourself.'

They saw the steep incline of a slippery hill with a deep gorge nearby. Everyone understood the import of Nitu's words. They had no difficulty in finding walking sticks as there were bamboo trees on all sides. But they couldn't find a rope. The women opened their boxes and took out some old, wet saris. They tied these tightly around their waists in rows of four. After that, the group advanced carefully at snail-like speed on that slippery incline, getting a grip with the help of their walking sticks. Their destination was Unthaw and it was still very far.

They came across a few streams on the way. Most of them were shallow, but their currents were strong. One of these streams was quite broad and deep. The travellers crossed the single plank of wood that served as a bridge carefully one at a time. The weak bridge swayed in the wind and the throats of the travellers went dry with fear as they crossed it.

Although it stopped raining at night, the water that had collected in the leaves of the tall trees and the thick mossy covering on the branches of the oak trees fell with redoubled force as the forest swayed with the wind. The darkness and stillness became more intense and frightening with each and every step. The growls and noises made by numerous invisible animals wafted towards them continuously. Rain stopped falling from the overhanging clouds which now began to settle in the deep gorges between the hills. A blast of cold air made the drenched travellers tremble and chilled them to the bone. The group was advancing somehow step by step like a herd of hungry, fatigued beasts. Just at that time, a cry of distress came from the front of the procession.

'Owww! I think I am dead!' Ballabh slipped, fell and hurt his waist and was now sitting with his legs splayed out on the mud. His terrible scream echoed for a long time in the darkness, and resonated with multiple cadences in the heart of the callous hills like an incorporeal spirit.

Ballabh's eyes widened in sheer terror after he was unable to stand up, despite attempting to do so twice. 'I don't think I can stand up' he said in a frightened voice.

Budhu, Ballabh, Chinti and Haricharan were tied together in a row. Once Ballabh fell down, the others couldn't move either. Nitu came near Ballabh and tried to loosen the knot in his waist.

'What are you doing? Do you plan to throw me away?' Ballabh grasped Nitu's hand tightly. In spite of the darkness, his eyes were shining brightly like those of a vicious tiger. 'You can't leave me alone here to die like this. If I die, we all go together', he gasped. He was foaming at the mouth.

'He has a terrible fever' the tall priest checked his brow. 'I guess he may have fractured a bone or two from his fall.'

'What are we to do now?' a look of perplexity was visible on Nitu's face.

'He is probably going to die here. We should leave him behind', Haricharan began cackling.

'We will all die; you shut up!' Kalu said irritatedly.

'Who is going to die?' Ballabh had begun dozing where he sat, but suddenly woke up and shouted loudly. 'I won't die, you will. My wife and children are in India. I have to go.' He held Nitu's hands and began sobbing loudly. 'What will happen to them otherwise? They must be waiting for me with such hope.' His gaze was now fixated on a peak in the distance, as if he saw his family there. Then, he fell unconscious, face down on the ground with a thud.

'Come on, let's do something', Budhu said impatiently.

'Hold him...two of us can carry him in a sort of

hammock. Once we reach some plain ground, we can start a fire and give him a few hot presses', Nitu said.

'Will he survive for such a length of time?' Budhu responded, looking at Ballabh's unconscious form.

'He will, he will! He is a bloodsucking merchant. He won't die so soon', Haricharan said and cackled again. 'He will have to suffer from hunger and fatigue for a few days.'

'Hold him, what are you looking at?' Nitu ordered Budhu. 'And Hari…carry his box.'

One of Ballabh's limp hands was still holding on to the box. 'Oof! This is very heavy', Haricharan lifted the box and said. Throwing his walking stick away he muttered, 'And here I can't even carry myself'.

'It isn't very far. Come on, you can do it', Nitu said. 'We should rest once we get to some level ground.'

'He is trembling a lot', Budhu said lifting Ballabh's head, and hurriedly picked him up with Nitu.

After an extremely labourious downhill descent of about a mile, they saw a river in between the hills. There was a small piece of level ground by its side, filled with rocks and teak trees. At this late hour of the night, the river glittered like a silver ornament in the moonlight. It was impossible to cross this river at that time; therefore, the travellers stretched out and rested on the rocks.

Their feet were swollen and flayed. Water had entered their footwear and puffed them up as well. They couldn't manage to open the tightly fitting shoes despite many attempts. Their feet and toes had cracked open at various places and blood streamed out from their shoes. A mixture of water and blood squished out of their shoes at every step.

'I think we will have to cut and prise open these shoes' Budhu said, squirming in agony as he tried to open his shoes.

'No, you don't have to. Let it remain stationary for a while. Open it when the swelling in your feet subside', Nitu said. 'If you cut open your shoes now, will you get another pair later? You have no inkling of the road that lies ahead—without shoes, you will die.'

In normal circumstances, no one would have paid heed to Nitu's last words. But in this moment of acute crisis, the word 'die' made everyone's hearts tremble with fear. Ballabh's body, lying on the rocks with his face pointed up, was trembling and moving agitatedly. His face and eyes, assaulted by a terrible fever, were as red as beetroot. Although he was unconscious, he kept muttering something incomprehensible.

'Do you know the name of this river?' Gurcharan asked Nitu. The river was quite wide and would prove difficult to cross. Nitu pretended that he hadn't heard the question and looked at the priest.

The tall priest checked Ballabh's pulse, took out some tablets from his box and gave them to Nitu. 'It seems like he has malaria. Give him these two tablets right now. We have to give him two more after four hours.'

'Who knows where we or Ballabh will be after four hours?' Nitu thought and sighed. He brought some water from the river and helped Ballabh swallow the two tablets. The journey hadn't even lasted ten days and one person had already fallen. Ballabh probably wouldn't be able to make it either. Even if he didn't die, they would have to leave him behind. There was no one who could carry him for such a distance. On the other hand, others would die if they waited for him…and that shouldn't happen. Of course, they would have to wait and watch for a few hours. If he survived through that, he may yet live.

The group made arrangements to spend the rest of the night there. A few of them were sound asleep already. The rocks were damp and they did not have dry firewood with them. Although everyone desired a bonfire, they did not have the energy or patience to gather firewood after the hunger and extreme labours they had to endure throughout the day.

Unable to resist the lure of sleep and lassitude when the day dawned, the group kept lying down like corpses on the rocks and stared sleepily at the vermilion-hued clouds in the eastern horizon. Fixing their blank stares on that limitless horizon, this small group of people who had lost everything contemplated the significance of the earth and the sky. Although they were at death's door, a few images began unspooling in the mental theater of these people immersed in dreams of life: a green field replete with crops, a herd of cattle, a loving face and the joyous shouts of little children. The dream of setting up a stable homestead haunted these homeless people.

Wisps of smoke were visible in the distant hills followed almost immediately by a row of fires that popped up in the horizon. These weren't produced by bombs. These weren't the fires of destruction, but of peace—the procreative fire of jhum cultivation. Kachin farmers had cleared the forests on the hillsides and started the fires for tou-iya.

Lacchmi and Budhu's mother washed their faces in the river in the meantime. Chinti and Ramgobinda gathered some leaves and twigs and tried to start a fire. A lot of smoke was produced because they managed to gather only some green twigs and shoots. The rest of them were also stirring awake at this point. The two priests were lying close to each other and discussing something.

Ramgobinda cut two stalks of bamboo, filled them with water and placed them over the fire. 'We can boil some rice here', he told Lacchmi. He felt a sudden stab of pain when he saw Budhu's mother sitting near Lacchmi. He would never ever get the opportunity to feed his mother like this again. His mother was sleeping forever near the gates of hell with only dry leaves for a covering. She would never rise again.

'I soaked some rice in a towel', Lacchmi said. 'Our stocks of rice will probably last us only for another meal. Now just have this for nourishment.'

'What will you give to the boy…to Thanu?'

'I have about a handful of rice powder; he will have that.'

'It would be nice if he could have had a full meal of rice', Ramgobinda said dispiritedly. 'He hasn't had anything resembling rice for the last four or five meals.'

'This isn't the time to prepare rice or lament the lack of it', Nitu arrived from somewhere and said. He feared that if the rest consumed a lot of rice, they would feel drowsy. On the other hand, their stocks of rice would also diminish. They wouldn't be able to gobble a lot if they had only raw soaked rice or rice powder.

'I heard that there are allied bases at Pantha and Jigon. We will probably get something to eat there. At least, we will be able to boil some rice there. The main thing now is to move as quickly as we can', he said.

'Still, it will be good for us if we can have at least a handful in the morning. At least we won't have to worry about that during the day', Chinti replied.

Ramgobinda walked to a wild tea bush nearby, tore a few leaves from the top and dropped them in the boiling water. 'That's fine' he said. 'We haven't had tea for a few days. Let us have some tea now.' No one had imagined that an ordinary bowl of tea could provide so much satisfaction in such conditions. For a moment, a sliver of a smile illuminated Ramgobinda's eyes.

Although the color was a dark red, the tea had a good aroma. However, it was difficult to drink it while it was piping hot. When the bamboo containers cooled after a while, the people either cupped the vessels in their hands and sipped the tea or drank the beverage straight from them. What enthusiasm, what joy! Such a rare, satisfying drink!

'Drink, drink! Who knows when we will be able to drink this again?' Ramgobinda said, pouring the beverage into the vessels of the others.

'I am not feeling very well', Lacchmi took Ramgobinda aside after she finished feeding Thanu. 'The lower part of my stomach hurts.' She lowered her head, mortified by pain and shame. She felt guilty for being the agent precipitating another extreme crisis that added to all that had already happened.

Ramgobinda's eyes widened with great fear and the veins on his head began throbbing. He was rooted to his spot as if struck by lightning.

'I think it will be easier for us once we cross Indawgyi hopefully without incident', Nitu said. 'Japanese activities aren't as intense on that side. At least, we will be able to walk on the highway.'

'We can't be certain', the tall priest said. 'What has happened elsewhere in this time is anyone's guess. We will however get to the newly built Stilwell Road once we reach Mogaung. It will be a different story then. Our troops have positions from Bhamo onwards. We may expect to get a vehicle or two there.'

'What's the name of this river? How much further to Mogaung?' Nitu asked.

'This must be the Mu river', the priest pointed at a spot on the map. 'There aren't any other big rivers marked near this spot. That means we are close to Indawgyi now.'

'When do we get to Indawgyi?' Budhu asked, simultaneously munching some raw rice. All his worries centered on his mother. She was the only surviving member of his family.

'We haven't reached Unthaw yet. It must be at least two days away. On top of that, we are walking on hilly roads and have to move slowly. If we keep on lazing about here…', Nitu halted as his eyes suddenly fell on something. Like a man who had seen a ghost, he shouted, 'What are those things over there?'

XII

Hearing him shout, eighteen pairs of eyes turned in the direction that Nitu was looking at. Two Burmese men advanced to meet the group from the thinly forested region nearby. The men were wearing japis on their heads. From their dress, the group understood that they were Kachins. They had bare, soft bodies, a short piece of cloth around their waists and spears in their hands.

'Who are you?' Nitu asked in a rough voice once the initial feeling of astonishment and fear had passed. Suspicion and fear were the primal human emotions evoked in such situations where trouble and uncertainty dogged every step.

In the meantime, almost everyone in the group surrounded the Kachins.

'We came here because we saw smoke', the shorter Kachin replied.

'Who are you?' Nitu asked them again.

'We are from Lesin village nearby', the taller Kachin said pointing towards the other side of the river. 'We were out hunting.' He showed them the sheathed *dao* hanging on his waist.

'What do you want here?' Chinti asked.

'We were checking. Many Indian refugees passed through this way in the past few days. They are escaping in droves towards their death either on the banks of the Indawgyi or in the Hukawng', the taller Chin said. 'It seems like they don't have places to die in Burma.'

The members of the group were stunned into silence.

'What is that to you? People will die where they feel like dying. What do you have to do with that?' Nitu asked.

'If you want, we can show you the way to Unthaw. There is a shorter route.'

Sitting on the other side of the fire, the two priests took some rice out from their bag and were soaking it in water.

'Which way?' the tall priest advanced towards them and asked.

'It's a road that cuts through the forest. You won't understand it if I explain it to you now', the taller Kachin said. 'There is a military base in Kaolin near Unthaw. They reward us if we direct Indian refugees there. It's even better if there are sahibs with them.'

'Why will the military reward you?'

'Burmese rebels infest the villages on the way to Unthaw. They rob Indians and hack them to death when they find them—that's why.'

'But you are Kachins. Aren't your people rebels too?' Nitu frowned and looked at the pair.

'If we are, we are—don't come with us then. Go wherever you want to. You will realise your mistake when you are hacked into tiny bits on the road. The Burmese are hunting people like deer near the jade quarries. They keep the shrunken heads till they are dry. After that, they string them like beads on a necklace and wear them. Your troubles will be over if you fall into the hands of savages like those.' The taller Kachin turned his back to the group and addressed the priest, 'The Burmese will be in seventh heaven if they lay hands on your head.'

Although it defied reason, trust began forming in the group based on the way the pair talked and behaved. They belonged to hill tribes who did not waste time on excessive verbiage. If they had some suspect intentions in their minds, they wouldn't have spoken so much. All they needed to do was to shout—the entire village would then throng there and take them prisoner.

'Is there any place here where we can halt for four to five days?' Ramgobinda queried. He was very worried about Lacchmi's condition. Thanu, too, looked spent. He was sleeping soundly from the very moment he arrived in this place and hadn't shown signs of waking up.

'You can stay in Lesin', one of the Kachins said. 'You won't have a lot of space. The houses are placed on bamboo stilts. Humans and livestock cohabit together. You may find it difficult.'

'So now you have the desire to stay behind. Have you fallen in love with Burma again?' Nitu asked Ramgobinda, and then halted when he saw the crumpled form of Lacchmi on the side. The tall priest too was looking at Lacchmi.

'What do we do with him now?' Chinti asked, pointing at the stiff form of Ballabh. Ballabh still hadn't regained consciousness.

'His box is very heavy', Haricharan said, looking at Ballabh. 'I am sure they are full of gold bars or other valuables like those clinking silver coins bearing the impress of the Empress.' Ballabh's limp hands were still in positions as if he was holding the box even though he was unconscious.

'You cannot leave anyone who is alive behind', Gurcharan said. 'All of us came together and will leave together.'

'That's why I am asking for a place of refuge. We can rest for a couple of days and then depart again together', Ramgobinda said.

'Then stay if you want to become a meal for the Burmese' Nitu said. 'We came out with the intent of escaping and will stick to our resolve.' He looked at the priests and the rest of the group for support.

'Who knows what's going to happen tomorrow? This road may become inaccessible as well', Chinti said. 'Maybe we won't be able to escape from this place because we delayed our departure by a couple of days. Then everyone will be stuck in a hole.'

'You will survive through it all if it is your destiny, my loves. If God wills, he will protect us from dying in the forest', Budhu's mother said, laying out some wet clothes to dry on the rocks. The old woman was very worried about Lacchmi. She considered Lacchmi, who was displaying signs of impending motherhood, to be like her own daughter. That darling just lost her mother-in-law the other day. Now who would take care of her?

'You don't have to scramble about in the villages of those untrustworthy Burmese at night', Budhu responded furiously. 'Haven't you seen how we had to leave everything behind and run away from our permanent foundations like mangy dogs?'

'Then just leave me and go' Budhu's mother replied, massaging her flayed legs which resembled a bloated banana tree. 'I can't even move my sluggish feet. I don't have the strength to go anywhere else.'

Budhu looked at his mother's feet and then turned towards Nitu. Nitu gave no response.

'A few of us can carry her in turns. But we don't even have enough people for that', Kalu said. 'Besides, all of us have a box or a bag each. The boxes have also become heavy because water seeped inside.' He somehow felt happy that his wife had succumbed to typhoid about a year ago. If she were still alive, that would have meant another burden. His wife was very sickly. She rescued herself when she died a year ago and also provided him some respite.

'Okay, whoever is prepared to leave needs to get ready right now; no point wasting time unnecessarily', Nitu said in a tone of authority. 'Those who cannot leave can rest for three to four days. Leave if the roads are clear; otherwise, it's your business.'

Ballabh was still lying on the rock trembling from the effects of a terrible fever. His eyes were still bloodshot and foam dribbled from the sides of his mouth. Occasionally he would move his head and mutter something deliriously.

'He won't be able to leave' Chinti said. Budhu looked at his mother. Ramgobinda looked at Lacchmi, who was squirming in agony and the sleeping Thanu and said nothing.

'The five of us will stay behind. You can leave', Budhu's mother said. 'In any case, I won't be able to travel such a distance. Just think that you had to abandon me here. You have already left one on the road...'

'You will get doctors and hospitals in the base at Unthaw. You can stay there for a while', Budhu said. 'It's just two days away.'

'We can't be sure of that', the tall priest said. 'You have already seen what happened to the base at Shwebo. What if Unthaw has suffered the same fate?'

'I hope they won't betray us?' Gurcharan said, looking at the two Kachins.

'Doesn't seem like it', the priest replied. 'But what do we know?'

'Won't you leave with us?', Nitu asked the priest and Gurcharan. He was beginning to feel concerned, judging the tenor of the conversation. If these people weren't leaving, the group would be severely diminished.

'The four of us are very tired as well', the tall priest said. 'These two are sick patients. They had to flee while they were still being treated in the hospital.'

'We were supposed to leave by train from Misina', the short priest said. The rest of the group was startled when they heard his deep voice. 'We weren't prepared for such a long, exhausting journey at all. We don't have a lot of food with us either. Therefore, we would like to rest for a while if we come across a safe, advantageous spot.'

'Hmm!' Anger and frustration were writ large on Nitu's face. 'That means only six of us are prepared to move ahead. Why did these people want to come here in the first place?' he looked with irritation at Chinti. 'Now argue with them as much as you want.'

'Let the women and children stay behind. The rest of us

can leave', Chinti replied, and immediately lowered his eyes when he met Ramgobinda's gaze. 'I mean…those who want to leave can come with us' he added hesitantly.

'Do you realise what you are saying? Where will they go later? How will they leave?' Budhu asked. 'Have you gone mad?'

'Aah!' suddenly Lacchmi screamed loudly, fell on the rocks and began to squirm in agony. Ramgobinda looked once at Budhu's mother and then at the Kachins confusedly. The Kachins had been standing in the same spot listening to the conversation in the meanwhile.

The tall priest rushed to Lacchmi's side, held her by the shoulders and looked at Ramgobinda. 'Her time has arrived. We shouldn't delay any longer.' The two priests lifted Lacchmi, holding her on both sides and gestured to the Kachins to lead the way. Budhu's mother and Ramgobinda followed them.

'What will you do now? They have already left', Chinti asked Nitu.

'Let's leave Ballabh and Thanu in the village and go our own way', Nitu said. 'Let's leave this pair of sick people with them. There is no other alternative. Do you want to die too by keeping them company?'

Whether it was because of the medicines or for some other reason, Ballabh had regained consciousness. The two sick people accompanying the priests were sitting beneath a tree and dozing. They were lying prone in the same position from the time they arrived in that location.

'What happened to you? If you want to go, get up', Nitu and Chinti shouted at the pair as they put Ballabh's arms around their shoulders and lifted him up. Haricharan lifted the sleeping Thanu and held the box in his other hand. The rest scrambled to get their belongings together. The sickly pair also got up. 'Hey! Hold these two boxes…' Gurcharan handed two boxes to them and the group began walking by the banks of the river to Lesin.

The village was located few furlongs away in a cramped space between two hills. There were about ten to twelve *changghar*s with walls made of bamboo and supported by wooden stilts. The roofs, constructed out of straw which had been procured from the hills, had sunk in alarmingly. A fire was blazing right in the middle of the wide courtyard which was fenced in from all sides. There was a crowd of people, both young and old, there.

A squinty eyed old man who was warming himself near the fire sitting on a wooden murha and smoking his pipe, observed the sudden entrance of the strangers suspiciously. The group with the priests had reached the village a little earlier. 'The Japanese and the nationalist Burmese will attack us if they learn that we provided shelter to these people', the old man told the shorter Kachin man who was now standing beside him.

A handwoven opaque cotton curtain was strung and attached to two bamboo poles on the other side of the fire. They could make out that a few Kachin women were moving busily to and fro on the other side of that curtain. Once they entered the courtyard, they could hear Lacchmi's screams of agony and the murmurings in the language spoken by the Kachin women. Letting Ballabh sleep in front of the fire, Nitu and Chinti paused for a breath.

Ramgobinda was pacing around agitatedly, beset with anxiety and foreboding. Sometimes he went close to the curtain and tried to discern what was going on, on the other side. 'Why don't you sit in the same place?' the Kachin elder noticed his activities and thundered. 'Why are you squirming like this? Aren't you a man?'

The two priests opened their shoes, kept them out in the sun and were now intently checking the blisters on their feet. One of them extracted something that looked like a leech or a slug from his socks and examined it in the sunlight. Suddenly everyone was shocked by a terrible scream emanating from the other side of the curtain. It was Lacchmi's scream. A weak, barely audible wail of a newly born infant also wafted into their ears. Budhu's mother emerged from the other side of the curtain and beckoned Ramgobinda. Everyone was sitting rooted to their spots. After a few moments, Ramgobinda came out into the courtyard. His face was pale and his manner grief-stricken.

'I had to leave Lacchmi behind on this destructive path too…' He looked at Nitu and, with his hands on his head, fell down with a thud near the sleeping Thanu. His eyes were tearless and not a single sigh escaped from his lips. The cruel mental trauma he suffered made him resemble a lifeless statue made of stone.

'What happened?' Gurcharan approached him and asked. Ramgobinda looked at him with a blank stare as if he were a stranger. It seemed like the query hadn't penetrated his consciousness. Maybe he felt no need to respond to an ordinary, brief question like 'What happened?' in this precarious situation and dangerous time. Maybe he had no answer.

'Lacchmi is no more', Budhu's mother came out wiping the tears with the corner of her sari. 'That unfortunate girl left us as soon as she gave birth to her son.'

'How is the baby?'

'He is fine', Budhu's mother said irritatedly. 'He swallowed his mother as soon as he was born. If he isn't fine, then who will be?'

The tall priest was sitting quietly near the fire. From Budhu's mother's words, he discerned that something terrible had happened. He jumped up and disappeared instantly behind the curtain, with the short priest following him.

Children were running around the courtyard creating

a din. The fowl and pigs were rummaging through the garbage looking for food. The Kachin elder was sitting still like a statue and observed the two priests disappear behind the curtain.

'There are women there. Why did they enter that space?' he asked, anger flashing in his eyes. 'Doctors… they're doctors', Nitu replied instantly. For these hill tribes, the women's chambers were off limits.

The short priest emerged from behind the curtain and asked Ramgobinda to come in. 'The woman isn't dead yet; she is merely unconscious' he said. 'The doctor wants to give her a shot. He also wants to give her medicine which unfortunately he doesn't have. He thinks she will recover if he gives her that medicine.'

'Where will we get medicines here?' Ramgobinda's face, which brightened momentarily at this news, once again furrowed darkly.

'What's the harm in looking for it? If there is a military base nearby, I am sure we can get the medicine', the short priest said.

The tall priest came out. He took out a piece of paper from his pocket, scribbled something on it and passed it to Ramgobinda. 'We'll need this medicine. Ask the Kachins… they may know something about the military base. I am sure there are a couple of military bases near Inleji or Gada.'

The Kachins heard what they said and shook their

heads at first. Gada was far away. There was a base at Inleji sometime during the beginning of the war. It was impossible that they would find a base at Inleji now. The road was a hilly one and the Japanese had destroyed the bridge in between. There were no boats there either and they would have to cross it with a raft.

'Still there is no harm in trying once' the tall priest said. 'We can't allow the woman to die without treatment like this.'

The tall Kachin whispered something in the elder's ears and then departed with the piece of paper.

'If she gets the medicine, will Lacchmi get better?' Ramgobinda asked. There was a lot of hope and expectation in his voice.

'I hope so. Everything is dependent on God's will', the priest held the cross shining on his breast and said. 'I have administered a shot. She will probably regain consciousness in an hour or so.'

The short priest was pouring some medicinal liquid down the pale-looking Lacchmi's throat. Trickles of red medicine flowed like blood on the sides of Lacchmi's mouth. Budhu's mother tore the front section of her sari, wrapped the infant carefully in it and let him sleep outside in the open air.

'There is no saying how long we have to wait here now', Nitu said. 'There is very little hope that she will recover soon once she gets that medicine or that she can move ahead immediately after she recovers. We will have to stay here for at least four to five days.'

'I told you earlier not to take them with us', Budhu said. 'Now where will you go with this bunch of sick people?'

'What needs to happen will happen. Let's curse our fate and sit here', Gurcharan said.

No one had paid any heed to Ballabh amidst this melee. He had regained consciousness and rolling his eyes around was trying to acquaint himself with the unfamiliar surroundings.

'His fever has broken' the tall priest checked his brow and said. He indicated to Nitu that he should give Ballabh the two remaining tablets.

The swelling in Ballabh's legs had subsided somewhat. Nitu gave him the two tablets and opened his shoes. 'These heavy shoes aren't good for a journey like this' he told the priest.' 'Actually, a long piece of cloth should be wrapped around the legs from the knees to the heels. The weight is substantially reduced, it doesn't press on the feet and they don't get flayed either. Leeches and ticks can be kept at bay as well' he laughed cheerlessly.

'By the way, do you feel ready to leave now?' Chinti asked Ballabh.

Ballabh shook his head and muttered something inaudible in reply.

Slowly, the sun assumed a scorching avatar as it rose high in the sky. The rest of the group felt impatient, sitting idly doing nothing.

Three young women with bamboo pins in their hair and a piece of cloth tied around their chest distributed some rice steamed on bamboo containers and a piece of smoked pork placed on some *sal* leaves to the visitors. 'Please eat' the Kachin elder said, turning his back to the sun. 'There is a shortage of food here. There is no salt at all. We haven't been able to send anyone to Manging Pung in the last six months because of harassment by the Japanese.'

Everyone was famished. They gobbled the boiled rice and the meat. The two priests cut some pieces of the meat and wrapping it in sal leaves kept them in the pockets of their overcoats. After a while, they were given some steaming red tea in small bamboo containers. The tea had been brewed in clay pots and smelled of earth.

'I wouldn't mind if we can rest here for about a day', Haricharan had stuffed himself, he released a few satisfied burps and stroked his belly. The tall priest finished eating, went once again to the other side of the curtain and then emerged from there looking at his watch.

'He won't be too long. He will get here very soon' the elder said, screening his eyes and peering at the sun. 'Please take some rest. Unthaw is still a day's journey away.'

'We could have moved ahead only if we found some

way to carry the sick people…' Nitu looked at the elder and said. 'Can some of you help us with this? At least till Unthaw.'

'You'll need to have a lot of strength in your bodies to carry people on this route', the elder shook his head. 'These two are the only able-bodied young men in the village. The rest have all left for tou-iya. They cleared the ground on Kiyakothin hill for cultivation. Next year, we will relocate Lesin village to that region. Our dwellings are dependent on where we go for cultivation—that's where our village will be as well.'

'Hmmm…then it will take a lot of time for these people to recover and leave' Nitu cast worried looks at both the priest and the elder.

'I can send one of them to show you the way. However, you will need quite a few young men to carry the sick' the elder said. 'There is a shorter route once you ford the river. You can decide what you want to do once you check it out.'

Nitu sighed and said, 'We can make arrangements once we reach Unthaw by any means possible. But how do we carry two sick people, two children and one old woman there?'

'Wait! Why are you so impatient? Let the two Kachins return. We can make decisions after that', Gurcharan said. Satiated by the meal of pork and rice, he was lying on the grass lazily.

'I see someone approaching us', Budhu looked at the pathway and said.

'Not one...many—maybe three', the elder stood up, took his pipe out of his mouth and peered at the road while screening his eyes.

The Kachin youth had returned with two military men wearing hats and khaki uniforms. 'The base at Inleji relocated day before yesterday. The allies have withdrawn from Gada as well. I didn't get any medicine', the Kachin said briefly.

It seemed as if everyone was prepared for this eventuality as no one displayed any emotion at the news. Ramgobinda was sitting with his head sunk on his knees. He raised it briefly only to let it sink back again.

'Who are these people? What do they want?' the elder pointed at the two men and said.

'They have come from Kalewa and are proceeding towards Mogaung', the Kachin said. 'There are only four of them in their jeep. They can take the women and sick people to Unthaw. They say that there is a big hospital there where they can receive treatment. Their jeep is parked on the other side of the river.'

'Where did you come across them?' the elder seemed suspicious.

'I waved and stopped them when I saw their jeep travelling on the highway. I was feeling exhausted after running for a while at that point. They let me get on their jeep. We talked there. They are Chindits and understand our language.'

'How long will it take you to get to Unthaw?', the tall priest asked one of the soldiers.

'It will take us about three hours if we go straight down the main road' the soldier replied. 'It's about fifty-sixty miles from here.'

'What is the condition of the road? Has it been bombed yet?'

'As far as we know, it's still pliable. Two groups left before us in the morning.'

'How many people can you fit in the jeep?' Nitu asked.

'There are four of us already. At most we can fit in three others' one soldier said. 'The other two are sitting in the jeep.'

Then let us send Lacchmi, Budhu's mother and Ballabh in the jeep.'

'If we start now, we will also reach Unthaw tomorrow morning', Chinti said. 'That is, if we do not stop anywhere on the road.'

'There is an infant as well', Ramgobinda rose and said guiltily. 'I can carry Thanu on my shoulders.'

'Where is your jeep parked?' the tall priest queried.

'In the sandbanks on the other side of the river. The highway isn't very far from there', the soldier replied.

'There is no point delaying any further then. Let's carry Lacchmi and Ballabh to the vehicle,' Nitu said. 'It will take us at least half an hour to ford the river.'

'We can cross the river together.' Gurcharan said.

'Who is going to carry the sick people to that spot? We can't even bear the weight of our own bodies.' Haricharan asked.

'Let the soldiers take one of them. The Kachins can carry the other', the tall priest said.

'I will carry the infant', the Kachin elder said. 'The rest of you can gather and arrange your stuff.'

'I can walk this short distance', Budhu's mother said.

'Can you carry Thanu?' Budhu asked Gurcharan. 'Ramgobinda has been carrying him on his shoulders the entire way.'

'I will carry Thanu on my shoulders', Ramgobinda clasped Thanu tightly and said. He didn't want to let Thanu get out of sight even for an instant. It was as if his world would be plunged into darkness without Thanu.

'She has regained consciousness!' the short priest shouted from the other side of the curtain, rushed out and halted seeing this unexpected congregation of people. Then he whispered in the tall priest's ears, 'She has regained consciousness.'

'She will probably survive this leg of the journey', the tall priest heaved a sigh of relief and glanced at his watch.

Ramgobinda dashed to the other side of the curtain. The infant began wailing.

'We should not delay any further' Nitu said hurriedly, slinging his bag on his shoulder. The tall priest scribbled something on a piece of paper and handed it to a soldier. 'Please give this to the surgeon at Unthaw', he said.

The group began their journey to the sandbank along the narrow, winding roads in the forest. The two Kachin young men lifted Lacchmi on a bamboo mat. The two soldiers carried Ballabh.

All of them lifted and helped Lacchmi, Ballabh, Budhu's mother and the infant across the wooden bridge. After that, the rest of them prepared to resume their journey. The two Kachin young men also accompanied them to show them the way. 'Don't worry' they commiserated with Ramgobinda. 'We will reach Unthaw tomorrow night.'

XIII

The narrow plain area of Inleji lay just across the Mu river. The hilly pathways resumed after they crossed that—undulating slopes full of black, slippery mud, dense jungles on both sides and tall grass below. Occasionally, they came across silver fir trees. Groups of grimacing hooluks were sometimes visible shouting at them from the gaps within the trees. One of the bandors in the group would screech *hulu-lulu-lu-u-u* when it noticed humans in the vicinity; immediately, the others would scream in unison, remove themselves from the way by climbing the nearest tree or branch, and wait and stare at the travellers from the other side of the road. The cooing of doves and pheasants, the entrancing tunes of the mynahs and magpies, and the tock-tock sounds of the woodpeckers mingled with the screeches of the hooluks. When these noises stopped occasionally, the forest became absolutely quiet.

The leaves of the taller trees enclosed the forest like a crown. The floor was dark even during daytime. The scorching rays of the sun could not penetrate the thick covering of green and reach the heart of the forest. The groups of owls sitting on the branches of these sky-kissing trees sat in huddles like the agents of fate and hooted occasionally. The sound of their hooting resonated like ululations in the trees of this somber forest. Multi-hued rhododendron and primula flowers bloomed in the open spaces in the elevations that the forest had not yet touched, and joyously heralded the changing season. The deep blue gentian and the sparkling white flowers of the pear trees were dancing ecstatically in the bright light of the sun. Groves of bamboo covered the hills in the distance; between these groves, the fruits of the *kolmou*s, cherry, green oak, crab apple and stubbled *bogor*s glittered like a carpet made out of flowers. Various types of greens like *dhekia*, ferns and clumps of long, sharp-bladed grass carpeted the forest floor. *Kopou phul*, *bhatou phul* and orchids of multiple hues hung from the branches in the middle. Sometimes they came across groves of pine, mahogany and sandalwood. Leeches, caterpillars, centipedes, wild spiders and other aggressive, poisonous insects ruled the forest floor. This unique natural backdrop was such a peculiar combination of violence and beauty!

'How much further do we have to travel from Unthaw to Mogaung?' Gurcharan asked.

'At least four days', the tall priest said. 'That too if we walk day and night without any breaks.'

'Even this journey of about half a day seems like an endless one', Budhu said. 'We'll have to take a long rest in Unthaw.'

'You only want to take rest', Chinti reprimanded Budhu and stumbling over an exposed tree root fell to the ground with an oof!

'It seems like this route which they advertised as a short one is never going to end', Ramgobinda said. The box in his hands felt like a sack of heavy rocks.

'We may have come across a jeep or two if we went and waited on the highway to Pantha', the emaciated sick patient who had come with the priests said. Everyone turned around and stared at him with surprise, hearing his high-pitched voice for the first time in days.

'The military is retreating from Kalewa. All their vehicles should be bursting with people now', the tall priest looked at the man and said in a soft voice.

'My legs are feeling like lead', the man said and kept moving by sheer force of habit. He was moving like a sleepwalker now.

'Throw your bag away', Nitu said, noticing that the man was staggering. 'It will be easier to walk if you aren't carrying any weight.' The man wordlessly threw the bag, which contained all his possessions in the world, down the gorge almost instantly.

'What did you have there?' Budhu asked looking in the direction of the bag that had disappeared in the forest below.

'Nothing! Just a few clothes' the man said hesitantly. His high-pitched voice sounded weak and slurry.

'If it had been Ballabh, he would never have thrown his box away in a jiffy like this', Haricharan said. 'I am sure there are a lot of valuable stones and gold in his bag. That's the primary difficulty of being rich', he explained to Nitu. 'If you hoard too much wealth, you suffer under its weight later…thankfully that box went in the jeep.'

'What's the worth of gold and jewels if we can't even preserve our own lives?' Ramgobinda piped in.

'No one knows whether he is alive or dead at this moment', Chinti added.

Dense forests that were dark even during daytime surrounded them on all sides. The massive teak and mahogany trees above were like a green umbrella in the sky. There was no way of guessing what lay beyond that. These tall trees exclusively enjoyed the light and heat of the sun at the expense of the short trees below. The tall trees were healthy, well-nourished and thriving. It was a futile effort for the middling trees to pompously compete with them by stretching their branches and pushing forth their shoots and leaves. Their struggle to glimpse just a ray of sunlight, to wallow in just a bit of warmth, was meaningless, fruitless!

Ramgobinda started suddenly and remembered Lacchmi when the matter of the jeep was broached. 'They must have reached Unthaw by now', he thought, and lovingly caressed the deeply slumbering Thanu's shoulders.

The sick person who had thrown away his bag was lagging behind. His knees were scraped badly. Walking slowly at the end of the line, he suddenly fell to his knees as he tried to step forward. He didn't have time to cushion his fall with his hands. He fell hard on his face and two streams of blood began flowing from the two corners of his mouth. In an instant, his knees suddenly gave way unable to bear his weight. He screamed, looking at all directions in disbelief, shock and terror. His legs were disabled forever. Recognising this terrible predicament, his entire body began shaking uncontrollably in fear. Like a victim of paralysis, the limbs below his waist lacked all sensation, although his animated eyes were inspecting the people who had encircled him. It was as if the fear evoked by the terrifying scenes he witnessed when he briefly peered through death's door had parched his inner being. It was a frightening, awe-inspiring scene; mute and meaningless. An inarticulate, poignant plea formed in his dying eyes. It was a grief-stricken plea of a person at death's door to a group of helpless people without means. His eyes communicated what his parched lips could not. Each member of the group experienced that call in his bones. 'Let me live—don't leave me and let me die in this place without refuge. This is my distressed prayer that appeals to your humanity.'

The tall priest retraced his steps and shook the fallen man by his shoulders. 'What happened to you?' he asked. The person fell back on the ground like a slowly melting candle in response.

'Is he dead?' Chinti whispered to the priest. Everyone was struck with fear. The hairs on their weak, exhausted bodies stood on end. No one had the courage to speak loudly in that moment of meaningful silence. It was as if their blood would chill if they dared to produce a sound.

'He isn't dead yet—but he will be soon', the priest checked the man's pulse and said. 'He will die within an hour.'

'Everyone will die! Ha, ha, ha! Everyone will die one by one!' Haricharan's unearthly laughter suddenly shattered the stillness of this deathly ground. His laughter resounded off the cruel, evil hills and re-echoed like the dictates of fate. The callous hills seemed to be mocking them by laughing in unison as bystanders. A flock of birds that had settled on a branch flew away creating a din.

'We can't waste an hour or an hour and a half like this', Nitu said. 'We'll have to think about other things too. Our predicaments will be the same if we cannot reach Unthaw quickly', he swallowed his spittle. Haricharan's words had pierced his heart like a spear.

'Haricharan has gone mad', Ramgobinda said and released Thanu from his chest. His shoulders too seemed to lack sensation due to soreness.

'I will feel very guilty if we have to abandon a half-dead man in a situation like this', the priest said. 'He will become easy prey for beasts and vultures if we leave him here.'

'Ha! Ha! Flocks of vultures are massing in the branches of the trees waiting for all of us to die. Now all we have to do is to die one by one. They will have a royal feast then', Haricharan said, looking at the hills ahead.

'You keep quiet!', Chinti pushed Haricharan away and said. 'We all have to die, yes, but if we waste time like this, there will be no hope for the living either.'

The tall priest glared at Chinti, 'That means you want to leave him here like this?' He pointed at the kneeling visage of the man whose face was smashed on one side and who seemed to be supplicating them with his hands folded, and asked, 'Will you say the same things if you are in a similar situation after a while?' The priest was furious. 'This man isn't related to you, he doesn't have any connections either. But he is still a man. We will become beasts ourselves if we treat him like one. I am not going to take another step till this man dies.'

'You are correct to say that troubles beset us on each step of the way. Anyone can succumb to such a fate at any moment', Ramgobinda said, and sighed looking at the way towards their destination.

'We still have two-thirds of the way to Unthaw left', Nitu said.

'That's fine, that's fine. In any case, we are running a little late. Let's wait for a while longer', Chinti said. 'We will be able to take some rest as well.'

The shadows of the travellers lengthened in the slanting light of the sun and were now seen moving in the clouds bubbling up from the gorges. When their gaze fell on these clouds, the people felt as if their shadows resembled ghosts and spirits. A couple of them pinched themselves for assurance that they were still alive.

The tall priest got down on his knees, laid out the sick man lengthwise on the muddy ground, straightened his arms and legs, and holding his hand tightly, checked his pulse. Two streams of tears flowed from the person's eyes, wound their way around the curves of his ears and fell on the ground. His dry lips were quivering slightly. There was no water with anyone to moisten his lips. There wasn't a stream anywhere in sight either.

The short priest tied two pieces of wood with some ferns in the shape of a cross. 'No one imagines that he is going to die till the moment before his death', he said in his gruff voice. 'Right at the last moment, the person is shocked; his eyes open wide in sheer terror. He believes that he will live till he has consciousness. Of course, death means freedom from all troubles and tribulations—the beginning of an everlasting peace!'

'What illness did this person have?' Gurcharan asked.

'Phthisis, most probably. We couldn't understand it very well either. He was admitted to the hospital just a couple of days prior to our escape. There is no medicine for that illness—he would have died anyway. The process was accelerated because of the circumstances. We couldn't begin treatment because the hospital closed in the meanwhile', the tall priest said.

'We will have to cover him with leaves and plants after he dies as well', Chinti said. 'There is no time to bury him with the attendant rituals. I felt bad thinking that vultures would feed on his still living body. But after he dies, we don't have to care whose food he becomes, do we?'

Ramgobinda shuddered when he remembered his mother.

'The Parsis leave their dead as food for the vultures', the short priest said. 'They neither cremate their corpses nor bury them.'

'I feel uneasy listening to this', Ramgobinda shuddered and replied. In the meantime, the rest of the group seemed to have relaxed a bit. Everything could be taken easily if one surrendered completely to uncertainty.

'He is dead!', the tall priest announced suddenly,

leading to the complete cessation of all the murmurings among the rest of the group. The short priest planted the wooden cross at the head of the corpse. 'We should cover him at least', he told his compatriot and got busy gathering some dry leaves.

The group resumed their journey in about an hour. Unthaw was not even a night's journey away. The red light emanating from the fast setting sun in the west appeared sporadically between the silvered firs and the other trees at that time.

The Kachins were advancing at a rapid pace. It was difficult keeping pace with them as they were used to climbing up and down the hills. The rest fell far behind.

'Where do you think it's best for us to go beyond Unthaw?' Nitu hurried ahead and asked one of the Kachins. 'We don't know the roads beyond Unthaw', the other replied. 'You will reach Mansi if you take the path through Indawgyi. You should find people who can guide you at the base.'

'I think it will be shorter if we walk to Mogaung, cutting through the jade mines', the tall priest added. He looked at the map whenever he got the chance. 'We will have to move in a circle if we walk through Mogaung.'

'Eh! He is thinking so far ahead' Chinti laughed drily and said. 'Let us first get safe and sound to Unthaw.'

The group advanced like puppets moving on clockwork.

The weight on their shoulders and arms was steadily becoming unbearable. Most of them didn't have the strength to support the weight of their own bodies. They had only two alternatives before them—either reach their destination successfully or to give themselves over to death's embrace. Slowly, they were losing their fear of death, as if this was an inevitable reality.

The night passed by with them forging their way at a slow pace on a difficult road. The group reached the Dungi river in the morning, guzzled some soaked rice sitting on its banks, and then continued their journey again. A few of them tore some green bamboo shoots and consumed them. Others found some wild bananas with seeds and some bels and munched them on the way.

It seemed like there was no end to the undulating, winding, rough pathway. The travellers were exhausted and cheerless. Darkness seemed to have descended before their eyes even during this peak period of the afternoon. The two Kachins tried to boost their morale with an occasional word or two, but no one had the strength to respond. Morning, afternoon and evening passed by—the group kept moving steadfastly. That same, slow pace; that same capacity for movement (*jangamata*) that humanity had gathered through the ages propelled by their desire for survival.

In the dying embers of the evening and from the top of the tall hills, they saw the town of Unthaw glittering on some level ground below in the distance.

A sliver of light in the midst of the all-enveloping darkness! A strange smile illuminated the faces of these zombie-like travellers almost immediately. That was the smile of true, unadulterated joy—the smile of accomplishment.

'There lies Unthaw! There lies Unthaw!' someone shouted. 'It isn't far away!' 'We are in Unthaw', one of the Kachins said.

With a lot of hope in their hearts, the group of travellers set foot on Unthaw's main road in the early hours of the night.

This was definitely Unthaw! The same Unthaw that made their hearts flutter with hope.

But…what a surprise! There was no movement on the main road, no sounds of cars or tanks, no congregation of people! It was lifeless and quiet everywhere, as if this was a ghost town awash in the illumination provided by many electric lights and the moon. The tiny straw huts were uninhabited. Their doors were wide open, but no sign of a single person anywhere. Unthaw was deserted, Unthaw was a funeral ground! It was as if the entire environment was playing a cruel joke on them.

'Oh my god!' the tall priest held his hand up to his head and sat down on the main road and looked at the pale faces of the bearded travellers in the moonlight. It seemed like even this religious, god-fearing priest had lost all faith and assurance in god's judgement, faced with a situation of such cruel disappointment.

No one responded or even discussed the situation. Not a single one shouted suddenly in despair, breaking the dam of their restrained emotions. At this instant it seemed as if the howling winds of a horrific incident had overturned and smashed into tiny bits the hopes and desires of a group of eager and anxious people. The feelings and expectations of these thunderstruck people seemed to have frozen suddenly. In fact, they didn't even notice the farewell and departure of their two Kachin guides who left for their village that same night.

XIV

'Can anyone explain what happened here?', the short priest asked after a while. 'Have the allies withdrawn from here as well?' 'That seems to be the case' the tall priest replied, putting his hands on his head. 'Maybe they have already withdrawn and entered Assam at this point. If that's the case, there is no hope for us.'

'What will happen to us now?' Gurcharan asked, almost bawling like a little boy.

'What happened to my Lachhmi?' Ramgobinda asked, unable to stifle a sob. Due to extreme despair, an all-embracing veil of darkness seemed to cloud his vision.

'I don't know anything—don't know anything.' The tall priest raised his hands to his head, stared at the stars in the sky and screaming like a madman said, 'I know nothing… only the creator of this world knows something.'

'All our suffering, all our hopes seem to have gone in vain', said Budhu. The certain, frightening visage of death arose before his eyes.

A light could be seen at quite a distance in the paved highway going towards Mogaung—illumination from the headlights of a jeep. The tall priest stood in the middle of the highway and, waving his hands, made the jeep halt.

'We are stranded', the priest told the two military officers who alighted from the jeep.

They learned from the officers that the allies had withdrawn from Mogaung after the Japanese had bombed Mansi. They were supposed to go to Mogaung via the Stilwell Road from here. A large camp for refugees had been set up in Mogaung. If the group managed to reach Mogaung, they could stay there for a few days. There were about four or five camps on the way to Ledo. That region hadn't fallen to the Japanese as yet. There were about fifteen to twenty injured soldiers in the jeep; hence, they did not have any free space…It was perilous to travel on the highway. No one could say when the Japanese would attack…The jeep left.

The darkness increased steadily. With no other alternative in sight, the group decided to spend the night in an abandoned hut.

'The allies must certainly have destroyed all the food and provisions during the time of their retreat', the tall priest said. 'The people from the neighbouring villages, too, must have fled by now. Maybe Unthaw will fall to the Japanese in a day or two…after that, Indawgyi.'

During the night, the group scrambled to find a few greens and the tender shoots of the tal tree, which they then began boiling. Their supplies of rice were almost over.

Ramgobinda, however, could not sleep despite all the tiredness and weariness. His mind overflowed with legions of worries. There was no way of getting news of Lachhmi. It was impossible to find her during the middle of the night. His mother passed away relatively easily; the burden of all the worries was now transferred to him.

Thoughts of his mother kept Budhu awake as well. There was no way of knowing what happened to those four people in the jeep or where they went.

Leaving everything to God and fate, the group rested in a hut in that abandoned city.

'Hey, are you listening?' Chinti asked, looking at Nitu, who was sleeping nearby. 'If Indawgyi too…'

'Say what you have to say in the morning, now go to sleep', Nitu said angrily. 'I am very tired. We should rest during whatever remains of the night.'

By this time, most of the people in the group had fallen asleep. Despite the din created by the barking of thousands of dogs and also the howling of foxes, deep sleep overtook them.

Chinti, waking up first, posed the question at the break of dawn, 'If Indawgyi has fallen to the Japanese, would it be safe for us to travel to Mogaung following that route? Moreover, there are no camps or even people here. I don't think it will be possible to go searching for Lacchmi, Ballabh and the rest'. He looked at the tall priest. Nitu was still fast asleep.

'It will be good if we can reach Mogaung via Indawgyi'—the tall priest said. 'At the very least, we will get some food and a hospital in Mogaung camp.'

'But what about our people who left in the jeep?' Chinti asked. 'Where will we look for them? What if they were taken to Mogaung?'

'Don't worry. Since they were in a military jeep, they will at least reach Mogaung, no matter which route they take. It makes no sense to travel to Indawgyi looking for them in the midst of a retreating, broken army and lakhs and lakhs of refugees. On the other hand, our path will also become very circuitous', the tall priest said. 'Also, there is no saying what we find there once we reach that place.'

'In spite of all that, it will be better for us if we follow the paved road', Nitu, who had woken up, said. 'I heard that the region around Indawgyi is very difficult and terrifying.'

'The fact is that it will take us two days to reach Mogaung if we walk on that paved road. In the meantime, we cannot say what may happen there', the priest said. 'If we see that Mogaung too has been bombed, then we will be delayed in our journey. Hoping for something good, we will be neither here nor there. You have seen already that Unthaw has fallen…'

'That's fine. Then we should move towards Mansi, cross Indawgyi and then go to Mogaung', Chinti said, supporting the priest's proposal. 'What do the rest of you say?'

Ramgobinda was thinking something with his head bowed; he said nothing. Gurcharan stared fixedly at the sun.

'How far is Indawgyi?' asked Gurcharan.

'Approximately one and a half day's walk, maybe even two', the tall priest replied peering at the map. 'However, it is a straight road from there to Mogaung. It will be a shorter walk for us.'

'That place is very dangerous', Nitu said. 'Lowlands submerged in water on all sides of that swampy region, lots of *char*s too. It is rumoured that the waters of that place are poisonous. It is avoided by birds as well. They die if they stop there. These are, however, rumours. The Burmese call Indawgyi the gates of hell. However, they tend to inflate the stories a lot as well.'

'What if Mansi too has fallen by now?' the short priest ruminated. 'In such circumstances, would it be safe to travel in that direction?'

'According to the officers we met last night, Mansi

hasn't fallen as yet', the tall priest replied. 'On the other hand, a pitched battle is going on at Mogaung.'

The sun was scorching hot in the morning itself. Hordes of stray mangy dogs were roaming around everywhere, creating a huge din. They moved in packs and kept barking and fighting. They were emaciated dogs ridden with scabies, gaping wounds visible all over their bodies. Just the mere sight of them was enough to make one feel like vomiting. Their necks were swollen due to malnutrition, epitomising the conditions of famine raging through the entire country. Some didn't have ears, some were lame, others blind. The hind portions of some of them were immobilised by paralysis. These dogs dragged their hind sections a fair distance when they attempted to move ahead with their forelegs. Clumps of blood rendered the road red.

These dogs weren't afraid of humans at all. They reigned supreme in the playfield of death. If attempts were made to shoo away one or two of them, they would bare their fangs and, growling aggressively, run towards people. A violent look was in their eyes, hunger in their bellies.

Unable to sit because of pain and agony, a paralysed dog repeatedly kept moving in circles and, suddenly, collapsed on the ground. Immediately, the other dogs began barking in unison, surrounded the prone dog, and, in an instant, tore it to pieces with their sharp fangs and consumed its flesh. The onlookers felt like throwing up in disgust at this horrific scene. However, the unquenchable desire, the limitless thirst for survival shone through even in the midst of all this savagery.

'I have heard rumours that the Chinese soldiers have resorted to cannibalism in the absence of food', the tall priest said, observing this scene. Creating a massive din, two fighter planes crossed them above. There was no way of ascertaining whether the two planes moving round and round belonged to the allies or the Japanese. The dogs banded together in the middle of the highway and began barking at the planes. Suddenly a jeep with a red frame crossed the highway at great speed. The dogs scattered pell-mell. A sick dog was sleeping soundly in the middle of the highway; it had no time to escape. The jeep flattened its hind portions and moved ahead. Not even a yelp of agony emerged from the poor dog. Attempting to rise by transferring its weight to its fore legs, it threw a mute, disgusted, meaningless glance in the jeep's direction, momentarily bared its teeth, and fell down on the ground with a thud. Within moments, the other dogs tore its still body apart.

The charred, half-burnt remains of shops and houses in abandoned Unthaw came into view in the harsh light of the morning sun. Occasionally, charred remains of a grove of large trees were also visible—denuded, ugly! Scores of vultures alighted on the branches of these trees.

Billows of smoke and fire were also visible on the other side of the city. The flames of the fires were still glowing red and dancing in the horizon. A blood-red sun rose in the eastern sky, bursting through the blazing illuminations of a thousand fires.

There wasn't any food left with anyone. Although some of them had a little bit of rice or other morsels in their bags, they gobbled these when no one was looking. Supplies of both puffed rice and pithaguri had run out a long time ago. Some of them took out handsful of gooseberries and edible seeds from their bags and ate. They had collected these on the road. Others collected young bananas and bamboo shoots from the roofs of houses, extracted their piths piece by piece and consumed them. Some of them even ate raw papayas with their skins intact.

'It's best that we move while it's still daylight. We can rest at night in Mansi', the tall priest said, carefully peering at his map. 'It will be difficult groping around for a place in Indawgyi when it's dark.'

While the group heard what the priest said, no one made any sign of movement. They had become somewhat handicapped because of the swelling in their legs. The unquenchable desire to survive that had dragged them to Unthaw began to lose its power and fervour substantially once they reached the town. Their will too had broken just like their near-disabled bodies. A drastic degree of disgust and hopelessness had rendered their existence still and purposeless. Their minds, too, were clouded with doubts and terror after the brightly illuminated light of hope had been extinguished.

'Does survival in the face of such privations hold any meaning? What is the point of living on?' lying on the ground with the pariah dogs, Haricharan asked, as if talking to himself. With a stony gaze, his eyes were transfixed on the sky. 'There is nothing ahead, there is nothing we have left behind; What do we have to worry about? All of us have to die one day.'

'It is unfair to give leeway to such thoughts. These are signs of cowardice', the tall priest said. 'Whether our respective duties are small or big, God has designated a role for all of us. Everyone will die one day: that is the truth. However, we were not just born to die. God has given responsibilities and roles to all creatures. Once we have fulfilled these responsibilities, God will take back the life that he has given. At that point, we cannot do anything. There is nothing left for us to do either.'

'I don't have a mother, father or brothers. I have a wife back home. She must have wiped off her sindoor already, if by this time she heard of the bombing of Mandalay' Gurcharan said with a smile on his face. His flashing teeth in that salt and pepper bearded face looked very unappealing. That wasn't the smile of a human being, but of a ghost; a smile of self-mockery produced by the brutal effects of hopelessness and futility.

'I started out with lots of hopes and expectations. I lost everything one by one on this cursed road', Ramgobinda sighed and said. 'I may survive, but it's futile to hope that my Lacchmi will return to me. Mother has already left me.' He looked at Thanu who was sleeping by his side.

The tall priest was worried that the spirits of the travellers had broken. 'What had to happen has happened. Now let us all take God's name and renew our journey', he said. 'Our only path is to fulfil our responsibilities. The goal is ultimately dependent on his will.' He touched the cross hanging on his breast as if he was trying to renew faith that was gradually slipping away.

'I have no desire to hear God's name anymore', Nitu blurted and then bit his tongue. Even in such circumstances, people lacked the courage to utter such words although they may have lost all faith in God and had become atheists.

'God is always there to help and protect troubled souls like us', the short priest said. Squinting at the rapidly brightening sun, he suddenly stopped dead. Immobilised as if he had seen a ghost, he gazed in the direction of a nearby hut.

A beautiful, fair, young maiden ran out from the hut towards them. Her silky, shiny, disheveled hair glowed in the bright sun. A bunch of colourful, artificial flowers tied to her hair was visible just above her slender, fair neck. She was wearing a maroon lungi extending below her knees and a loose-fitting white silk blouse. The tight bodice below was visible through the soft, transparent fabric of the blouse. With each step, her slender, beautiful feet rippled like electricity. The leather bag slung over her shoulders was also glittering.

The girl approached the group and stopped panting right in front of the tall priest as the stunned group stared at her with disbelief. 'I'll join you as well', she said panting, moving her hands back and forth repeatedly.

'Who are you?' the tall priest queried, keeping his composure intact and trying to hide his astonishment. It was indeed unexpected to come across a lone young woman in such a remote region with war and bombing raging on all sides.

'I, too, am a refugee', the girl said glancing at the odd-looking members of the group. The members of the group cast questioning looks in her direction. 'Actually I am a Karen girl from the Taungoo region. My name is Ma-Pu. I also have an English name—Mary', she explained, gesticulating with her hands.

This time, the priest looked at her, scrutinising her from head to toe. 'Why are you here?' the priest asked her. 'I am actually Anglo-Burmese—a Christian. When I was younger, I studied at a missionary school in Rangoon. My parents passed away a long time ago. I worked as a nurse for a memsahib at an English household in Rangoon after I graduated from school...'

The girl halted and looked at the others with a wary, frightened gaze. Joy filled the hearts of the group. No one seemed perturbed by the fact that their departure had been delayed.

'And after that?' the priest asked.

'The sahib and his family escaped towards the north as the Japanese entered Rangoon. We travelled by jeep in the midst of all the bombing. However, we ran out of fuel near the banks of the Kathar river. Rationing was going on; petrol was nowhere to be found. Actually, we were supposed to travel to Misina. However, we heard that Misina too was being bombed. Seeing no other alternative, we left the jeep where it was and began crossing the jungle on foot. We came across a lot of refugees. We joined a large group and crossed the Irrawaddy with them on two boats that were lashed together', the girl was gasping and stopped momentarily after talking continuously for a time.

The priest shook his head. 'What happened after that?' he asked.

'Suddenly a lot of people were afflicted by cholera. We fell behind in the forest, once my memsahib and her two sons fell ill. The memsahib died the following day. We reached Unthaw yesterday morning with the two sick boys.

The fires caused by the bombing were still raging here. There were no people or hospitals here either. The two boys died within an hour of each other yesterday afternoon.'

'Where did the sahib go?'

'He locked himself in a room for about two hours. He shot himself in the chest and died in the evening', the girl began to weep. 'I closeted myself alone with those three corpses in that house for around eighteen hours.'

'Why didn't you come out and search for help?'

'Whom should I ask for help? There was no sign of life here. A couple of military jeeps occasionally crossed the alley. However, I am terrified of military men', with a bashful gaze, the girl looked once at the priest, then at her youthful, matured body, and then lowered her gaze to the ground.

'Did you know that we arrived here last night?'

'Yes! I was watching your movement and activities from the window there in the moonlight.'

'Why didn't you come out then?'

'I was scared. This is an unknown place. I couldn't figure out what type of people you were either. I heard rumours that after the bombings of the cities and the withdrawal of the Allied forces, hordes of Burmese demons arrived with sharp weapons and proceeded to loot the shops and markets. Fires were raging in the households. Robbery was going on in full daylight. I heard that even the police forces stripped off their uniforms and badges and joined the rioting mobs. We saw the corpses of scores of soldiers on our way. Apparently, the Burmese hacked the isolated ones to death. Clumps of blood were still visible on the corpses. During such times, can you place even a smidgeon of trust on others?' the girl opened her eyes wide and looked at the priest.

'Seems like you weren't scared to come out now?'

'When I saw the two of you, I realised that you weren't some sort of demonic horde. On the other hand, I thought that maybe you are the last band of refugees travelling in this direction. Therefore, if I don't take my chances with you, I may be stuck in this place. There is no saying when the Japanese will arrive here either', the girl raised her endearing face and looked at everyone. 'I heard that they are very barbaric.'

'Aren't you Burmese yourself?' the tall priest said, checking the girl's profile once more from head to toe. 'What is the problem if you remain behind in Burma? Why do you want to escape?'

'From my childhood, I have been raised close to British families. Burmese life and customs are alien for me. I am not conversant with them. I am not used to that form of living', Ma-Pu replied with a sorrowful face. 'I have no attachment to the Burmese way of life. Even though I am Burmese, I hardly know that way of life.'

'What do we do now?' faced with this unprecedented situation, the tall priest turned towards Nitu.

'It will be very difficult if we have a woman with us on this route', Budhu said.

'Be that as it may, but how can we abandon a lonely girl like her in this place?' like a wise man, Chinti responded. 'Would we have abandoned our sisters like this? Could you leave your mother behind?' Chinti felt strangely attracted to this helpless girl when he saw her for the first time. Expecting support, he looked at Nitu.

Nitu did not respond. It was as if his powers of thinking had stopped functioning after he had laid all his expectations at fortune's feet and stumbled at each and every step. 'Whatever is written by the fates will happen anyway.' At that moment, each member of the group felt the same way.

'Whatever you do, do it quickly. Don't waste time', Ramgobinda said, looking at the sun which was now high in the skies. He was constantly assailed by thoughts of Lacchmi and the infant.

'You mentioned something about your sahib committing suicide with his pistol…', the short priest asked in his deep voice, his deep-set pair of eyes twinkling. 'What happened to the pistol?'

'It's still…in the clenched fist of the corpse', Ma-Pu replied.

'Does it still have bullets?'

'I don't know. I haven't checked that.'

The short priest looked at the rest. 'It will be useful to have the pistol with us, what do you say?' He said that and made a gesture to Ma-Pu to retrieve the pistol. Ma-Pu quickly went into the house, and emerged in an instant with the pistol and a bag of bullets in her hand.

'The sahib's box is also lying there. There is a lot of jewelry there, maybe some money as well', she said.

Everyone was suffering from fatigue and lacked the strength to carry any weight. No one showed any enthusiasm when they heard about the box and the jewelry. What was the value of wealth and jewelry for people engaged in a struggle for life near death's doorway? They were like valueless, meaningless burdens on a donkey's back for these people who were anyway unable to bear the weight of life.

'Is there any food there?' Kalu asked.

'No! Whatever was there ran out a while ago. We had to abandon some provisions in the jeep', Ma-Pu replied. 'We were planning to buy some provisions here.'

'There aren't too many bullets, but they still will be of use', the short priest checked the pistol carefully, and placed it in the pocket of his overcoat. He also slung the bag of bullets on his back. 'An American pistol', he explained to his tall compatriot.

The group resumed their trek around nine in the

morning. This time their destination was Indawgyi via Mansi.

Once again, that same journey with an unknown destination! This journey was an unending procession of a group of uprooted people in search of safety and a new life through a perilous, extremely difficult road.

XV

Manku's quiet, quotidian existence became terrifyingly sombre after the departure of the Indian families. A couple of nights passed by as the aged Ba-Mao lay in bed contemplating myriad issues. Unlike other days, the old man showed no inclination to wake up his two sons, who often slept late, at the crack of dawn. The season for cultivation, however, was nearly at hand. Seedlings of rice were about to sprout. They were supposed to wake up early and tend to the fields. As he agitatedly turned and tossed in his bed at night, Ba-Mao attempted to keep the recurring nightmares about war and terror at bay by repeatedly trying to turn his thoughts towards his fields and matters of cultivation. However, despite all his attempts, he was unable to stave off the naked truth of the cruel realities of these terror-filled times that kept dancing before his weary eyes. The terrifying spectres of war and destruction returned repeatedly and convulsed the peaceful, stable conditions of his everyday existence.

'How long can we go on like this?' he asked himself. Two days had already gone by. The rebels were already moving on the path lying between Pakokku and Manku. The Japanese would probably arrive any moment. Yesterday, a band of youthful rebels were in Manku inquiring about the Indians. Oh my dears! You poor ones arrived two days late! Even in the midst of all these worries and travails, Ba-Mao cheered up when he thought of how the Indians managed to get out of Manku safely. 'In all probability, they must have crossed the dangerous portions of the route by now', he thought. The rebels said that in the meantime Mandalay had been conquered. Misina too had fallen.

'How much longer?' Ba-Mao got no answer as he posed this question to himself while turning around in bed. Whatever happened, it would be good to have some certainty; nothing could be achieved when they were kept dangling like this. Consternation took root in the mind then. On the other hand, the time to weed the rice seedlings and till the soil had also arrived. If the seedlings weren't weeded right now, then the planting could not be done in time. Everything would be ruined if the rains arrived early as in the previous year. In a few days, the glittering rice seedlings would turn green. Smearing *thanaka* powder on their hands and faces and singing songs of cultivation in tune with the beat of drums, the young women of the village would need to plant the seeds in groups. 'But what an evil time has now afflicted the country...?'

Suddenly, Ba-Mao's unpleasant contemplations were interrupted by the tapping sound of a walking stick outside his door. He pricked up his ears to guess who it might be. It was evident from the sound of the footsteps that it must be Jayanao. Why was he here so early? Something terrible must have happened! Ba-Mao got up from bed in a trice. His mind was racing with fear, as if some terrible nightmare was about to unfold.

Jayanao had just reached the verandah. When he saw Ba-Mao, he leaned on the pillar and let his walking stick fall on the ground.

'What happened?' Ba-Mao asked as calmly as possible, adjusting the knot on his lungi. He voiced his question calmly and did not betray even a hint of worry.

'Nungnao—', Jayanao said and letting go of the pillar bent down to pick his wooden stick from the ground. 'They murdered Nungnao!' the words were ejected like bullets from Jayanao's mouth, probably shrouding the thousand tempests that were raging in the recesses of his heart. 'His bloody, battered corpse was flung into my courtyard last night.' Jayanao bowed his head and paused.

'How inhuman! How cruel!' Ba-Mao said. Even though

he anticipated ill-tidings, he wasn't prepared for such tragic and unexpected news. With extreme disgust, he spat out a gob of spittle very volubly on the ground.

'He is gone—my hirsute boy is gone forever', Jayanao lamented. 'I am not saddened by the fact that he has taken leave of us. Everyone has to leave when their time is nigh. Who can hold them back? But to be hunted down like an animal—!'

'Do not give way to grief', Ba-Mao said, placing his hand on Jayanao's shoulder. 'These are the evil dictates of fate; humans have no say in this.'

'Of course, this is the deserved fate for such people, their behavior was so wicked', Jayanao said. 'My boy fell into bad company at such a tender age. He had always been stubborn and quick-tempered. His mother spoilt him a lot when he was growing up. She would not let even the shadow of punishment come near him', remembering his wife, Jayanao sighed. 'Thank goodness, the woman isn't alive to see what happened today. She must have witnessed it. Wherever she is, she must have witnessed it too.'

'Come, let's go over there. You are giving way to sorrow.' Ba-Mao said. The two aged men crossed the long courtyard and stepped outside. 'What is gone is gone; however, we need to conduct our duties responsibly.'

'It's his good fortune that his death took him away from this devastated country. Who knows how many misfortunes will still beset the living? Who knows what will happen to us in the coming days?' Jayanao said.

Ba-Mao's eyes began smoldering like raging stars. 'Who is responsible for this terrible thing? Whose well did he poison, that little boy with milk still drooling from his mouth?'

'Must be someone from his group; who else can it be? Who else knows him or has heard about him? He had connections, a deep intimacy, only with this band of rebels.'

'These rebels who lack any semblance of rationality or conscience should be caught and impaled one by one on stakes.' Ba-Mao said.

'I will have my revenge', it was as if the tide of Jayanao's repressed emotions began swelling suddenly at Ba-Mao's words. His voice trembled betraying the tremendous force of his emotions. 'I will take revenge on each and every Burmese rebel. I will wreak my vengeance on Burma!' The lines on Jayanao's face hardened as he reiterated this harsh promise. The firm grip of his left fist tightened even further after it trembled incessantly for a while.

'Mark my words, the lives of each Burmese rebel will be the only recompense for every drop of Nungnao's blood...'

'Keep your calm, don't give way to emotion. You shouldn't fall apart at this hour of crisis', Ba-Mao said, shaking Jayanao's left shoulder. 'The time for revenge will come. If you give leeway to emotion at this time, it will cloud your judgement. Make a decision only after you have deliberated on it calmly, rationally.'

Nungnao's blood-spattered, battered body was lying in the courtyard. Pools of blood surrounded his body. The two elder sons of Jayanao were sitting on the ground and staring fixedly with their heads in their hands at the bloody, unrecognisable face of their brother. They were all dry-eyed. They were neither wailing and giving vent to grief nor showing any sign of weakness. They were absolutely silent. They resembled a group of corpses who had lost their lives instantaneously when thunder struck them from the skies, and were now sitting frozen in a circle surrounding another cadaver.

'He had done a lot for the group of rebels. And this is the reward he gets!' Pointing at the corpse, Jayanao said to Ba-Mao, 'He was charred in the fire of the rebellion.'

'What, according to you, is the reason for this?' Ba-Mao asked, looking carefully at the marks of torture on the corpse. 'Why would the rebels inflict such cruel treatment on one of their own without any significant cause?'

'What else could be the cause of this? He helped Manku's Indians escape and made arrangements for that himself; isn't that reason enough?' Jayanao responded. 'In their hierarchy of crimes, betrayal is foremost. When he agreed to help them the other day, I knew that something terrible would happen.'

'So, does this mean that the other rebels did not agree with the arrangements made to help the Indians cross the Irrawaddy?'

'How can they agree to a proposal like this? They are a bunch of bloodsucking vampires, a group of barbaric demons deranged by the intoxications of nationalist sentiment. They require raw blood, they desire revenge! They are a group of young men with no conscience. He had to bear the brunt of their fury when they couldn't find the Indians…it is my misfortune that my Nungnao dallied with such a group of savage beasts. He was a very simple boy. He could be swayed by anyone's words. He couldn't fathom wicked intentions disguised in that whirlpool of noxious, divisive speeches that made the pulse quicken', Jayanao said.

'How do you know that the group didn't agree with the arrangements made to let the Indians escape?' Ba-Mao queried.

'On that day, he told me that the other members of the group had disagreed with him after he got home from the meeting. I advised him to keep himself at a distance from them because of these eventualities. He said that he was about to do something.' Jayanao clasped Ba-Mao's hand tightly and spoke in a faltering voice. 'I never dreamt that my darling son would do something so drastic.'

'When did he leave home? The people from our village left that evening itself, didn't they?'

'On that evening, he opened my safe and disappeared from the house with silver worth about two hundred in currency. I knew what he was doing, but didn't question him about anything. I realised that he had taken that money to bribe the boatmen.'

'You should have stopped him then. It's dangerous to go against the will of the group in this fashion', Ba-Mao said.

'That's true! But I didn't have the will to stop him. I didn't feel like stopping him once I thought of those desperate people trying to escape to save their lives. Moreover, would he have listened to me if I stopped him? He made a promise; there was no way he would turn back from that. I had counseled him earlier as well. The astrologer said a long time ago that there were evil omens in his horoscope. However, he was a hot-blooded, stubborn young man—why would he listen to anybody?' Jayanao fell silent.

In the meantime, a few peasants, ready to till their fields with their ploughshares, had gathered in the courtyard.

'Must be the doing of the Japanese', one of them said. 'Those Japanese don't have a shred of mercy in their hearts.'

'No, not the Japanese!' Jayanao shouted passionately once these words reached his ears. 'The Japanese are foreigners. Whom do they know here? This is the doing of his fellow Burmese young men; his comrades thrust this blazing fire in my heart.'

'Please be patient! There is no point giving way to rage

now', Ba-Mao said. 'We'll have to do what we are supposed to do. You cannot change the dictates of fate. It's important that we conduct our responsibilities in a calm manner now.'

'The Indians have left—they have been rescued from this. Even beasts don't club a person to death like these demons did', Jayanao lamented. 'We won't be able to survive for long in this devastated country. Ah! Our countrymen, our friends, our own flesh and blood have now become our greatest enemies.'

'He was a rebel. Couldn't he have been killed by the British or the Indians?' one of the bystanders asked.

'His corpse would have been thrown into the Irrawaddy if the British or Indians killed him. They wouldn't have speared me through the heart in this fashion, casually throwing his corpse in my courtyard after piercing him repeatedly through his chest as if he were a cornered deer' Jayanao said. 'I have no doubt that this was the doing of the Burmese.' He pointed towards the corpse. 'Only the Burmese are capable of such cruelty—cutting up the face of a corpse so brutally!' Covering his face with his hands, Jayanao stood up.

'However, we should not let the Indians off the hook either', one of the farmers said. 'They are landlords who charge a lot of interest; they can consume people alive. I have also heard that they have become very violent now that they are facing the situation of leaving Burma.'

'Apparently, day before yesterday, they rioted and set Burmese houses on fire after Mandalay was bombed', another peasant chimed in supportively.

'I heard that many Indian spies, disguised as beggars, were captured in front of the Arakan pagoda…'

'Keep quiet, you lot! I know the truth', Jayanao said.

Gusenpung, who had slept in late, arrived out of breath. 'I ran here as soon as I heard the news', he said. 'What a terrible tragedy!'

'I don't know what to say', a peasant said by way of consolation. 'Such rotten fortune has afflicted the aged Jayanao in his dying days! I feel very sorry at his predicament.'

'I saw an astounding dream last night', said Gusenpung. 'A light as red as vermilion was streaming out of the crest of the Shwedagon pagoda. That means…' Noticing that the peasants weren't paying any attention to what he said, and were streaming out of the courtyard with bowed heads, he stopped and looking at Jayanao who was standing right in the middle of the courtyard, blurted, 'I just received the news now'.

'There is no point letting the corpse lie in this manner here. We have to perform the funeral rites as soon as possible', Ba-Mao said.

'Oh my darling motherless child!' Suddenly Jayanao began wailing loudly giving vent to his suppressed emotions, and covered the corpse's face with a white shroud. The veins in his face seemed swollen; his pale face had turned red like vermilion. However, he controlled himself suddenly with tremendous effort and looking at Ba-Mao said, 'Let's do what we have to do soon. My Nungnao is gone; it is futile clinging to his beloved form'.

The corpse was buried in a pit dug in one of the elevated grounds dotting Manku. Nungnao's attractive visage slept peacefully forever under three feet of soil.

'The British, Japanese or Indians aren't our enemies; our most formidable enemy is ourselves', Jayanao said, looking in the direction of his eldest son. 'Keep this bit of counsel in mind. I don't expect to survive much longer. The poisonous weeds of division have begun sprouting. Everyone will have to partake of its poisonous fruits in the future.'

'The same crisis that has befallen the Indians will also afflict the Burmese soon. Poison has entered the minds of people. Very soon, this poison will proliferate throughout Burma and splinter the country into tiny, tiny pieces' Ba-Mao said. 'People will desire that evil befall others, petty selfishness and self-centred thinking will take root. These are the signs of erosion, of destruction. Since the poisoned seeds of division and differentiation have taken root, it will be difficult to turn the clock back. They will squeeze the life out of this country.'

'Why can't everyone in this country stay united like brothers, as we do in our own families?' Jayanao said, his head collapsing in his arms. 'The entire country can be at peace then.' Glancing at Nungnao's grave, he pressed his left hand to his chest.

That night, the entire village was in mourning. Unlike other days, no one stepped out of their households to exchange a word or two with their neighbours in order to relax their minds. A dark, ominous shadow that exceeded the terror caused by war and bombings shrouded the entire village.

XVI

The journey from Unthaw to Mansi was a repetition of the old story once again. The only difference was that the elevations and descents on the road increased along with the density of the wild foliage. The path wound its way along an unending line of remorseless hills. These cruel, frightening hills were covered with tall trees. From tiny insects to small plants and bushes—an incessant battle for survival was waging underneath the cover of the thick forest. The band of refugees carefully avoided the Burmese villages that occasionally came into view at the foothills. The influence of the Japanese was very strong in these northern hills. They were also afraid to advance too close to the railroads and the highways. The Japanese concentrated their attacks on such places. Besides that, they couldn't say when a particular region would fall under Japanese control.

Therefore, it was preferable to advance following these winding pathways using the thick cover provided by the forest as a means of camouflage.

The people were advancing steadfastly with one aim in mind…simply advancing! Everyone was occupied with their own worries. A few of them plucked gooseberries hanging in bunches on the thorny shrubs at the edge of the pathways and ate large mouthsful of these fruits or stuffed them quickly in their bags. The narrow pathways were covered by trees and leaves and resembled tunnels. The forest was astonishingly quiet; not even the sound of birds to be heard anywhere. The thorny shrubs would clasp and jerk at their clothing. Their clothes were slowly being shredded to pieces. The scissor-like sharpness of the tall jungle grass that grew as tall as their heads clawed at them, and left stinging wounds on their bodies. The clumps of blood drying on the blotches of grass made them glitter even more. A few clumps of grass were scattered around in mounds. Hordes of flies laid their eggs there. Spotted leeches attached themselves at will to the bodies of these half-dead travellers and fell away on their own after fattening themselves on their blood. Not a single one of the travellers tried to get rid of the leeches that were stuck to their bodies. Occasionally, the thick webs of wild spiders got into their faces and mouths. They were also sometimes startled by wild creepers that wound themselves on their bodies, as if they were some sort of green serpent. The fear of death infiltrated the minds of the startled travellers—the oldest fear persisting since creation. This fear didn't abandon these people even on this final journey through death's road.

The group proceeded steadfastly hour by hour, stumbling, slipping and falling repeatedly on the black, clayey soil of the continuously ascending and descending slopes. A few members of the group, moving at a slow pace like a flock of half-dead beasts, suggested briefly that they would like to rest awhile at night. However, the others didn't agree. They should keep advancing although their pace was slow, as uncertainty and danger shadowed them. It would be safer for them if they could cross this treacherous forest in Northern Burma as quickly as possible as even a minor delay could result in death. Seeing no other alternative, the group kept going forward.

Soon it was morning. Jhum fields glittered like dewdrops in the morning light, appearing occasionally in the smoke-hued, massive valley dotted with hills. After a while, the twisting currents of a swollen river came into view. Tall hills on either side—kissing the skies, invincible!

A path that twisted like a snake along the hillside disappeared near the river. 'From now on we probably have to advance keeping close to the riverbanks. It will be impossible to climb up the edges of the hills', the tall priest said, peering at his map and glancing at the hills in either direction. 'This is the Meja river. Its currents are very treacherous. If we follow the straight pathway, we will have to cross this river a number of times. We will also have to wade through the river in a couple of spots.'

Multi-hued round pebbles and fishes of various shapes and sizes cavorting fearlessly and consuming algae were clearly visible in the bed of the crystal-clear river.

'The water isn't very deep', Gurcharan girded his loins and stepped into the knee-deep river. 'However, the current is very strong and the water is ice-cold.'

'We shouldn't have any problem with this current flowing downstream.' Nitu said. The other members stepped into the water. Occasionally, the depth of the river increased sharply in the pockets between the hills. There were a few whirlpools moving at slow speed in these regions as well. The tall trees on the hills on both sides covered the river with a leafy canopy and rendered those portions dark even in daytime. The swollen feet of the travellers became pale after walking continuously for hours in a row in the freezing water. Blood oozed out of their skins that had begun fraying due to the cold.

By the afternoon, the height of the hills on their left side became progressively smaller. After a while, they noticed a small clearing of dry ground near one of the foothills. There was a paddy field on the other side of the clearing. Beyond that was a village. The group clambered up the banks.

Their exhaustion and sorrow increased a hundred-fold when their eyes fell on the village. They were deeply affected by the sudden consciousness of the distress and hunger that had accumulated over time.

'It is impossible to go on…', Budhu stretched his legs and flopped on the grass. 'It is infinitely better to die by the bullets of the Japanese or the machetes of the Burmese than to pass away after surviving in such a pathetic fashion.'

They realised that the habitation ahead of them was a Kachin village as soon as they noticed the *machan* at the entrance of the village. The machan was decorated with the coloured skull of a wild buffalo. Dried flowers and leaves were strewn beside it. A number of skulls of smaller animals were strung on the pillars of the machan.

'There is no way that we can avoid this village now. There is no other road. We have to go right through it' Chinti said.

'Does anyone know who these people are? Can we know something for certain?' Nitu asked. 'We should keep our guard up from the very beginning.' He cast a meaningful look in the short priest's direction. The priest put his hands in the pocket of his overcoat and fingered the pistol.

'The Kachins aren't rebels', the tall priest said. 'Therefore, these people should not harm us. However, nothing can be said for certain.'

'Whatever is written in our fates will happen', Gurcharan said. 'In any case, there is virtually no hope that we will survive after traversing the long stretch that lies ahead. If we have to die, let us die here.' His eyes, which had sunk deep into his shaggy face, began glittering like dim stars when he said this.

'There is nothing that they can snatch from us in any case', Budhu said. 'Of course, if they can't find anything, they can always take our lives.'

Some sort of celebration was going on at that point in the open ground in the middle of the village. A group of ten to twelve young maidens, wearing colourful clothing and placing their hands on their hips, were dancing to the beat of drums and bamboo clappers. Their singing and dancing ceased once the travelling group reached that spot. The villagers surrounding the group of dancers stared at the stragglers with a great deal of curiosity.

Noticing that one of the villagers was approaching them, the tall priest said, 'We are refugees.'

'We are trying to reach Assam. We have to take the road that crosses Mogaung *en route* to Ledo.'

'Mogaung is very far', the Kachin said. Probably he hadn't heard of Ledo at all. 'You have taken the wrong route. You should have gone to Mansi via Thayetkan. A lot of refugees have gone through this way though', he continued.

'We are extremely tired', the tall priest said. 'We don't have any food with us either. We have been surviving on gooseberries for the last two days. Our hunger is acute. Can you help us?'

The Kachin man scanned the group of sick, half-dead people. 'You cannot stay here. The Japanese have set up camp in Bonmok nearby', he said. 'If they learn that you are here, they will kill you and won't spare us either.' He stopped, looked in the direction of the villagers who massed behind him for a moment and said, 'We don't have food here. The soldiers came twice, looted our granaries and left virtually nothing for us.'

One by one, the people watching the dance slowly began milling around the group. Looks of hopelessness were visible on the faces of the refugees.

'We have a vat or two of *saku*—we can offer that to you. Drink that and please leave this place quickly', the Kachin said. 'The Japanese are advancing towards Mansi. If you cannot cross Mansi quickly, you will fall into trouble.'

The refugees gulped down the saku served in bamboo holders, rested for a brief while, and then resumed their journey again when the sun's rays began to slant. Glimmers of hope began forming once again when they spotted Mansi from the top of a hill in the evening. Their morale received a boost when they noticed a glittering sign, written with lime on a plank of wood saying, 'Welcome to Mansi' when they reached the outskirts of the town at dusk.

There was no sign of people in Mansi that had been bombed just two days ago. They witnessed smoky and ashy remains and broken, gutted houses everywhere. The teak pillars of some of these houses were still standing upright and burning. The smell of burning matter pervaded the town; the streets were completely deserted. The inhabitants had scattered pell-mell locking all the shops—a silence devoid of breath and isolation reigned supreme in this town whose life had been throttled very suddenly. A couple of military jeeps proceeded speedily with their headlights turned off on the main road in the early hours of the night. Proceeding through the wide road of the city, the group noticed a signboard hanging on a gutted house that read 'Mansi Hotel'. The signboard seemed to be holding its head up with pride even in the midst of all this destruction. The group entered the building, hoping to find something to eat. However, the kitchen and dining room were completely empty; not a single drop of water to be found, no sign of people anywhere. A pen and a letter that hadn't been completed were lying on a table in the large, razed room in the center. The tall priest picked up the letter from the table and read, 'My darling, we have lovely weather in Mansi this time of the year. The Japanese haven't attacked this region in Burma as yet. Don't believe the terrifying news about Burma that the newspapers are carrying. You shouldn't believe and needn't worry about such ill-tidings. I am doing very well. In all probability, I will be able to return in a few days and hold you and the baby in my arms. There is talk that we will get a longer holiday next month. I haven't even seen the baby yet…' A melancholic smile formed on the priest's face. 'This unfortunate person wasn't able to finish a letter to his faraway beloved. Maybe if they receive this letter, it will give some measure of consolation to the surviving members of his family.' He carefully folded the letter and placed it in his coat pocket.

An uncountable number of corpses and dismembered body parts were strewn on the road. A lot of dead bodies were visible inside the houses as well. Apart from a few ragged pariahs, even the dogs were dead. The surviving pariah dogs were gnawing at the corpses lying on the sides of the road.

Finding a relatively secure spot in a destroyed house, the group decided to spend the rest of the night there. There was a large well right in front of the house. 'At least we will have some fresh water' the group thought. There was simply no way that they could proceed without taking some rest. The fear of death seemed to have evaporated completely for them.

To be sure, dark forebodings filled the minds of each person. The stretch between Mansi and Indawgyi was extremely difficult; beyond that were the gates of hell of the Hukawng. There was no certainty who would survive and ultimately reach their destination. Besides the threat from people and disease, they still had to contend with the lack of food, the steady weakening of their bodies, and this unending, unendurable, exhausting journey.

A piercing, melancholic sigh escaped Ramgobinda's lips when he noticed the curled up figure of Thanu sleeping deeply in a corner of the house. Thousands of black mosquitoes covered Thanu's body; however, he did not stir at all. Occasionally he would mumble something or change his position agitatedly in his deep slumber. 'I have carried him so far tying him very tightly to my chest; his tender body must be aching by now!' Ramgobinda thought. His limbs seemed to belong to an alien entity due to the pain he experienced. Every joint and socket of his body was aching. 'I should also give the boy something to eat', he thought. He didn't have a single grain of rice or a morsel of food with him. He asked his compatriots if they had some rice or pithaguri with them.

'Rice?' Nitu laughed drily. 'Where do you expect to get rice? Have some berries or fruits.'

'No, I wasn't asking for myself. Thanu hasn't eaten anything since yesterday afternoon. I couldn't find anything for him in the morning either.'

'No, there is nothing! Rice, puffed rice, pithaguri—everything is finished. No one managed to get anything in this town either', Nitu replied in a distressed tone. 'I don't know if anyone is still hiding something. I don't have anything with me.'

The tall priest approached them and asked, 'What happened?' Ramgobinda mutely pointed in the direction of the exhausted Thanu curled up in a corner. The priest went close to Thanu and checked his temperature. 'He is suffering acutely from hunger', he said. 'Does anyone have anything to give him?'

'Nothing!' Ramgobinda said, and with extreme self-reproach began to chastise himself for the handful of rice that he had wasted in the previous days. He clasped his head tightly in his arms and fell with a thud on the ground.

Budhu, Chinti and Kalu banded together and got a fire going at the other end of the room. 'We can roast bamboo and banana shoots in the fire and eat them.' Kalu grinned and said, noticing the tall priest approaching them. The white teeth flashing in his bearded face looked very unappealing.

'Let's see if we can find a kettle lying somewhere. We can consume anything if we boil them well', Budhu said.

'I noticed a lot of wild arum plants near the doorway—dig those up and bring them here', Chinti said while attempting to fan the fire. 'Our throats will itch; however, they will satisfy our hunger. There is no need for salt and oil when one is hungry.'

'We made a big mistake', the short priest addressed his compatriot from where he was sitting. 'We could have detonated a grenade in one of those crevices in the river and killed some fish. That thought never occurred to me earlier.'

'Our lives were on the line during that time. Who remembers such things at those times?' The surviving sick man who had come with the two priests said. He was leaning on the wall and dozing.

'Does anyone have rice with them? I just need a handful of rice', the tall priest addressed everyone in a loud voice. 'The tiny tot is dying of malnutrition; where will I get a handful of rice?'

Everyone looked in the priest's direction. They never imagined that a small boy and an ordinary handful of rice could precipitate such a crisis. People needed rice to survive; however, survival itself had become an irrelevant question now. Where was the need for rice? There was no ground for consternation if someone died because they did not get any rice. Let that person die! In any case, thousands of corpses were strewn everywhere. Their numbers would merely increase by one—was there any loss in that?

'Rice…Ha! Ha! Ha!' Haricharan, suddenly waking up in the corner where he was lying, began screaming like a madman. 'I, too, want rice. Where is it? Give me some rice, right now. I, too, am about to die.' He clutched his shrunken stomach with one hand and flopped face-down on the ground. His eyes were extremely red. In the flickering light of the fire, this long-haired and densely bearded person resembled a frightening spectre. 'Death, death is everywhere! Everyone will die! One by one, everyone will die! Death is better than this. You will die only once—your troubles then are over.' He cackled frighteningly once again.

'Maybe we will find a handful of rice if we search outside', Nitu said. 'However, there is no sign of life anywhere. We don't know the place either.'

'What will people who are counting the moments leading up to their deaths whilst waiting to be bombed have with them? Apparently, the Chinese army also crossed through this town. They must have cleaned and consumed everything in this place like locusts', the short priest said.

The tall priest and Ramgobinda went out in the direction of the marketplace. Noticing the dim light of a hurricane lamp casting its rays through a crack in the wooden door of a small house in the other corner of the closed marketplace, the tall priest halted and knocked. This house must have been a shop. There was no sign of life in the beginning. After he knocked several times, a short, pale man, with a lamp in his left hand and a revolver in his right, peered outside with the door slightly ajar. Most probably, he was assured by the priest's outfit and stepped outside.

'What do you want?' he raised the lantern to the priest's face and asked in a rough voice.

'We are out looking for a handful of rice to feed an ailing child', the priest replied, without standing on ceremony.

'I knew that you had come here in search of food', the short man said. 'However, I have nothing here. They robbed and looted everything from here. They must have hidden it somewhere.'

'Who are the "they?"'

'Demons, low-life scum, robbers', the man lowered his revolver and spat on the ground. 'You won't get food anywhere here. They came last night and looted everything. They even injured the few people who remained behind. They will come again tonight.'

'Who are you talking about? Who are the "they?"', the priest asked. 'Why will they come again?'

'Wow! I don't know where you think you are?' the short man said, with disgust writ large on his face. 'They are all going to come again. Robbers, policemen, Chinese soldiers—they will descend in hordes. Everyone is the same in these times. They will burn houses, fire their weapons, loot everything in their way! The Japanese destroyed us with their bombs; these traitors will complete the destruction and increase our misery manifold. Hordes of rebels are crawling out of the villages. Robbery reigns supreme. In fact, they took away rings and jewelry after chopping off the fingers and necks of the corpses', suddenly, the short man went inside and slammed the door shut. In a trice, the lamp was extinguished and the weak light emerging from the crack on the door also disappeared.

'I am sure that they have some food with them', Ramgobinda told the priest as they were returning. 'They won't give it to us.'

'Why should they?' the priest replied. 'In these terrible days, a handful of rice is equivalent to a life, far more valuable than riches or jewelry.' They were now approaching the bonfire lit by their group.

'We just need a handful of rice' the priest's voice was trembling with emotion. 'We have to save that little boy's life; however, a handful of rice is such a precarious resource now.'

Ma-Pu came closer to the fire from the room on the other side. 'No rice? I, however, have a few crumbling loaves of bread in my bag. Will that do?' she asked. 'They have been stale for several days though.'

The priest nodded his head. 'Bring them quickly', he said. Ma-Pu went inside the room quickly and brought a few loaves of bread wrapped in newspaper. Green fungi was visible in the several days old bread. They also had a strong, stale smell.

The priest took two slices of bread and began toasting them over the fire. He returned the rest to the girl. 'Keep these remaining loaves of bread with you…we may require them later', he said. 'Please bring the boy closer to the fire.'

'I also want bread. I want to eat bread before I die.' Haricharan began screaming from where he was sitting. His blazing eyes resembled those of a famished dog. He suddenly jumped up and tried to snatch the bread from Ma-Pu's grasp.

'Beware!' In a trice, Chinti was at Ma-Pu's side and pushed Haricharan to the ground using all his strength. 'Please put the loaves of bread in your bag', he said, gazing at the frightened, terror-stricken eyes of the girl who was rooted to her spot.

Thanu opened his eyes after swallowing some of the toasted bread which was further softened in warm water. 'He has fever', the priest said. 'Let's observe him tonight. Most probably, he has malaria. We will have to give him quinine tomorrow.'

Ma-Pu was holding one of Thanu's hands very affectionately. Although he opened his eyes, he didn't have the strength to move his body. He just coughed occasionally and his thin chest affected by fever, rose and fell periodically. These were the only signs of life in him. Ma-Pu covered him with an old lungi she took out from her bag, and kept tousling his hair with her fingers. A little further away, the trembling figure of Ramgobinda, praying with his head raised to the skies, resembled a ghost in the crackling light of the fire. Only that unfortunate being knew what he wanted from the god whose name he was invoking with such sincerity.

'Mother! Mother! Where is Mini? My Mini?' suddenly Thanu shouted while changing his position. Ramgobinda came close to him hearing his voice and placed his hand on his forehead. 'We will take Mini with us', Thanu said agitatedly in his sleep. 'Mother, please tell father about it.' Once again, he slunk back into the deep recesses of sleep.

'His temperature is rising', Ma-Pu said worriedly, continuing to tousle his hair with her fingers. 'The fever has nearly reached his brain. We have to apply compresses to his forehead.' The boy's body was on fire. His face had also become red. Occasionally, he would start in his sleep and move his hands as if he were searching for something. His lips were dry. Sometimes, they would move, but no sound emerged from them. Ramgobinda froze in his spot like a statue. Ma-Pu rose, immersed a tattered rag in water, and then placed that on Thanu's forehead.

'I don't think we will be able to leave tomorrow morning if his fever rages on like this', the tall priest said. He broke a white tablet into four separate pieces, and giving them to Ramgobinda said, 'Let him have one quarter every two hours. We will have to be up and alert all night. The fever may break in the morning; however, the boy is extremely weak.'

Ramgobinda's mind repeatedly returned to his mother and Lacchmi. His heart was bursting with grief and sorrow. All his hopes for this life had been dashed. The only one among the remaining that he could call his own was this little boy. There was no guarantee what would happen to him. The story that Ma-Pu narrated of the sahib who committed suicide kept returning back to him.

The members of the group were munching the partially boiled shoots of banana trees and arum sitting together around the fire. Ma-Pu began retching, rushed outside and vomited after she ate a few roasted shoots of bamboo. After they were done eating, the group just lay down wherever they were sitting and prepared to go to sleep. Some of them bent their knees and slept in a fetal position. Ramgobinda dozed, leaning on a wooden pillar. Although he tried his best to remain awake, he fell deeply asleep within minutes, still sitting and leaning on the pillar. Ma-Pu sat close to Thanu's head and regularly changed the compresses on his forehead.

Ramgobinda woke up with a start at around four in the morning. He looked everywhere and noticed that everyone was sleeping soundly. Only Ma-Pu was up with her hands on Thanu's forehead. The boy was muttering something deliriously.

'He should have one half of his tablet now, no?' Ramgobinda yawned and muttered as if speaking to himself.

'I have already given him two pieces, only one remains', Ma-Pu glanced at her watch and said. 'We will have to give him the last piece in half an hour. You shouldn't worry—please sleep for a while longer, I am awake.'

Ramgobinda felt ashamed. As the father, he was sleeping so comfortably, while this unknown girl had sacrificed her sleep and was giving Thanu medicine. He rose and sat near Thanu. A pair of eyes was glowing in the dark on the other side of the room. Ramgobinda went closer and saw that it was the kitten, Mini. She had curled up near Thanu and occasionally licked his fingers.

'Thanu loves this kitten very much. It became very tame and lived close to our house', Ramgobinda explained to Ma-Pu, not finding any other topic to begin conversation. 'She left Manku with us, but disappeared somewhere on the road. She has reappeared again now—she keeps appearing and disappearing periodically, as if she is some sort of ghost.' Ramgobinda attempted to laugh drily.

'Actually animals have a more loving nature than human beings, they understand love very quickly as well', Ma-Pu smiled shyly. Ramgobinda once again felt embarrassed.

In the meantime, the tall priest had also woken up. He came near them and checked Thanu's pulse. 'The fever has broken…' he said. 'Has he taken his medicine?'

Ma-Pu nodded her head. Ramgobinda looked at her and then lowered his head. A feeling of attraction suddenly developed in him for this Anglo-Burmese girl he had come across just a few days ago. He felt a tiny, inexpressible ache somewhere in the cockles of his heart. He felt as if God had sent Ma-Pu to take Lacchmi's place for Thanu. He felt as if there was some form of intimacy between him and the girl as soon as this alien attraction took shape in his mind.

It was now morning. There was a huge difference between the morning in Mansi and the mornings in the uninhabited areas of the forest. The morning resounded with the tumultuous din of the *xalika* and sparrows and the harsh cawing of the crows. The colorful sun seemed to be exposing itself shyly between the thin, wispy clouds surrounding the peaks of the majestic hills. Hills everywhere! Tall and short, rising and undulating hills, with visible marks of glittering soil in between their blue and green facades.

The leaves of the casuarina and tal trees were swaying noisily in the soft breeze. Once the sun was out, the refugees woke up and began making preparations for the journey ahead. A few mango trees near the house they had visited the night before had begun blossoming. Plucking the raw mangoes hanging in bunches on the trees and throwing their stems away, the travellers gobbled these down by the mouthful. Some said that consuming raw mangoes would result in dysentery, but no one heeded this advice.

'The boy needs good treatment and care', the tall priest

checked Thanu's temperature and said. 'It would be nice if we could take rest in some sort of safe refuge for a few days.'

'I am not sure whether anyone will agree to stay here for a while', Ramgobinda replied. 'I have heard that Mansi may be occupied by Japanese forces at any moment now.'

'Yes, getting to Mogaung by hook or by crook seems to be the topmost priority for everyone now', the priest said. 'If we continue like this, we should be able to get there in about three days.'

'What's the point of remaining here?' the short priest said. 'No hospitals or medicines...a shortage of food. It's best that we keep moving.'

With thoughts of Lacchmi and the infant on his mind, Ramgobinda did not want to delay the journey any further. 'The boy's fever has gone down', Ma-Pu said while Ramgobinda nodded. In the meantime, the rest of the group was already prepared to set off on their journey again. Because they had run out of rice and food, their bags were also considerably lighter. Only a few clothes, a couple of pieces of jewelry and some money which had been saved for later remained in those bags. They had thrown away the heavy objects and unnecessary clothing a long time ago. Many of them had donned some of those clothes and kept the money in pouches tied to their waist; the boxes had been dispensed with in the hills long before they reached Mansi.

The tall priest pulled out the map printed on silk from the pocket of his overcoat and plotted a straight line between Mansi and Indawgyi. 'The journey is going to get progressively harder from here to Mogaung. There are no rail lines or highways as signposts either', he said. 'There are very few villages or dwellings on the way. On the other hand, this pathway is the lair of wild elephants and panthers.'

'It will be safer if we all band together and remain alert', Nitu said.

'Didn't the Kachins talk about allied camps somewhere nearby? Where are they?' Ramgobinda looked at the map and asked. Even though he didn't understand anything in that map, his sole worry was to get Thanu safely to Mogaung. He was very perturbed by the boy's illness. Pain, anxiety and terror at the prospect of losing everything were evident in his helpless eyes.

The group crossed a hilly stream named Songi with great difficulty. The relentless journey continued unchangingly after that, that same debilitating procession. These uninhabited hills resembled a deathworld without signs of life anywhere—between them, a procession of corpses moving ahead at a slow, funereal pace. Above them, the tall, sky-kissing leaves of the tal trees formed a canopy and blocked the hills from view. Occasionally, they came across the stunted trunks of trees charred by lightning. Diversely shaped wild plants and creepers had taken refuge under these and formed their own assembly there. Creepers had wound around and were hanging luxuriantly on a bent tree trunk; a massive dead tree trunk that could not shake off the intricate embrace of dependent forms of life. Besides the infinite number of mosquitoes, leeches and flies in the spaces below the trees, there were millions and millions of minuscule ticks and fleas. Once these vermin alighted on their bodies, they bored holes in the flesh and travelled right up to the bones. The spectacular, unspoiled beauty of the forest was all around. Occasionally, the appetising aroma of unknown types of fruit carried by the winds wafted their way into their nostrils. The echoing sound of thousands of cicadas was everywhere.

The group reached the flat lands of Longton, which was buffeted constantly by the poisonous winds from Indawgyi, after travelling continuously for half a day crossing many crevices, elevations and hills *en route*. They found a stretch of flat land in this forbidding landscape only in the evening, after crossing what seemed like an endless stretch of forests and hills. This flat expanse was fenced on all sides by rows and rows of rubber trees.

'We are in all likelihood near Indawgyi', the tall priest said. 'Quicksands abound near the lake. We need to advance very carefully.'

'The waters of the Indawgyi are poisonous', Nitu raised

his hand and spoke as if he were some sort of fortune-teller. 'Don't drink the water here even if you are dying of thirst.' He had heard that, apart from a couple of species of fish and a few snakes, no other form of life could survive here. Apparently even the fishes here were poisonous.

The group was overjoyed to see a grove of jackfruit trees at the edges of the flat expanse of land—at least they would now have something to eat. All of them began plucking jackfruits from the trees. Some of them gobbled the fruits with their skins intact. Groves of rubber trees lay towards the south and the east. The Bukit Hantu hills were towards the north—these hills were haunted by ghosts and demons. A couple of denuded rocky hills occasionally dotted the green ocean on all sides. These hills glittered fiercely when viewed from a distance. They were hard, dry! Once the sun set, the group came closer to the vast water body of the Indawgyi whose waves were sporting with the moonlight. This massive lake was the genesis and the culmination of numerous rivers. Its boundless expanse looked terrifying. The throats of the witnesses went dry with fear.

'Once we reach Longton, we have to keep moving north along the banks of the lake', the tall priest said. 'I can't figure out where we are now though.'

The group sat under a massive rubber tree. An elevated platform had been constructed in the tree. Someone climbed up to the platform only to see the massive expanse of the Indawgyi glittering even more terrifyingly in the moonlight. Water everywhere, as far as the eye could see—spectacular, fathomless! The horizon on the other side seemed merely like a dark blue, undulating line. It seemed like this was an ocean of violence designed specifically by nature to take revenge on human beings.

Ramgobinda was extremely fatigued after carrying Thanu on his shoulders for such a length of time. His heart was palpitating; each and every part of his body seemed to have declared war. At times, the thought that it would be best to commit suicide with Thanu tied to his chest crossed his mind. The other members of the group too seemed to advance semi-consciously, as if they had been hypnotised like snakes in a trance. Their injured, semi-paralysed legs seemed to be advancing mechanically, step by step only by the sheer force of habit.

Ramgobinda carefully laid down the sleeping Thanu on the patch of grass below a large tree. The weak, fatigued boy's head had begun drooping. The leaves of the trees in the open area near the lake were falling rapidly because of the howling wind. Tearing the jackfruits they had carried with them with their teeth, the people began gulping them down. The tall priest took a few loaves of bread from Ma-Pu and fed Thanu without toasting them. He munched those weakly whilst sleeping. 'He doesn't have a fever now', the priest said, placing his hand on Thanu's forehead.

'Ballabh had it good!' Nitu said, massaging his flayed feet. 'Although he may be lying in some hospital now, he was saved from all these hardships. At least he didn't have to walk till he dropped like us.'

'I wonder if he is still alive to enjoy his period of rest in the hospital', Haricharan said. It was as if someone had stabbed Ramgobinda through his heart.

'He is alive! I am sure he is alive!' Nitu said, glancing at Ramgobinda. 'He must be in some military hospital in Mogaung.' Like a fortune-teller, he closed his eyes. He was elated to be able to relax for a while.

'Many refugees are rumored to have died on the banks of the Indawgyi', the tall priest came near them and began caressing Thanu's head. 'Apparently corpses of people who succumbed to cholera or dysentery have piled up on the western banks. The corpses of innumerable people who could not advance any further are also strewn about like pieces of paper and have covered the entire expanse.'

'I don't know what will happen to us once the rains begin. Thankfully, the monsoon has been a bit delayed this year', Chinti said, looking at the clusters of white clouds gathering in the skies from his prone position.

Budhu walked ahead and sat at quite a distance from the group. He had procured a few pieces of dried pork from Lesin, which were still in his bag. Although the meat had begun to rot and tasted sour, he could not keep the acute pangs of hunger at bay and began munching them.

'I am sure he has some rice in his bag', Nitu noticed him munching something and whispered to Kalu. 'Just look at how he is munching something sitting at a distance.'

'There are a lot of big *bamuni-bhokola* in this lake', pretending that he hadn't heard Nitu, Kalu proclaimed loudly, leaning comfortably against that large tree. He still had a few remaining handful of rice in his bag. 'If we can catch a few of these fish and take them with us, we will have something to eat at least for a meal or two.'

This particular place was uninhabited and as quiet as a funeral ground. The occasional croaking of a group of frogs only served to accentuate the muted ambience of the locale. There were no signs of birds or nocturnal animals. The emaciated, dirty people sitting and sleeping on these banks resembled otherworldly beings in the illumination of the weak moonlight. Clad in coarse, tattered rags, their bodies raggedly covered with long, unkempt hair and beards, these people wouldn't be able to recognise each other if one of them appeared before them suddenly.

Although the pangs of hunger were intolerable, exhaustion and agony compelled them to close their eyes. Ramgobinda had just lain down beside Thanu; in an instant, he was fast asleep. A couple of them clambered up the raised platform and slept there. Chinti and Ma-Pu, along with the short priest, leaned and snuggled comfortably in a wide seat-like space in between two massive, exposed roots of a tree. The howling wind was progressively getting chilly. Carefully covering Thanu with a tattered lungi, the tall priest too stretched out near the little boy.

'I have heard that huge snakes inhabit the Indawgyi lake', the short priest sat up leaning on the massive root and curled his knees. 'I hope this tree is not a lair of snakes.' He gazed at the stars shining in the sky. 'However, what can you do if this is a lair of snakes? We still have to sleep.'

'Yeah, when you wake up in the morning, you will see that you are dead. Your hands and feet will be stiff', Chinti said, and began laughing loudly. Even though he was younger, he did not indulge in mindless humor unnecessarily. He was embarrassed by this sudden, unthinking burst of laughter and looked shamefacedly in Ma-Pu's direction.

Ma-Pu had wrapped a woolen shawl around her body, and was sitting with her legs stretched. 'Everyone is terribly exhausted', she said. 'It is very essential that we get complete, uninterrupted rest for a few days.'

'Have we come across a safe place to take rest as yet?' Chinti said. 'There is a trail of destruction wherever we have gone. Maybe if we found a military camp, we can at least rest for a day or two without worrying.'

The short priest had already begun dozing. 'Rest, at least some rest', he muttered.

'I don't think we will come across any other town in our

route', Ma-Pu yawned and said. 'I wonder if any military camp is still standing.'

'I don't know for sure…I have heard that there is one at Mogaung. But we still have to travel quite a distance to get there', Chinti replied. His voice was slurred with sleep.

'Go to sleep now! Who knows what difficulties lie in store for us on the road tomorrow?' Ma-Pu said, sitting up and leaning on that massive root of the tree.

'I have this burning desire to smoke a bidi…' Chinti smiled at Ma-Pu and said. He was experiencing attraction for this Anglo-Burmese girl who was sitting leaning on the tree next to him, with her body draped by a shawl and her bare feet stretched out. He felt as if he could chat with her the entire night keeping his exhaustion and sleep at bay. He wanted to watch her fall asleep, tousling her shiny black hair with his hands. He felt a strong desire to kiss her slender, delicate fingers. A medley of thoughts began to course through his mind despite him being enmeshed in the web of sleep. He was just an uneducated, ordinary peasant. She was very educated; there was a huge gulf between them. However, those factors held true only in mundane reality. Today, both of them were refugees. The similarity in their condition had shattered the differences wrought by such divisions. Both of them were humans—humans without any differentiation. They experienced similar pangs of hunger, the same tiredness in their bodies, and had been reduced to the same skeletal frames because of malnutrition. An equality wrought by the misfortunes of catastrophe, the lack of differentiation experienced in the lap of death. There was no distinction between rich and poor, educated and illiterate in this domain of wild nature—everyone was equal, the journey of each person was oriented towards death, a tremendous *jangamata* geared at preserving life!

However, his courage failed him. The short priest was snoring loudly. Chinti peered at Ma-Pu with his sleep-laden eyes. She was sleeping soundly. The calm waters of the Indawgyi were in front of him, a chilly wind was blowing in the moonlight, and an uninhabited expanse of nature lay behind. Even then, he could not gather courage to run his fingers through Ma-Pu's unkempt hair. He wasn't able to clasp her hand and draw her closer to him. She was so near, yet so far. What he imagined was in the realm of possibility, but was still impractical. As he slowly slunk into the web of sleep, Chinti began dreaming. He dreamt that he was holding her close and caressing her. Millions of romantic, disjointed dreams danced in front of his eyes in this accelerating union of fantasy and sleep. Most probably these dreams would forever remain unattainable fantasies for him.

Despite himself, he was soon transported into the realms of deep slumber.

XVII

As soon as it was dawn, the massive, placid, and yet terrifying expanse of the Indawgyi materialised in front of their eyes. The lake seemed like a limitless ocean without boundaries. All the curses of cruel nature seemed to have gathered around to inhabit this body of water.

Ramgobinda checked Thanu's brow—no fever now. He heaved a sigh of relief quietly. To be sure, the temperature was always under control in the mornings. It was difficult to wend one's way with a sickly boy tied to one's chest. Moreover, the boy had become virtually immobile—there seemed to be very few signs of vitality in his body. 'Oh God, please let my son get through this journey', he prayed quietly.

'We should get ready', Nitu looked at the rest and said.

'I am hungry, I am very hungry. My empty belly is

aching with hunger', Haricharan shouted, baring his teeth. 'I have to eat something first.' He looked at Nitu with blood-shot eyes, as if he would eat him if he got the chance.

'It's better to eat something before we leave', Chinti said. 'We won't be able to stop once we begin our journey. If we eat something now, we don't have to worry about food during our journey.'

'You are correct. But what can we eat?' Nitu said. 'We don't have anything with us. We will waste a lot of time if we go out in search of food. Let us move ahead instead. We'll eat whatever we find on the way.'

'The train line going to Mogaung valley must be around sixty miles to our east', the tall priest looked at the map and said. 'Unsurmountable hills lie in between. It is impossible to advance that way. We should go north following a straight line.'

After dropping their belongings one by one on the way to reduce weight, the travellers now had their fatigued, emaciated bodies as their only remaining possession. Besides a couple of bags swinging on the shoulders of some, the rest had nothing with them. They had not experienced any agitation or hesitation in carelessly throwing away, like mere pieces of garbage, the objects that they had preserved very carefully all their lives. On the way to Indawgyi, as the weight of the silver coins with the impress of the queen on them began feeling burdensome, the refugees took them out from their boxes and pockets and just tossed them away pell-mell. After that, they had to hurl the boxes away as well. They wore whatever remained of their jewelry on their bodies. They continuously kept emptying the clothes in their boxes, and kept casting off those that had been reduced to tattered rags on their bodies. Now that they didn't have anything with them, they got ready for the journey in a jiffy.

Although the fields with black, clayey soil on the western side of the Indawgyi were flat and open, they were filled with waist or knee-deep water under which lay sharp clumps of wild grass. In the dry areas, they came across a number of streams curving and wending their way with the Indawgyi as their destination. Occasionally, they noticed small settlements in the elevated areas on the banks. These were the villages of workers in the rubber plantations. Once they crossed these settlements, they reached the hills again. They saw an endless horizon of hills whose peaks sported with the wispy white clouds—cruel, unconquered!

The elevation of the hills steadily increased once they left Indawgyi. After climbing up a few shorter hills following a forested path for a few hours, they stood in front of a forbiddingly tall hill. During the afternoon, the group straggled up and reached the top of the Kawabumu. They noticed that dense jungle lay ahead on all sides. There was a winding pathway that connected one hilltop to another. The slopes of the hills descended sharply into the Karaika plateau. Tou-iya fields were visible on the slopes and edges of the hills. Although masses of white clouds enveloped the tall, forbidding hills, not a drop of rain or water could be found anywhere. The thirst experienced by these exhausted travellers beset by the difficulties of the road increased manifold when they heard the gurgling sound produced by unseen hilly streams somewhere in the distance. They were unable to articulate any words because their lips and throats were very parched. Thick forests full of bamboo surrounded the small pathway on both sides. Colourful flowers were blooming in those wild, thorny groves of bamboo. The travellers gathered the white bamboo flowers that had fallen from the trees and were strewn on the sides of the pathway by the handful and stuffed these in their clothes. A few of them also filled their empty bags with these flowers. Some of them immediately began gobbling these flowers whole. The whitish juice of these flowers mingled with the blood oozing out of the sores in their mouth, and this concoction dribbled out in streams from both corners of their maw. The fruits in the wild banana trees in the foothills had ripened and become red. Chasing away the hordes of hooluks that surrounded these trees, the refugees tore off these bananas from the tree with a jerk and began guzzling them. Unable to consume the bananas whole, some of them peeled the skins off and softened them by pounding them with a piece of bamboo. These wild bananas were full of seeds and bereft of taste. However, for these famished people, these bananas were akin to nectar from heaven. In fact, as they descended the hills, they even consumed the seeds of the prickly eggplants growing in clusters of short, thorny bushes.

The group reached the Karaika plateau at dusk. Once they crossed this region, they would come across a line of tall hills again. The cloud covered crown of the Namting hill was the apex of this cluster. After that, only hills and hills, seemingly innumerable and endless! They came across quite a few streams in the Karaika region. Their waters were muddy; however, suffering acutely from thirst, these people paid no heed to that and gulped handful after handful of water greedily. Coming across flowing water after a long time, the group halted for a while, splashed water on their bodies, and also drenched their clothes like little children. They would have to climb those parched, dry hills in a while. They drank as much water as they could. They had no means of taking water with them; none of them had the strength to carry water in any case. A few fires were burning in the dry, stubbled fields of the Karaika plateau. The half-burnt, black stubbles of rice along with the cracks that had opened up in the dry ground due to the intensity of the heat made the fields resemble the hide of a spotted leopard. The tall stalks of the clumps of elephant grass in the middle of the fields were green and glittering in the harsh afternoon sun.

After crossing a number of hills during day time, the group reached Namting in the evening. Slippery red soil covered the foothills and slopes of the elevation. They were exhausted almost to the point of death by the time they reached the top of Namting. In the distance, the majestic peaks of the Laimiya Bum range, crowned by clusters of clouds, stood proudly erect as they surveyed the green kingdom in front of them in the flickering light of this starry night.

'We should not relax now', Nitu said, gazing at the smoky cluster of clouds in the distance. 'We are fortunate that the heavy rains haven't begun as yet. Even a passing shower will render these muddy pathways impassable. Therefore, we should proceed although it will be extremely difficult. I don't think it's worth wasting our time sitting and resting.'

'I heard that there are quite a few Japanese camps near Laimiya Bum', the tall priest said. 'It isn't safe to walk in daylight. We have to advance hidden during the night.'

The travellers were more wary of the rains than the Japanese, and hence did not disagree with the priest's proposal. What Nitu said was also correct. It was already drizzling… these were just a prelude to the heavy rains. After that, it would begin pouring buckets, the waters in the river would begin rising, and the streams would begin to overflow. The red clayey soil would be transformed into mud rendering it difficult to walk on the pathways. Therefore, no one opposed Nitu's proposal. Moreover, it was also possible that no one had any strength left to dissent. The group merely proceeded forward at a reluctant pace, again looking very much like clockwork dolls—no one knew where, which way and why.

Night crept up slowly on them as they climbed up and down numerous hills and followed the pathway across forested areas densely covered by teak trees. An uninhabited, dark kingdom! Although the moon was out in the sky, the moonlight could not pierce through the thick leaves of the teak trees. Their swollen, flayed legs rose, fell and sometimes lost balance in the slippery mud of the forest floor. A couple of them kept slipping, lifted themselves as if they were in a trance, and then kept advancing again. They knew that the dire consequences of falling behind could be very dreadful.. A few of them kept dozing off while walking; no one seemed to have any vitality left in their bodies. They moved slowly, hesitantly. The group kept advancing as if it were a procession of dolls and in this manner reached Laimiya Bum in the morning.

'We should rest if we find a safe place somewhere here. It's just a day's journey to Mogaung from here', the tall priest said to Nitu, observing the pitiable condition of the travellers. He was in a bad shape himself. 'We should also find something to eat', he said.

'What will you eat? What is there to eat here?' Gurcharan flashed his teeth and laughed. 'The pulp of the toko tree, the stems of the banana tree or bamboo shoots?' Although he was terribly hungry, he felt like throwing up when he remembered what they had to eat a day earlier. 'Or will you boil the flowers from the bamboo tree as they are?'

'There is no food left. It is impossible to move ahead with empty bellies. We may all die due to lack of food', Chinti said.

'No point running scared now. We should check if there are any Burmese villages nearby', Nitu said and looked in the direction of the short priest. 'If they don't give us food willingly, then we will have to put your two grenades to use.'

'We should have gone through one of the main roads. Maybe we could have come across a military vehicle or two. We may also have had something to eat…' the short priest said, moistening his lips with his tongue and trying not to heed what Nitu said. He glanced at the tall hills glittering on all sides in the soft light of the morning.

'How can we travel via the highway? You'd meet either the Japanese or the rebels. Moreover, the route becomes very circuitous if we followed the highway. Also, can we be sure whether the highway is still standing?' the tall priest said. 'The military are busy escaping; they don't even know what's going to happen to them. What help can they offer us?' He took out the map from his pocket. 'There is a sign here for Shaduzup which is near Laimiya Bum. This means that there is an allied camp there. But I wonder if it's still there or not? Maybe we will find that the camp has shifted location once we get to that place. All our labours will go in vain then. I think its best we keep going straight following the horizon; what happens will happen.'

'Is there any certainty about the situation in Mogaung either?'

'Mogaung is still a fair distance to the north. The Japanese are advancing via the direction of China. No one can stop the Japanese if they overrun Mogaung—they will have a free hand over Assam then.'

'Then the allied forces must have concentrated all their energies in Mogaung.'

'I think you are correct. General Stilwell must also be somewhere in this region.'

'Forget your General', the short priest blurted, and then fell quiet when his compatriot threw a sharp look in his direction.

The peak of Laimiya Bum had begun glittering in the harsh glare of the sunlight. The travellers suffering from hunger, thirst and exhaustion looked anxiously at the foothills for a safe place where they could at least rest for a while. They could survey the landscape a fair distance from the hilltop.

Chinti noticed it first—a trail of smoke was visible in between the thick rows of teak trees at the foothills. As they peered carefully at that spot, it became evident that there were around twenty to twenty-five bamboo dwellings in that spot at the center of the grove of teak. Definitely, this must be a village. The travellers were astounded, yet reassured, when they noticed this village in this thickly forested foothill region. The travails and terrors of war, then, had not as yet singed this relatively inaccessible village. The group had no time or patience to consider whether this village would be friendly or hostile to them. The hunger in their bellies and the exhaustion of their bodies took priority over everything else as they began to descend the slopes of the hill slowly.

A group of Kachin girls were filling their long bamboo vessels with water from a stream at the foothills. A couple of them were lounging on the flat rocks and were playfully splashing their bare, stout feet in the swiftly flowing waters of the stream. A few of them tied two of the bamboo vessels with ropes and were carrying them on their heads. The partings in the hair of these girls were visible and glittering due to the weight of the vessels that they balanced on their heads. Shocked by the sight of the group of refugees one of the girls screamed in terror, which led to the others abandoning their vessels and instantly fleeing towards the village. Besides lungis wrapped around their waists and extending to their knees, these girls had no other clothing on their bodies. As they fled, their large, bare breasts periodically falling and rising were visible for a while. After that, they simply disappeared into the dense forest nearby.

The village was full of tall, cramped *changghar*s constructed out of bamboo. Chickens and swine were housed in the empty spaces below the platforms of these changghars. When the refugees entered the village, the courtyard was deserted and all the doors and windows of the changghars were shut. Although there weren't signs of life anywhere, many eyes observed their movements secretly from the small gaps in the bamboo walls of their houses. The refugees felt like a group of bandits when they observed the barred doors and windows of the houses from their vantage point in the middle of the wide, empty courtyard.

'I think this is an appropriate place to detonate one of the grenades', the short priest said, pointing in the direction of a few fowl wandering around without a care in the world, simultaneously putting his hands in the pockets of his overcoat. We will get at least twenty chickens if we detonate the grenade.'

Suddenly, they heard the creaking of a door from one of the nearby houses, and saw a couple of Kachin youth advancing rapidly towards them. Immediately, the creaking door slammed shut.

'We are refugees', the tall priest said in fluent Burmese when the two young men approached them, and fell silent immediately after this brief introduction. There was a puzzled, interrogative look in the eyes of the two young men and signs of incomprehension in their faces. They looked at the group and then began talking among themselves in their own tongue. After that, they looked at the tall priest and gestured in the direction of the distant hills.

'Most probably they are asking us to go our own way', the tall priest said, looking at his short compatriot. 'They are suspicious and distrustful of us here.'

The short priest slowly produced the revolver from his overcoat and began examining it calmly. Probably noticing that, one young man disappeared into a nearby house twice as rapidly as he had arrived, while the other person began to explain something to the tall priest in his language. For a while, the sounds of an intense argument conducted in loud voices also wafted into their ears from inside the house. The young man then emerged with an elderly person in tow.

Once the old man made an appearance, the doors and windows seemed to open like magic and very soon a large group of people, both young and old, clustered in the courtyard. The old man stood in front of the group and began surveying them from head to toe with a piercing gaze. Then, he asked them in broken Burmese, 'Who are you? Where do you come from?'

'We are refugees. We come from the direction of Mandalay', Nitu advanced and replied. As soon as he heard the name of Mandalay, the old man folded his hands and placed them on his forehead. 'Mandalay is very far—a very holy place. The royal throne, royal umbrella and the royal sceptre are in Mandalay', he said.

The refugees were somewhat reassured at this temporary solution of the barrier of language.

'What do you want? Why are you here?' the old man asked in a harsh voice.

'We don't have any food with us. We are also extremely exhausted', Nitu replied, articulating each word slowly and steadily. 'We are looking for a place to rest for a brief while.'

The old man once again stared at the group. His gaze rested on Ma-Pu for a while and then traveled to the crucifix hanging on the tall priest's neck. 'Are you from the military?' he asked.

The priest shook his head. 'We are refugees looking for shelter. We are not robbers.'

The wizened face of the Kachin elder suddenly brightened. He smiled at the priest's words, looked at the two young men, said something to them in a foreign tongue and sent them on their way.

'All of you can rest here. But you have guns with you', the old man told Nitu after the young men departed. 'Those are dangerous objects. Don't take them out here.

The villagers here are simple peasants. They are scared of guns and weapons.'

'He has that revolver with him just for safety… to protect us from trouble if the need arises', Nitu said. 'We haven't come here with guns with the intention of wreaking terror. We are just poor peasants escaping from war.'

'Our people are terrified by the military men. Thc other day, a group of deserters from the military passed by this way, bashed two boys from the village mercilessly and left them lying on the road. They did this because they demanded food and we couldn't give any', the elder said. 'The deserters looked just like you—thick flowing beards, clothes torn and shredded to rags.'

'We aren't deserters', Nitu blurted, unable to find words to articulate anything else. 'We were just searching for a little bit of food and a safe refuge where we can rest awhile.'

The refugees slumped on the floor of the courtyard. After a while, the two young men brought them tea brewed from sun-dried leaves in bamboo beakers and some ripe bananas. In the meantime, the sun was shining very brightly high up in the sky. One of the young men escorted the group to an unoccupied changghar.

'I am very happy to see that the curse of this destructive war hasn't affected your village as yet', the tall priest addressed the elder, noticing the peaceful environment around the village. 'I hope that you can live in such a peaceful fashion among God's creations forever.'

Hearing the mention of god, the elder folded his hands and touched his forehead. 'The man from Misina who used to come here every Sunday to talk about God stopped his visits', the elder sat cross-legged near the priest and said. 'A lot of people from the nearby villages used to congregate here earlier to hear his sermons. After the war began, he hasn't been seen in the area…for about six months now. No one comes here from the nearby villages to hear the word of God either.'

There were three rooms in that expansive changghar whose walls were made of bamboo. The floor was intricately woven with bamboo and was covered with a layer of earth. The floor stood firm when they walked on it. The dwelling didn't look like a changghar. A fire was burning in a tall, earthen foundation in the inner chamber. A dry vessel for boiling tea was placed over blazing coal kept in two thick urns made out of tree trunks. 'Don't let the fire go out', the old man said. 'Fires like this are kept constantly on in all the houses here. Suddenly it might get very cold. Then everyone sleeps around the fire.'

The roof was made out of sturdy toko leaves. The ridges were woven with thick grass. A few seats made out of cane and wood were strewn about in a disorderly fashion inside. Thick centre stems of the leaves of plantain were hanging on the walls. Handwoven, colourful mosquito nets made out of thick cloth had been dumped in a pile in one corner of the room. A strange loom with a half-woven piece of cloth was visible in the verandah at the back of the house. Although the dwelling did not have any windows, a considerable amount of light and air streamed in through the gaps in the bamboo walls.

The refugees slumped on the floor as soon as they entered the dwelling. A couple of them began examining the welts and wounds on their legs and feet sitting near the fire.

'The village is so tranquil, as if all the peace in this world has gathered only in this oasis', Ma-Pu told Chinti, who was sitting beside her. 'The world around us is caught in the vice-like grip of war. However, these troubles seemed to have passed by this village. Time seems to have stopped here.'

Although he didn't understand everything Ma-Pu said, Chinti too had quietly experienced the tranquil atmosphere of the village. 'Didn't the old man say that deserters from the army had beaten up two young men from the village? Where is the peace you are alluding to?' he said.

'Tigers and leopards often kill one or two stragglers on the way in this region. This isn't a big deal for these people', Ma-Pu said, leaning against the bamboo wall.

'The important thing here is that such incidents impel these simple, unsophisticated people to lose their faith in humankind. Suspicions begin to take root in their uncomplicated minds and difficulties arise in their otherwise simple lifestyle...' Noticing that Chinti was dozing, her voice trailed off.

In an hour or so, some of the villagers brought rice steamed in bamboo vessels, smoked chicken and saku, and left them with the group. Although the meat was a little tough, it tasted good sprinkled with rock salt. The saku was sour and fermented; but everyone had their fill to their heart's desire. The group felt very sleepy after drinking about a cup or two of tea. Their bodies felt very heavy. After satiating their hunger, all of them fell asleep wherever they were. Once twilight began erasing signs of bright sunlight, a shroud of silence enveloped the entire village. However, the travellers were unaware of this and rested like the dead in front of the dim light cast by the fire. The tiredness, the lassitude, the deep sleep—as if these would never cease!

The night thus passed by. After partaking of some tea, steamed rice and pork in the morning, the group once again began preparing for the journey ahead. Everyone in the village gathered in the courtyard to bid them farewell. Hale and hearty, half-naked children wearing tiny loincloths, with tiny tufts of hair and snot streaming out of their noses, bare breasted young women wearing bamboo bangles and colourful, short lungis, a group of middle aged women with baskets on their backs and infants in their laps, aged men wearing hand-woven shirts, a group of Kachin youth wearing lungis and elaborate headgear with a quiver full of massive arrows slung on their backs and a Kachin dao each in their hands—all these people surrounded the departing group of refugees.

However, everyone was silent. It seemed as if these homeless people had become part of the village only in a day. That message was communicated by these people mutely with their moistened eyes.

'We will now take our leave', the tall priest said, gazing at the tall hills in the distance.

'Yes', the Kachin elder said. 'One day we all have to leave.'

The group commenced their journey again. As they made their way across the hilly, heavily forested pathway from Laimiya Bum to La-ungga, hordes of black monkeys bared their teeth and screeched at them aggressively. Although the travellers had rested for a day and refreshed themselves, they experienced aches and pains in each and every joint in their bodies. It was still very difficult for them to walk rapidly. Of course, besides a few bumps and ascents, this portion of the pathway to La-ungga did not pose a lot of problems for them. After wading across a small stream of the Nambu river right in the middle of the road, they crossed a wooden bridge and once again began traversing those twisting pathways.

Steadily following the pathway, the group reached Laungga in the evening. Suddenly, after climbing the winding pathway leading to the hilltop, they saw some hammocks tied to the trees on both sides and also a few tree-houses constructed of leaves and branches. Before they could comprehend anything, a group of about forty soldiers armed with bayonets came out charging and surrounded them on all sides.

A military officer dressed in a clean khaki uniform emerged from one of the tree-houses.

'Who are you? Where have you come from?' he asked the tall priest. After the priest briefly explained everything, he went inside one of the houses without a word, emerged with another person and asked the latter to check whether the sores on the feet of the travellers were authentic or not. After that, they faced a volley of questions: when did they leave, which road did they take, where did they stop on the way and so on. The officer smiled at them once he was assured that the group was truly a band of refugees. 'This is the Mogaung border post', he said. 'The activities of spies and rebels have increased tremendously here. Just yesterday, a group of rebels bayoneted six of our own in the back and threw their corpses in the forest. Therefore, we cannot trust anyone. Please don't mind.'

'No problem, no problem. You are just performing your duty; why should we mind?' with the possibility of safety emerging with the appearance of the army after so many days, the tall priest smiled contentedly.

'Now we only have the battalion at Mogaung left—that's why we are extremely careful. A number of Japanese and Burmese have entered Mogaung via these hilly pathways, and have attempted to cut off the routes supplying us provisions and food. The Japanese have a lot of bases nearby…' Suddenly he spotted Ma-Pu, and surveying her from head to toe asked, 'Is she Burmese?'

'She isn't Burmese, but Anglo-Burmese…' The priest replied almost instantaneously, and began nervously twitching the cross on his neck for fear of discovery. 'She was a nurse in our hospital and is a refugee like us' he said. 'There is nothing to fear or suspect about her. She has been with us for many years.' The priest silently asked God for forgiveness for speaking this untruth.

'Hmm!' the officer said contemplatively. 'However, you will have to certify her credentials before you leave. The rest are fine—they can just sign in their names.' The priest heaved a sigh of relief.

'There will be four military guards assigned to your group', the officer told the tall priest, scanning the form that the latter had just signed. 'First, a security briefing. The Japanese have embedded themselves here. Therefore, the Burmese people here are not to be trusted. Second, your identities. If I don't document where you have departed from and the route that you have taken, you may be harassed at the Mogaung post. There is a shorter way to Mogaung through the forest. It will be difficult for you to find that route at night.'

Dusk had become night by the time the group left La-ungga with four guards in tow *en route* to Mogaung. After they descended the hill, they reached a level road. They noticed a few Burmese villages in the distance across the cultivated fields. The dim lights of the lamps burning in these households pierced through the darkness and the distance.

The group moved steadily despite the all-enveloping darkness. Suddenly, they halted at the signal of the military guards. Almost instantly, they heard a few voices talking agitatedly in Singpho. Three Burmese young men were advancing in their direction.

'Hands up!' A guard suddenly jumped in front of them holding his gun. Immediately, the young men raised their hands and stopped where they were. Even with the dim illumination, scornful smiles were visible on their pale faces.

'Who are you? Where are you going?' The military guard questioned them in a harsh voice.

'Why do you want to know who we are and where we are going?' a young man, dressed in a Hawaiian shirt and trousers, asked in return.

'We demand that you tell us. Don't you know there is a war going on?'

'We know. You have started this war and are now suffering because of it. We are peaceful village folk. What do we have to do with war?'

'Are there any Japanese in these villages?' The military guard came to the main point.

'We don't know. We haven't seen anyone', another young man replied.

'I am sure you know, but aren't saying anything.'

'We don't know anything.'

'Tell us the truth. Otherwise you will be shot dead', the military guard said gravely.

'You have the revolvers and the capability to take our lives. You can do whatever you want', a young man replied with comparable equanimity. 'We don't feel the need to answer your questions.'

'You are Japanese spies', the guard bellowed in anger.

'No', the young man replied in a calm, assured tone.

'Tell us the truth! Tell us how many Japanese are hiding in these villages.'

'We don't know', the young man with the Hawaiian shirt said. 'Let us go. Why are you harassing us without evidence?'

'The three of you have to provide an oral testimony to the sergeant major of the La-ungga camp.'

'This is unjust!', suddenly one of the young men began shouting. 'Look at how these bloodsucking white monkeys strut their authority over our ravaged motherland!'

'Don't you have any power of reasoning?' another one said. 'You are guests in Burma. You rooted yourself here without invitation. Since when did you become owners of this land? Move from our way and let us go', the young man moved furiously towards the soldier. In an instant, a volley of bullets from three guns rendered him lifeless. For a brief moment, the two other young men were stunned and stared at the corpse, as if they could not believe their own eyes. Almost immediately, they turned back, began fleeing and were cut down by another hail of bullets. The three corpses lay in a prone position on both sides of the narrow pathway.

'What happened?' the tall priest asked emerging from the thick jungle on the sides.

'Spies…they were spies for the Japanese. There are scores of Japanese in these villages', a guard said, scanning the three corpses.

'That may be the case—however, it is still unjust', the priest said. 'If the Japanese are indeed present in the village, it is your responsibility to find out. But, to kill these three defenseless young men for that reason…'

'Shut up, father!', a guard replied rudely. 'Your job is to preach and talk about religion. Let us conduct our duties in our own fashion.'

'Why don't you oppose the fact that these Japanese are killing lakhs and lakhs of innocent people by dropping bombs, eh father?' another guard queried. 'See, you too are escaping to preserve your own life. If your humanity and sense of justice impels you so much, then please go in front of a Japanese encampment, raise your hands and say that this war is unjust. Before you complete your sentence, thousands of bullets will riddle your body. There is no morality in war, father. The only morality that reigns here is the preservation of one's life', the guard said, fury writ large on his face.

The priest dragged the three bloody corpses to the side of the road, laid them flat on the ground and then kneeling down looked up and began muttering a prayer.

The guards were getting impatient. 'There is a long road left, priest. Be quick about this...we are getting delayed', one of them said.

'Wait, I too have my responsibilities to fulfil. Don't place impediments in the fulfilment of my duty', the priest said gravely. The impatience and hurry displayed by the guards was no match for the grave demeanor of the priest. They slung their guns on their shoulders and waited for him. The priest took off the cross dangling on his chest and placed it on the neck of the corpse placed in the middle. 'The Archbishop of Canterbury gave me this crucifix' he told the guards. 'I think I have been successful today in carrying out God and the Archbishop's will in this distant corner of the world.' He gazed mournfully at the three bloodied corpses for a while, then suddenly stood up, wiped the tears from his eyes and said, 'Let's go!'

They saw a few lights glimmering in Mogaung during the latter half of the night. They moved expeditiously with lots of hope in their hearts. When they reached Mogaung at midnight, this town which represented new hope for these devastated refugees was enmeshed in the web of sleep. Only the occasional piercing shouts by the guards of the camp and the dim light of the flickering lanterns welcomed the exhausted and weary group of travellers to this long-awaited dreamland of hope.

XVIII

There was no military officer present at the Mogaung checkpoint at that time to check the identification papers of the travellers. Seeing no other alternative, the group spent the night at the checkpoint. In the morning, two military officers interrogated both the group and the guards accompanying them for a long while and then allowed them to enter the premises of the camp. Two soldiers carrying guns accompanied them to meet the major.

The major talked with the group for a bit. They learned from him that a large relief camp had been set up for refugees moving towards Assam two miles away from the military encampment. The camp had sufficient facilities for shelter and medical relief. Thousands of refugees were already in the camp. There were lots of camps like this on the way from Mogaung to Ledo. Large groups of refugees streamed in to Mogaung from all over Burma and then crossed the Hukawng region to reach Ledo. Although the camps were relatively well-equipped, occasionally outbreaks of cholera and other contagious diseases as well as the effects of fatigue and exhaustion killed large swathes of people. Food, moreover, was very scarce. A bowl of boiled red rice along with a pinch of salt—the camps were unable to provide anything beyond that. Most probably these supplies wouldn't last for more than a few days. Bridges had been destroyed in various places. The river had to be crossed by ferry or boat. The hilly roads were riddled with potholes and were extremely muddy at a few places. Even jeeps couldn't cross some of these roads. Meagre provisions carried on the backs of mules were all they had. It was a problem feeding thousands of people with these steadily depleting rations. Furthermore, fleeing Chinese soldiers were also swelling the numbers in the camps. Therefore, arrangements had been made to help the refugees cross the Towang Hka river by ferry and to transport them by military jeeps to Ningbwiyang after they had rested for a day or two. After that, they were left to their fate. Jeeps could not traverse that stretch of the pathway. Trains ran from Ledo to the west. The Assam Oil Company had set up a number of refugee camps in and around Ledo. Good facilities for medical treatments were to be found there.

Therefore, their worries would come to an end once they arrived in Ledo somehow. The major scribbled something quickly on a piece of paper and gave it to the tall priest. 'Please hand this paper to the manager of the refugee camp and he will do the rest for you', he said. 'Of course, it isn't safe to stay for a long time in Mogaung. Food is extremely scarce here.' Although the major could not give them any tidings of Lacchmi or Ballabh, he wrote down their names and made a note to himself to inquire about them in the hospitals and camps nearby.

They noticed the hectic occupation and movement of the troops as soon as they emerged from the camp. No one had any time for leisure or relaxation. Hurried movements and noise everywhere. There was a rumour that the Japanese were advancing. Thousands of military trucks and jeeps were arriving and departing. There was knee-deep mud everywhere on the motorways going in and out from the camp.

The sheer excess of movement meant that the stationary refugees could not find anyone to ask directions to the relief camp. A few soldiers in khaki uniforms were loading canisters of gasoline on a military truck parked near the main gate of the camp. They asked a guard stationed there and he gestured silently towards the east. After walking east for about two miles, the group reached the refugee camp at about one in the afternoon.

It was less of a camp and more of a wide, open space where an uncountable number of spacious dwellings constructed out of thatch and bamboo were lined in rows. A number of trenches, some of them deep and the others shallow, dotted the edges and the center of the field. Due to the incessant drizzles the trenches were full of water while the field had become very muddy. People kept streaming out of the sheds. The place resembled a sea of people who were homeless, sick, skeletal, filthy and haggard. They were moving slowly and resembled millions of micropscopic objects. Some of them slept in the mud without a care, others dozed off leaning on the walls, and many more hurried to and fro in a futile manner. There were leprosy-like wounds on the limbs of the sick people and marks of drying blood shining on their exposed, red, raw flesh. Many Burmese, British and American troops were busily moving around examining the refugees. Groups of sick people were waiting for first aid besides the trucks marked with red crosses.

The group took refuge in a large room in the dwelling pointed out by the manager and after a meal of a bowl of salt and rice lay down on the earthen floor intending to rest awhile. A group of around six to seven people were already occupying one corner. The travellers experienced stiffness in their limbs, weakness in their bodies and a general breakdown in morale. Their existence seemed to be defined by agony and exhaustion. After many days, their exhausted bodies and minds had garnered a smidgeon of rest and peace in this refugee camp in Mogaung. Dreams produced by deep slumber had just begun unspooling rapidly like a film reel, driving away the terror-filled realities when suddenly thousands of sirens began a massive cacophonic din on all sides. The people sat up suddenly, the web of dreams enveloping them shattering in an instant. Stunned by the noise and frenetic movement, they began examining their unfamiliar surroundings confusedly.

'*La-byiyo! La-byiyo*!' The Chindit and Kachin soldiers guarding the refugee camp suddenly began shouting in unison. Suddenly there was chaos and tumult everywhere. Unable to make sense of anything, the occupants of the camp began scattering in all directions as if the gates of a madhouse had suddenly been opened. The upper garments of mothers suckling babies at their breast fell away as they made a mad dash for safety. People who had dozed off leaning on the walls and were still enmeshed in the web of sleep suddenly jumped up, began running, and fell to the ground as they bumped into others. Small children suddenly separated from their parents began to wail loudly. Sick people who could not get up began supplicating their gods loudly from where they were. Suddenly, the terrifying drone of the Japanese bombers pierced the skies and blotted out the tremendous cacophony created by the screams of afflicted humanity and the screeching, sustained noise of the wailing sirens. Scores of people jumped into the trenches. Quite a few of them stumbled in the stampede and lay where they fell. Some of them were quite close to the trenches, but couldn't get in and laid face-down wherever they were. A lot of them remained rooted to their spots in confusion. Others ran out of the shelters, and not knowing what to do, went back inside once again. Nitu's group too ran out of their shelter and scattered in all directions. Everyone ran, with the only intent being the preservation of their own lives.

The bombers suddenly swooped down like eagles and flying in a zigzag fashion began dropping bombs, first on the military encampments and then on the refugee shelters. The soldiers responded with anti-aircraft fire which probably missed their targets. Within a minute, the bombers completed their orgy of destruction and disappeared into the skies.

Smoke and fire had enveloped the refugee camps. Loud screams wafted in the air as the bombs exploded one by one. The scorching light of many fires were visible all over. The world seemed to have churned within the space of a minute. After wreaking destruction on the Mogaung military camp and the refugee settlements in a jiffy, the Japanese planes disappeared in the horizon of the hills lying towards the east.

The sirens began wailing once again, but this time they were the sirens of peace.

People began streaming out like hordes of tiny ants from the trenches and the other places of refuge. Lots of them had died or were injured badly. The dead and the injured lay where they were. A crescendo of wails and screams of terror arose. The soldiers and medical personnel were busy carrying the injured soldiers and civilians from the trenches to the ambulances with red crosses standing nearby. The military men had to drag some people out from the trenches. Whoever was in the mouth of the trenches inevitably died. Many in the trenches died due to suffocation from the sheer weight of people pressing on them from above. Some were lying unconscious. A few people were still inside the burning shelters. Firemen sprayed water on these sheds with their long hoses and were trying to rescue the people trapped inside. The refugees who were safe were extremely busy, moving to and fro. Hectic movement and tumult everywhere—a veritable kingdom of chaos!

At the sound of the sirens, Ramgobinda woke up and looked in every direction with a stupefied gaze. His limbs had frozen for an instant with terror. After that, he noticed that people were running panic-stricken. The desire to preserve his life and find a place of refuge forced him to move almost unthinkingly as he plunged into the sea of people. Holding Thanu tightly, he ran out of the shelter and somehow, after receiving many bumps and scratches and being swept away by this swelling tide of human movement almost without volition, he tried to jump into a trench. Only a small portion of his body entered the trench, the rest remained suspended outside. Just at that instant, the earth-shattering noise of the exploding bombs reached him. His spirit seemed to be sapped of any vitality by the terror that arose from the shrill screams that wafted into his ears. He clasped the unconscious Thanu tightly to his chest and trying to stop the onrush of the panic-stricken crowd with his other hand, fell to the ground. Lots of people fell on top of his body. Closing his eyes and suspending his breath, he saw a wave of darkness crashing against his shut eyelids. Silently praying to God, he thought that this probably was what the end was like.

However, the expected end did not arrive. The siren wailed again and the people who had fallen flat on the trenches began rising up. A smidgeon of fresh air revived some of them, while the rest remained where they were. A few of them stumbled around in the crowd trying to find people they knew. A lot died, many were injured, others were crippled for life. The people who were alive though instantaneously went about with the business of the living. The others were irrelevant for them.

Placing Thanu on his shoulders, Ramgobinda climbed out of the trench and looked in all directions. The field was strewn with dead and half-dead people. The injured were screaming in agony. Others were unable to even scream because of acute pain. Fragments of a bomb had lodged themselves in a soldier's stomach. Shiny, red blobs were visible in the stomach of this soldier whose face looked upwards. When they tried to lift him on to a stretcher, he whimpered piteously in pain. His helmet had been dented badly. A captain came over and rearranged his helmet on his head with great care. The injured soldier opened one of his eyes and flashing a pathetic smile at his captain, gasped and whispered amidst great pain, 'I performed my duty, didn't I captain?' Tears welled up in the captain's eyes. He tried to curve his lips into a smile and nodded his head. The soldier probably did not have more than an hour to live. 'At least he will be able to garner some satisfaction and have a sense of accomplishment in the hour of his death', the captain thought.

Corpses of two soldiers were lying side by side in the muddy field. The stunned and terrified gaze of one of these corpses stared fixedly and emptily at the sky. His hands were still clasping his gun tightly. A strange calm was manifest on his face despite a sliver of blood flowing from the corner of his mouth—the peace attained only in the lap of death. The uniform of the other soldier was still on fire. He too was sleeping peacefully, with his entire body ablaze. Bodies with amputated limbs were laid out in one corner. There weren't enough ambulances to ferry the wounded. The green grass by the side of these bodies was coloured red with blood. In another spot, a charred, yet still alive soldier was screaming in agony. His entire body was burnt. The flesh had fallen off in a few places from his charred body and the bones were visible. He was still alive though and was screaming and wriggling in unbearable pain, 'Why did we come here to die? To save the oil companies or the teak tycoons? Look at me…look at what I have become. Who began this damned war? For whom?…' Clasped tightly in the embrace of death, this man was still screaming at the top of his voice. He suddenly fell quiet in the midst of all that screaming. His quivering hands became immobile. Another insignificant life had been sacrificed in this carnival of destruction. No one, however, had the time to contemplate what he gained from suffering so terribly, from eventually sacrificing his life. Everyone was busy preserving their own life. Death was irrelevant, momentary, forgettable.

Such destruction! What massive destruction! Ramgobinda could not find a place to sit and rest for a moment. There was no sign of the other group members. Everyone had scattered pell-mell in the moment of crisis. It would be futile to go in search of them. He didn't have enough strength to move around. Lifting the weakened Thanu on his shoulders, he slowly made his way to the makeshift kitchen of the refugee camp.

That kitten once again! Mini! Amidst all this chaos, she was sitting in the ground just below the eaves and calmly licking her paws. Once she saw Ramgobinda, she ran up to him and snuggled at his feet. Ramgobinda felt an immense outpouring of love for this little kitten. For a brief moment, he felt very close to this kitten that was now licking his feet, for reuniting with them in the Mogaung refugee camp after facing so many tribulations on the way. It was as if this kitten was their only constant companion. She had appeared only fleetingly during their dangerous journey without ever leaving their side and was now their only guide and companion. He sat down and began petting the kitten on her head. Thanu did not have the strength to speak. He extended his feeble hands and Mini began to lick his fingers. An exchange of thoughts and feelings that transcended language was conducted between two beings. Both of them understood each other. Suddenly, Ramgobinda again remembered Lacchmi and the infant. He was amazed that he still experienced such love, attachment and weakness towards that tiny, wailing infant who hadn't even nestled in his lap and whom he had seen for less than an hour. When did such love take root in him for that infant he hadn't had the time to know properly? How did it take root?

He met the tall priest and Nitu when he was wandering around aimlessly in the crowd during the evening. The dwellings in the camp had by now been reduced to heaps of ashes. The denizens of the camp were lying about here and there under the open sky. After the corpses, the sick and the injured had been taken away by the military, and a bit of clear space had opened up in the fields.

'We don't know when Mogaung will fall into enemy hands,' the priest said, placing his hands on his head. 'According to the major, the allied forces are contemplating withdrawing into Assam. Although Stilwell sahib is in Shaduzup, he won't be able to help us from there. There are very few forces stationed there. On the other side, the retreating Chinese soldiers have also crossed into Mogaung.'

'It will be best if we keep proceeding towards Assam', Nitu said. 'They said that they would transport us by jeep to the banks of the Towang river. We should probably make our move this evening itself', he said, contemplating awhile. 'We cannot guarantee what the situation will be like tomorrow. Since the Japanese have already rooted themselves here…'

'I have heard that there is no bridge across the Towang river', the priest said.

'Yes, they said there is no bridge there. However, there is a military ferry—we will have to cross the river on that', Nitu said. 'The bridge was destroyed a long time ago.'

'How much more do we have to travel once we cross the Towang?' Ramgobinda asked.

'Vehicles are said to be plying on the road from Towang to Shingbwiyan. After that, those hills again and that same journey. Nearly sixty miles or so', the priest sighed and said. 'That entire region is full of hills and crevices—a tough, terrible route! I have heard that even the military mules haven't been able to cross that region.' The priest took out his map, 'There is definitely a ferry running across the Tarung Hka river. If we cross that, we may be able to hail a military jeep to travel to Nathkao…at least till Sawgni-ga.'

Ramgobinda was assailed by worry. He was planning to stay in Mogaung for a day or two to inquire about Lacchmi and the child. He would need a lot of time to find some news of them in this vast sea of people. 'It would be nice if we could stay here for a day or two', he said hesitantly. 'I had no time to find out anything about Lacchmi, Ballabh and the rest.'

'Maybe we can stay behind…' the priest contemplated. 'But after seeing the conditions here, I don't think it is advisable or possible to stay here for longer.'

'However, if they are still alive, who is there to take care of them?' Ramgobinda said, stifling a sob. 'They don't have anyone. We sent them away when they were unconscious in an unknown military vehicle…'

'I have the utmost belief that the allies will transport the sick, the needy and the womenfolk to Ledo by hook or by crook at the slightest hint of danger.'

'What do the rest of the people in our group say?' Ramgobinda asked.

'We haven't met anyone as yet. We have no idea as to their whereabouts', Nitu said.

They met Budhu, Gurcharan and Kalu together as they were walking amongst the crowd.

'Haricharan sustained a head injury. They took him away in an unconscious state to the hospital', Budhu said. 'The sick person who came with the priests was also taken away.'

'Most probably they have been admitted to the hospital', the priest heaved a sigh of relief. They could not find the short priest, Ma-Pu or Chinti anywhere. There was no time to look for them either. In the meantime, a posse of about eight to ten military jeeps parked in a line in the middle of the field to take the refugees who wanted to leave for Towang.

The banks of the Towang Hka river.

At dusk, the banks of the river were teeming with an uncountable number of refugees and soldiers. Besides Ramgobinda, six members of the group travelled in the same jeep to the banks of the river. These were the banks of a hill river—therefore, there were no wide, expansive sand coves and no grass-filled groves of jhau trees either. A few steps had been cut out in the surrounding hills. One could clamber down to the water below using those. Slippery mud everywhere; the stairs were also winding and slippery. A plethora of thoughts coursed through Ramgobinda's mind as he carefully descended the steps with Thanu on his back. Surveying that infinite sea of humanity with hopeful eyes, he wondered if he could get some sign of a beloved face among them. However, his hopeful gaze was thwarted every time. Hopelessness and frustration began taking root in his mind. Despite that, he repeatedly admonished himself for the dark thoughts that constantly brought images of horrible eventualities that could have beset Lacchmi and the infant.

'There is a large camp at Ledo; I am sure I will find them there.'

Nearly two hundred people were crammed in the narrow space that led to the ferry. Among them, many military men in green and khaki uniforms were trying to push their way through and get in front. The captain of the ferry, his cap inclined on one side, stood in the doorway and gesticulated wildly with his hands begging the people not to board it, 'The ferry is going to return in two hours. Everyone will be able to leave. No one will be left behind.' However, no one paid any heed to what he was saying. The stream of people flowing by his side and even over his head had filled the ferry to the brim. The red border of the ferry was already under water due to the weight of the passengers. The currents were also very strong. The jeeps were steadily bringing more and more people to the banks. 'The ferry is going to sink', the captain said looking at the side that was tilting over. 'Before you bring more people, please arrange for more ferries.' Despite that, people kept streaming in as if this was the final journey for this ferry.

They noticed the short priest, Chinti and Ma-Pu standing in one corner of the ferry. Ma-Pu was leaning against a railing. Somehow the tall priest and Nitu waded through the sea of people and reached their side. Ma-Pu held the priest's hand, pulled him near the railing, and moved from her spot slightly so that he could lean against the railings. In the meantime, Ramgobinda, with Thanu on his back, and Gurcharan also came closer.

'Where will the ferry take us?' the tall priest asked the short one.

'I don't know. Apparently, there is a small harbour near Ritu. Most probably they will take us there', the short priest said.

'I don't know. They may take us a short distance and let us off at Taihpa Ga', a soldier standing nearby said.

'Will the ferry be able to get there with the sheer weight of the passengers in it?', another soldier said skeptically.

'We looked everywhere for you', Chinti said. 'However, with the chaotic clamour to clamber into the jeeps, there was no way we could have found you in the melee.' He tried to smile, 'Where are the others?'

'Haricharan was injured in the head by fragments from the bombs. He was taken away to the hospital', Nitu said. 'We don't know about the rest. We didn't come across them.'

Thousands of people everywhere! Shifting Thanu to his shoulders, Ramgobinda stood on one side. There wasn't any space left to fit even a tiny ant. There was no place where he could put Thanu down either. It was impossible to move with the sheer weight of people all around. After haranguing the passengers repeatedly, the captain somehow managed to shut the door of the ferry pushing it with all his strength. Immediately, the horn of the ferry blared twice. The ferry began to move. The wooden plank attached to the ferry fell down as soon as the ferry began to move. The people on the plank fell into the river and began bobbing up and down in the water.

Ramgobinda peered into the crowd surrounding him searching for someone. His empty gaze whirled around the elevations on the banks, the strong currents of the Towang, the trees at the edges of river, the sea of humanity on all sides, the steam emerging from the boiler, and numerous other nondescript objects before finally resting on a wooden beam above him. That adorable kitten once again! She was sitting on the beam, curled up into a ball, occasionally licking her paws, and surveying the ocean of humanity before her warily. When Ramgobinda's gaze met hers, she released a soft meow almost as an acknowledgement and then went back to surveying her surroundings warily.

After floating for a while on the strong currents of the Towang, the tilted ferry slowly began to pick up speed. Darkness was then beginning to settle in the heart of the river. Suffering from the incredible heat inside the ferry, the passengers tried to breathe deeply by raising their heads upwards, also hoping thereby to get a whiff of cool breeze. The ferry was swaying in the strong currents and kept tooting its horn periodically. Maneuvering its way across the many rocks rising up from the heart of the river, the ferry finally reached the western banks of the Towang in about an hour. They noticed a long sand bank extending to the Melsuwa river on the west once they docked in Ritu. The ferry halted at a spot where the water was knee-deep. Immediately, the travellers began to jump out of the ferry, not caring whether they landed in water or on the sands. Around half of the people on in the ferry had already reached the banks before the wooden plank used as a platform for alighting was taken out. The people who jumped into the water were thoroughly drenched. Feeling the weight of the people behind them, the young children standing at the head of the wooden plank began screaming in terror. Nearly two hundred to two hundred and fifty passengers dismounted from the ferry and spread across the sandbank in the midst of all the chaos and bedlam. It was as if they had arrived at a place of refuge, as if this were the end of the journey with nothing ahead.

But, that wasn't the end. Sticky mounds of sand from the river mixed with sharp, tiny pebbles paved the path ahead which ran for about half a mile. The Tabaunga wasn't far away; after that, the Patkai hills. Innumerable rivers, hills, mountains, ascents and descents! They had only traversed a minute segment of this massive natural sakrabehu. The most formidable segment at the heart of the horrifying Hukawng valley still lay ahead.

Once the travellers alighted on the sandbanks, they once again dispersed into smaller groups. The groups began moving in different directions. No one knew which route to take; their only thoughts were those of escape and constant movement. They just had to advance in a ceaseless journey with a lust for life. Where, how, through which route?—these were irrelevant questions.

A group of five advanced along with Nitu's group. They caught up with the group once all of them had clambered up the sandbanks. The family in the group constituted a couple, a young man and an infant girl in the woman's lap. The family was from Walaw-bum, not too far from Mogaung. There was a middle-aged man from Chaukang as well. These new people didn't seem to be too exhausted from the arduous journey. Actually, it hadn't even been two days since they had begun their journey.

'It will probably be good for us if we can follow these American military men', Nitu said. 'They seem to know the way and can also help us if there is any trouble.'

'Will they agree?' the tall priest asked? 'I asked a couple of them, but they said they were on duty. Moreover, they may not like travelling with a band of refugees.'

'Most of them are crippled', the short priest said. 'They are only walking through this route because no jeep or vehicle can traverse this segment. They will walk for a short distance and once again get on their jeeps.'

'That's for later—if that is the case, then we will follow our own path. We have travelled so far; what more is there to fear?' the tall priest replied, and walking with long strides, began talking with the military officer standing at a distance. The officer had ten to twelve soldiers with him. After talking to him for a few moments, he gestured to the group with his hands from the elevation where he was standing.

'We can travel with them to Ningbwiyan', he said. 'They will stay behind there. But I have gathered that it won't be very difficult for us to advance ahead from there. In fact, we may come across another unit marching towards Ledo. Apparently, travellers keep coming and going through this route.'

'Ningbwiyan, of course, is just a military base. However, if we move ahead, I've heard that there is a camp for refugees in Shingbwiyan', the military officer said. 'It will be safer for you to move with us at least on this stretch of the road. Once we reach Taihpa Ga, which is a short distance away, we will also have to cross the Tarung Hka river. If we don't know the exact bank, it will be difficult to cross the river.'

Lots of corpses were strewn around on the sides of the narrow hilly road between Ritu and Tarung. Many corpses were clad in expensive apparel and also had bags strung on their shoulders. Suitcases, bags and small boxes were lying about in a disorderly fashion around many of these corpses. Clothes, intricately made with silk and with golden threads, were hanging on the gooseberry bushes and waving in the wind. The colourful apparel appeared to mock the corpses with their smiles. Valuable bags encrusted with jade and silver coins with her majesty's stamp on them were scattered everywhere. Torn rags bespeaking of poverty were also visible, streaming out of the many tin boxes and dirty bags lying about in this region. These rags accompanied the rich clothes in their merry dance in the wind. The corpses were half-buried in the earth after the rains had rendered this pathway slippery and muddy. The cruel embrace of death had destroyed any differentiation between the rich and the poor, the high and the low, the rulers and the ruled. The boundaries separating the corpses had collapsed as all of them fell in this place. Their journey ended in the middle of the road. However, thousands of refugees who had begun to resemble the living dead ignored their presence and advanced forward, continuing their ceaseless movement. The distressed cries of the tall trees whistling in the wind was like a dirge accompanying this ghastly procession of life as it wound its way against a backdrop of death.

The travellers were exhausted.

'I think it is probably best that we spend the night here', the military officer said once they reached Taihpa Ga. 'If we can begin our journey very early tomorrow, we can cross Tabaunga when there is still light and reach Ningbwiyan before evening.'

However, they did not find any facilities for rest in Taihpa Ga. There was no sign of life in that tall hill covered with dense forest. There were no signs of human habitation there either, save for a few corpses. The small huts constructed to oversee tou-iya were also overflowing with corpses.

'It's better that we keep moving ahead rather than spend the night in this terrifying place', the tall priest said. 'If there is a camp in Shingbwiyan…'

'Yes, yes', the military officer interrupted him. 'I have also heard that North sahib is there. He is said to have established a large refugee camp with a hospital there. Check the facilities there and then decide what you want to do.'

The group kept moving during the remainder of the

night, crossed Tabaunga and reached Ningbwiyan when it was twilight. After making inquiries in the military camp there, they learned that it would be best to move ahead to Shingbwiyan for refuge and treatment. There were no facilities in Ningbwiyan. A small military contingent was posted there and they were trying desperately hard to defend this outpost. There was no food here. The stuff distributed via airdrops had also fallen all over the place and were difficult, if not impossible, to find. Even mules couldn't cross the tall hills lying between this place and Shingbwiyan.

The travellers passed the remainder of the night in hunger in Ningbwiyan, and resumed their journey once again when it was dawn. Straggling across the steep, muddy and slippery pathways, they reached Shingbwiyan when evening had begun descending.

XIX

Shingbwiyan!

A narrow region surrounded on several sides by hills located at the borders of Burma. By the time Nitu's group reached this region, this tiny area was teeming with ten to fifteen thousand refugees. Many British, Indian and Chinese troops were also among these refugees. These troops were evacuated from regions like Misina, Mogaung and Sumpra-bum about the time of the Japanese attack. A lot of them took their fortunes in their hands and preemptively escaped from their hospitals. With hope in their hearts, these people travelled from afar, and after crossing the mountains and hills facing many privations *en route*, gathered in this place. They were very sick and skeletal. Most of them were wounded. Hundreds died in the camps, much like mass deaths in a plague, while waiting expectantly to get admitted to the hospitals. On certain days, fifty to sixty people died together. Since it was virtually impossible to bury these corpses, they were dumped in the deep gorges between the hills. There was a severe shortage of space in the camps—they were teeming with people. Cholera, malaria, dysentery, typhoid and *kala azar* made their imprint known here. There wasn't enough medication to treat these diseases in the hospitals. Most of the bundles of medicine that were occasionally air-dropped flowed away in the rivers. A lot of these bundles were lost in the gorges in between the hills.

Political Officer North could not be found. A lower ranking political official made arrangements for Father Berry and the group to stay in one corner of the refugee camp. Separate arrangements had, of course, been made for the soldiers. They learned later from North sahib that the Indian Tea Association had established around sixteen shelters alongside the densely overgrown pathways used by opium traders lying between Taikhan Jup and Lekhapani. As far as possible, arrangements for food had also been made in these camps. These camps, of course, were supplied intermittently by drops made by airplanes. Resources were scarce; somehow they were getting by. At least there was the partial satisfaction of hunger as a single ration of rice and salt was received per day by everyone; otherwise, they would get a packet each from the military rations. It was virtually impossible to maintain contact with the world beyond

Shingbwiyan. Occasionally, a smidgeon of news arrived from Mogaung with a postman. Of course, every day lots of refugees arrived via different routes. Although they weren't bearers of accurate news, they passed on a few rumours.

Nitu's group rested in Shingbwiyan camp for two days. Ramgobinda, of course, didn't get time for rest. He roamed across the camps and hospitals searching for Lacchmi and the infant. They were nowhere to be found. Two days went by. In fact, this time he didn't even notice the kitten. Gathering the meagre provisions of food that they saved in the previous couple of days, the group began making their way to Nathkao after crossing the Tarung Hka by ferry on the morning of the third day. Aside from the difficulty of the journey and the threat of illness, there was no major reason to be worried. The Japanese were far away. At least they now had the opportunity to get shelter and rest in the refugee camps on the way. Provisions for a meal could be found here. A tiring, treacherous path, enriched however by the light of hope, illuminated by the promise of safety.

Of course, once they crossed Nathkao, there was the treacherous region of the Hukawng valley extending up to Namiya-Ra. After that, the terrifyingly dangerous death-world: the gates of hell to Hukawng, extending from Namiya-Ra to the region beyond Pangsau. The journey would come to an end once they crossed the mountainous pathways of Pangsau. Beyond that was the kingdom of refuge, the empire of happiness, joy and peace. The refugees were suffused with unexpected joy with the knowledge that they did not have too far to travel.

Even though the distance wasn't great, the pathways were still very steep. It was almost evening when the group reached Nathkao. There was no food in the Nathkao camp either. The group ate whatever little they carried with them and rested there for the night. There was no other alternative. No one was brave enough to wend their way across this segment of the Hukawng pathway at night.

Ramgobinda had given way to despair. There were signs that Thanu was once again catching a fever. He was running a temperature and his face became extremely red. There was no opportunity for any treatment either as there were no medicines to be found when they arrived. The boy did not eat anything that night and Ramgobinda spent the entire night tossing and turning agitatedly. As the night progressed, the boy's temperature began to rise steadily. While checking his temperature, even the lean face of the tall priest became pale for a moment.

'It is imperative that he receives medication very soon', he looked skywards and spoke as if he were communing with God. 'However, there seems to be no option of that here.' The rest of the group ventured nothing in response.

Ma-Pu changed the cold compresses on Thanu's forehead the entire night. At one time, she managed to get some warm water from somewhere to wash his feet. The boy was lying down, speechless with fatigue, and occasionally muttered something unintelligible.

They spent the night beset with tension, worry and anxiety. Actually, no one slept. The next day, the group resumed climbing the hills as soon as it was daylight and by evening reached Namiya-Ra. They repeatedly climbed up and down—that same exhausting journey! The day was cloudy and dark. The sun never revealed its face because of the dense jungle and its own inability to pierce the thick covering of the clouds. In the meantime, black clouds also gathered clod by clod in the gorges between the hills. Due to the wet, cold wind, these clouds became visible in the light that flashed and disappeared intermittently. Quite frequently, the floating clouds also surrounded the densely overgrown pathways and made breathing difficult for the travellers.

There weren't a lot of people in the Namiya-Ra camp. The group settled in an empty dwelling pointed out by the caretaker of the camp.

'The monsoon is probably upon us', the caretaker said, looking at the cloud-covered sky. Everyone felt apprehensive at the thought of the difficulties they would face if heavy rain fell on this stretch of the road. Ramgobinda's thoughts, however, were elsewhere. Although Thanu's fever wasn't very high during the daytime, it shot up when evening descended. Ramgobinda looked at the priest in distress.

'Is there a doctor anywhere here…and can some medicine be arranged for him here?' The tall priest asked the caretaker.

'No doctor here, no medicine either' the caretaker said. 'Actually this is not a camp, only a few roofs made of straw have been erected here so that the refugees can rest awhile. We are somehow tiding through the days here with meagre provisions.'

'Don't the refugees stay here?'

'In the last few days, approximately three thousand refugees have travelled past this place. Everyone rests for an hour or two and then makes a move ahead. Everyone stops near the Nong-Jong river—after that, the hilly pathways of Pangsau.'

'Couldn't people cross the river? Or do they stop there for some other reason?' the priest asked in an apprehensive tone. Anyway, there were signs of approaching rain and that was a cause for worry.

'It's a hilly river with very strong currents. In the twinkle of an eye, the water can rise up to eight or nine feet', the caretaker said. 'One can't even imagine the terrible conditions the travellers will face once the rains begin.'

The people were chilled to the bone by that tingling cold weather. A wave of cold wind just before the onset of the rains produced a tumultuous wave that made the grass and trees of Namiya-Ra quiver. Folks were talking without inhibition, sitting around a bonfire in an empty room in the refugee camp. The dreams of life seemed to be reanimated and glittered before the eyes of these despairing people after many days. The light of new hope illuminated their interior horizons just prior to arriving at their desired destination. An extremely difficult stretch of the road still lay before them. In spite of that, thoughts of the future were springing up in the conversations between them. Such thoughts were the constant companions of these people who were still alive. They imagined what tomorrow held despite not knowing what would transpire today!

'Where are you all planning to go after you reach Ledo?' Nitu asked, stretching his legs closer to the bonfire and looking up at the other members of the group.

The murmur of the voluble crowd ceased suddenly. This was an unprecedented question—no one had thought about this at all! A new problem that hadn't sprung up in their minds in the preceding days! This was an unsettling question for these people who had dragged themselves and moved here by the sheer force of the irresistible desire for life. No one was prepared to give an answer to this. The tall priest raised his head and gazed at the bamboo lathes supporting the roof of the hut constructed with toko leaves. Ramgobinda opened his eyes wide, looked at Thanu, and then stared fixedly at the bonfire with a blank gaze. Chinti looked in Ma-Pu's direction and then turned his eyes towards the walls. Gurcharan looked at Nitu with a melancholic gaze, as if the question hadn't penetrated his mind as yet. The short priest, in the meantime, was lying down with his eyes shut. He continued to lie down like this.

'We'll go wherever fortune takes us', Budhu replied briefly on behalf of the entire group and looked at Ramgobinda. In the meantime, the new members of the group began to get ready to sleep. The young man was running a high temperature. The infant girl in her mother's lap was crying loudly and incessantly. The two middle-aged men from Sagaing were in another room. They were staying apart from the group, suspecting that the boy had kala azar.

'When do we leave this place?' Ramgobinda asked after a long while. He was almost beginning to lose his wits worrying about Lachhmi.

'A very difficult road lies just ahead…no point staying here for a long time', the tall priest said. 'The way the clouds are gathering, it may rain any moment. We will suffer more when the rains begin. Besides that, there aren't a lot of facilities here either.'

'It's better if we start tomorrow morning itself', Nitu said, baring the teeth in his shrunken face. 'We will have to travel across this pathway during daylight. We will be alright if we can take shelter in the refugee camps at night.'

'Will we actually get shelters like these?' Kalu, who was dozing near the fire, woke up with a start and asked as if he was speaking to himself.

'Stop that!' Nitu scolded him, 'you shouldn't talk like that. We managed to come so far, now we will cross the remainder by hook or by crook'. He turned his head towards the wall. He didn't have any conviction in his own statements.

There was no food to be found in the camp. 'We haven't eaten anything in the previous couple of days either', the caretaker of the camp said with a dejected laugh. 'The rations from the airdrops couldn't be found in the jungle.' He sighed deeply and chimed melancholically, 'On others are we dependent, in the jungle are we resident!'

The rain indeed began pouring at midnight. Even though the weather cleared up in the morning, slippery water and mud surrounded the camp due to the rains. The group set out at the break of dawn. None of them had any belongings. They didn't have any food either. The family of four also began the journey along with the sick girl. The middle-aged men decided to proceed after resting for two days. They had a little bit of food with them.

'I pray to the Almighty that you may reach your destination without any impediment', the caretaker of Namiya-Ra said and sighed looking at the lofty hills in the distance. 'I hope that luck and success follows you every step of the way.'

'We would like to convey good wishes to you too', the tall priest said.

'People come and go. They rest here for a night, and then leave; we, however, remain in the same place. We remain stationary in this vast theater of movement (*jangamata*). We welcome people and take care of them. We get joy from their company for a day or two…that's it! We can't give them anything, we have no capacity to distribute anything', tears began welling in the eyes of the caretaker.

'Once you cross Pangsau, you will find a large refugee camp with a hospital in Nampung…', the caretaker continued, wiping away his tears. 'Please take some rest there. You can also treat the two sick children there. Good luck!'

The red, clayey soil in the undulating pathway between Namiya-Ra and the Njang Yang river had become very slippery. In that steep incline, it was difficult to get a foothold while climbing or descending. By the afternoon, a mass of black clouds covered the sky and the peaks of the hills. Darkness fell during daylight; it was as if the world in front of their eyes was shrouded in a veil of darkness. After a while, it began drizzling. It became difficult for the travellers to press forward. In that unfortunate situation, the travellers scrambled and wound their way with wooden sticks in their hands. An uncountable number of corpses lay prone in various positions in the spaces between the pathway and the edges of the hills ringing it, and also in the fields that had been cleared for jhum cultivation. They seemed to be flashing their teeth and grinning at the travellers. Almost all the corpses were swollen and puffed up, and scores of brightly-coloured butterflies illuminated them further, covering them like a shroud. There was no other sign of life in those virtually unsurmountable hills other than those butterflies. In fact, birds too were absent and no encouragement could be found from them either. The butterflies did not move away even when the travellers moved closer. They had no knowledge of humans, and hence no fear of them. They had absolute monarchy in that field of nature! There were no signs of any villages or human habitations in the blotches of open areas cleared for the purposes of tou-iya that they encountered sporadically on the way. A thin layer of green vegetation had grown and yellowed in the older fields used earlier for jhum cultivation.

In that cloudy weather, the deepest part of the Njang Yang river emerged glittering in their field of vision, and appeared like a vast winding entity when viewed from the peaks of the Tandun hills. Occasionally white rays of light shone through the bosom of the clouds even though it could not be said with certainty where the sun hid itself behind the black clouds. Signs of ground cleared for tou-iya were visible in the peaks of the hills which were now a playground for the clouds. Tall platforms were visible in each patch of cleared ground. Frighteningly tall hills on every side, tableaus of death and destruction visible with each and every step! A group of uprooted people were proceeding through a territory that even wild animals had abandoned after losing a titanic struggle with nature—as if this was nothing but a cruel joke! An exhibition of shiny jewelry, priceless rubies, jade stones and expensive apparel in the numerous bags and trunks lying open near the corpses seemed to be going on; however, the innumerable refugees who travelled through this pathway did not even stop to cast a backward glance at these. In fact, the wild bloodsucking butterflies did not attempt to alight on these objects even momentarily. They were busy in the search for nourishment. Life, only life—in this endless journey, inertness and stillness were of no value. This was just a carnival of movement, to halt meant death and futile, meaningless silence!

The people began to be divided into groups while traversing the winding, twisting pathways. Ramgobinda tied Thanu tightly to his chest. Chinti did not leave Ma-Pu's side. He was gradually falling deeply in love with this Anglo-Burmese girl who was becoming increasingly distressed by the tiring journey. Chinti felt an unexplained, unspoken attraction to this simple girl with whom he had hardly exchanged words. He walked by her side apprehensive that she may lose her footing on that slippery pathway. The travellers did not speak to each other or display any emotion on their faces, advancing in a line at their own pace.

A number of huts and roofs constructed of thin, wild bamboo could be seen in the cleared areas on the top of the hills at the edges of the pathway they used to ascend the Tandun hills. It could be garnered that scores of refugees had taken refuge under these roofs before the Namiya-Ra camp had been set up. Since many families could not move any further they survived under these roofs for quite a few days, and then, without any differentiation or discrimination, fell into the jaws of death. The entwined corpses of a mother attempting to breastfeed an infant in her lap were leaning on the pillars of one of these houses. Thousands of black ants clung to the flesh of the infant. The flesh of the mother, too, had begun rotting. Under an unoccupied roof, the rotting fragments of a half-decayed infant's corpse had become indistinguishable from the remaining bits of another mother's cadaver. The infant's bones were visible in certain places. Termites had constructed a mound on the mother's head. Crosses, hastily constructed out of the branches of trees, were seen in the hands and bosoms of the rotting cadavers. They came across many corpses clasping the holy images of Mary and Jesus Christ in the skeletal remains of their hands. Termites had consumed the flesh and cotton apparel of the corpses of many a dead soldier. Caps made of colourful wool and down tightly fitted their grinning skulls. The flashing bits of flesh occasionally stuck to the remaining bones of their skeletons made them appear even more gruesome and disgusting. In the meantime, the forest proliferated luxuriantly in the oncoming rains, and covered most of the huts and the roofs. Cruel nature was busy in its irresistible quest to transform bodies forged out of earth back into dust once again.

After crossing the Saugni Ga hills, the group reached the Njang Yang river just as the sun began going down. Thousands of refugees had crowded on the slightly elevated banks of the river. With the touch of the rains, the river began gurgling and resembled a lively youthful maiden of the wilds. Underneath, wood and bamboo came floating by, carried by its forceful currents. Many refugees were expectantly waiting, with hope and despair ebbing and flowing periodically, on the high inclines of the hills by the banks of the river. Thousands of people had been waiting hopefully like this for the past four or five days. They hadn't managed to cross the river. Packets of food airdropped by the allies either fell on the other side of the river or were carried away by the strong currents. Many people jumped into the river to grab hold of these packets. Many tried to cross the river despite the speedy currents and powerful flow. These people disappeared without a trace. An uncountable number of people died in the sharply descending, precipitous banks of the Njang Yang river. The heavy airdropped packets fell on the bodies of some; others died of cholera. Many died due to malnutrition and fatigue accumulated during the difficult journey. No one had the strength to check who lived and who died. Uncertainty and fear dogged them at each step. After the incessant rainfall of the past four-five days, the vegetation grew luxuriantly all around and assumed a terrifying appearance. If this situation continued, it seemed as if nature would swallow people alive where they stood. The pitiful cries of scores of people waiting for a morsel of food and the curses and sighs of hundreds of corpses haunting that horrifying setting ridiculed even the merciless cruelty and terror of the loathsome Hukawng valley.

It started raining heavily again during the darkest hours of the night. The level of the river also began to rise. Many travellers had erected some low-lying coverings. The rain-drenched occupants shivered because of the cold despite setting large stacks of wood on fire. The coverings leaked—the resounding rain constantly assaulted them. Flashes of lightning and the harsh sound of thunder juxtaposed with the tumultuous whiplash of heavy rainfall and the howling wind struck fear in the hearts of each and every person. Lightning tearing the sky above the hills illuminated the lofty, heartless peaks on all sides making them occasionally come into view. It was as if a group of pitiless murderers surrounded the hapless people on all sides. On that fateful night of their funereal march, thousands of people stranded on the banks of the Njang Yang river experienced the sheer insignificance of human strength and power and the pitiless anger of unconquerable nature. Lightning and massive drops of rain fell relentlessly on the people suffering from acute hunger. However, even this could not elicit any response from the bodies of the weak, semi-conscious refugees.

Although the weather cleared up a little in the morning, the level of water in the river did not subside. Rain was still pouring in the distant mountains. With hopeful gazes, the people stared fixedly at the horizon in the clear light of the morning. Maybe a plane would arrive and airdrop stuff, maybe they would get something to eat? But food didn't arrive. The emaciated, weak people mentally prepared themselves to spend another day on an empty stomach. Sick Chinese soldiers had snatched away the tiny morsels of food that remained with a few refugees from the airdrops a couple of days earlier. Threatening the people with their guns and bayonets, they grabbed their goods and took them away. The ten or twelve British soldiers that remained were reduced to skin and bone because of malnutrition and the struggles faced on the road. In fact, the wild spotted leeches could hardly find a drop of blood in their bodies. Unable to carry anything heavy, they threw away their big rifles and all their bullets. Some of them tore open their star-studded uniforms and hurled them down the gorges.

The day passed by in this fashion in the midst of hope, hunger and expectations. Ma-Pu managed to steal a small portion of food from the minuscule rations of a group of British soldiers in a tent nearby and fed Thanu with that. She experienced an inexplicable outpouring of love for that little boy. Once evening set in, the level of the river suddenly receded, and within an hour, tiny pebbles were visible glittering in the knee-deep water at the heart of the river. People began walking on the slippery, moss-covered pebbles lying at the bottom of the ice-cold water of the river and heaved sighs of relief when they reached the other side just before dusk set in. A few boxes of food were found strewn pell-mell when they climbed the steep bank on the other side of the river: dry meat and other rations among them.

However, nature's cruelty returned a thousand-fold again after the briefest of pauses. Heavy rain began falling again. The hilly pathway just above the banks filled with knee-deep mud once evening turned into night. After travelling a short distance on that steep hillside, the travellers had to halt again. Heavy rain battered them a little less when they took shelter beneath the tall trees. The rain-drenched travellers spent that night standing under those trees. Of course, there was no question of advancing in that dark night in the midst of all their woes. There was some mild rainfall the following morning; however, the refugees began wending their way once again while there was still light.

A silent procession of approximately a thousand people—a silent, lifeless pace, indolent steps, marks of extreme exhaustion. The group progressed together. The hearts of these weak, emaciated, pale travellers, however, were suffused with hope.

People who stopped on the road stayed there. There was no point feeling sorry for them, the people thought, 'This world is only for living beings. The dead belong to the cremation grounds.' They felt upbeat sensing the journey's end despite their extreme tiredness and fatigue. Now only the hilly passes of Pangsau stood on their way. After that, the journey would be over. This new lease of life and enthusiasm kept pushing them forward on that road still strewn with many dangers.

From the top of the Pangsau pass, an unbroken kingdom of mountains extending up to the snowy, white peaks of the Himalayas in the distance emerged before the traveler's eyes, just above the groves of trees decorated with myriad colours. Below, numerous streams advanced rapidly in the midst of the alternately thin and thick greenery, resounding loudly and busy with an aimless flow.

These streams were swift and well-nourished by the rains. oceans of beauty glittering in the bright afternoon sun. Despite that, a peculiar sensation arose when the travellers stood on those sky-kissing, lofty peaks. These hills were the silent memorials to thousands of people. So many Indians, British, Chinese and Anglo-Indian men and women, children and aged people had fallen here. These hills—the graveyards of innumerable soldiers! The skeletons and bones of thousands of people were interred in their icy tombs here. Anxiety, terror, courage and cowardice, illness from malnutrition, hopes and expectations, struggles—in this place, everything merged with nature's immense beauty and vanished without a trace! Many stories reached their conclusion here; nature enveloped an infinite number of lofty dreams in her peaceful lap. How many agony-ridden cries fell silent for eternity here? How many elated gasps of breath merged with the winds here?

It was as if the unfathomable silence in the hilly pathways of Pangsau resembled the eternal quietude of death, as if a merciless curse of nature reigned supreme in this isolated region, as if this silence was like the thundering roar of *mahakaal!*

XX

New hope and enthusiasm dawned in the hearts of the travellers even though they were extremely exhausted. After facing many trials and tribulations, they had reached the Kumlao plateau after crossing the Pangsau pass. Nitu's group felt as if they had traversed the kingdom of death, labeled Nampong, the exit gate of hell. Food was available in the row of refugee camps that the Indian Tea Association had set up between the Pangsau pass and Tipong. Good facilities for the treatment of sick soldiers and refugees were also available in the large hospital established in Nampong camp. Doctors, medicine and options for treatment were available to a large degree here. This stream of humanity that came floating by on the destructive currents of the great war after crossing massive swathes of dense forest, climbing myriad hills and mountains, and constantly being assailed by agony, the labours of the journey and by numerous unknown diseases, suddenly came to a halt at this spot. This region was like another world altogether, brightened by the illumination of a limitless horizon of hope, a new creation engendered by the vibrancy of life.

Most of the travellers were in no condition to move any further. Exhaustion and lassitude after arriving at their desired destination had enveloped their entire being and rendered them virtually disabled. The refugees rested for a long while in the row of camps dotting the way from Pangsau to Nampong. A lot of them, of course, slowly proceeded ahead after having their fill in these camps. Others contemplated moving ahead only after spending a good few days in the camps.

Nitu's group did not halt in any of the camps on the way and proceeded straight ahead to Nampong. The two sick children needed urgent medical attention. There was also a possibility of proceeding ahead to Lidu or Lekhapani (Ledo) from Nampong. Walking at a slow and steady pace for a day and a night, Nitu's group reached Nampong refugee camp.

Ramgobinda somehow got through the night and went out in search of Lacchmi and the infant early in the morning. However, he couldn't find Lacchmi, Ballabh or Budhu's mother among the thousands of the sick and the infirm in the hospital. Acute tiredness and hopelessness set in after he spent the entire day futilely, searching for them in the hospital and the neighbouring camps. While it was highly probable that the infant must have died by now, he was unable to reconcile himself to the fact that Lacchmi, Budhu's mother and Ballabh had vanished without a trace on the road. On the other hand, Thanu had a raging fever. He was also very weak and didn't have the strength to utter a word. It wasn't easy either to walk tying Thanu on his back. He returned once during the afternoon and left Thanu with Ma-Pu. After that, the same, frantic round of asking doctors, nurses, majors and guards in the hospital all ending up in nothing. In the latter half of the day, the tall priest also accompanied him in his search. The rest of the group lay slumped on the floor of their shelter.

They gathered that a number of sick refugees had been transferred by trolley to the main hospital in Lekhapani. It was probable that the lost ones may be among them. No one knew anything about the jeep or where it had gone. There were a number of possibilities. If the jeep had gone up to Mogaung, it was very likely that it had fallen prey to the bombings. Just two days after the jeep had left, Mogaung sustained intense bombing. Another possibility was that some accident had occurred on the way. Maybe the military men had abandoned them on the way, failing to find any hospitals or medical facilities in Unthaw. The priest remembered the numberplate of that jeep travelling from Lesin; however, his difficulties were magnified because he did not remember the names of the military men. If they had been left behind, it was virtually certain that these sick people couldn't have completed the journey. Their death was then inevitable.

Budhu, too, began making inquiries in the evening. After searching for news the entire day, the tall priest managed to garner a sliver of information at dusk. Checking the records of the vehicles travelling to and fro from Lesin to Unthaw, a military officer said the vehicle had been involved in an accident that same night on the way to Mogaung. There were no records about the fate of the military officers and the passengers. Mogaung was being bombed relentlessly during that time—who had the time to keep track of such things? It was virtually certain that the sick passengers must have passed away by now.

'If the infant was still alive, he would have been nineteen days old today…' Ramgobinda counted silently and with a sigh looked at the sleeping Thanu. Probably the priest was correct—Lacchmi was no more. It made no sense waiting expectantly for them any longer at Nampong. He placed his hand on Thanu's brow and tried to gauge his temperature. His own limbs ached severely. His body resembled a dried bit of wood. Other than noticing that Thanu was still trembling, he couldn't figure out anything else. Budhu had spent himself with grief. Ma-Pu and Chinti approached

Ramgobinda and sat by his side.

'He too will die', Ramgobinda told Chinti while looking at Thanu who was convulsing due to the fever he suffered from. 'He will die now, right in front of my eyes.' He began bawling. 'Everything is finished. I don't have anything left now.' Beating his chest, he crumpled on the floor. Chinti held Ramgobinda in an embrace. White foam began flowing through the corners of Ramgobinda's bearded face.

'He has a very high fever', caressing Thanu's head, Ma-Pu spoke to the tall priest. 'He got drenched in the rainfall last night. His temperature immediately shot up after he had some rice gruel.'

'We should take him to the hospital right now', the tall priest said, checking Thanu's temperature. 'Chinti, look after him. We will go to the hospital now', the priest pointed to the unconscious figure of Ramgobinda lying on the floor and lifted Thanu up.

After examining Thanu for several minutes, the wizened, bearded doctor in the hospital stared at the tall priest for quite a while. 'Serious infection!' he said. 'On top of that, he is very weak. He will require an extensive spell of treatment. For the moment, I will administer a shot. I hope you have no objections?' The doctor reached out towards the rack where the needles were lined up.

'No, no! What objections will we have?' the priest said without hesitating. 'It must be malaria, isn't it?'

'It begins as malaria. But it's a terrible fever that rages incessantly for a few days', the doctor said. 'Have you given him any medicine in the meanwhile?'

'No, we didn't have any medicine. Last week, I gave him the two tablets of quinine that I had with me—that's it', the priest said.

'Are you a doctor too?' The doctor prepared the syringe and looked at the priest.

'It seems I know you from somewhere', the priest looked at the doctor and said hesitantly. 'Aren't you Doctor Shimray?'

'Yes! Oh yes!' the doctor said, placing the syringe on the tray. 'I too was wondering all this while. Father Berry, I presume?' The doctor embraced the priest. 'How did you get here?'

'I will tell you everything', the priest smiled and said. 'But first please tend to this boy.'

'Sure, sure!' Doctor Shimray washed his hands after administering two shots to the feverish Thanu. 'I have no idea whether the people we knew from earlier are still alive or not. There is so much I have to talk to you about.' The doctor checked Thanu's pulse.

'My worries won't cease until this boy is completely healed', the priest said. 'The boy's father has almost lost his wits. They are the only two survivors from their family—at least, that's what we know for certain.'

'We don't have a lot of nurses in this hospital', Doctor Shimray said, placing a blanket on the sleeping form of Thanu. 'We have to do everything ourselves, from administering shots to changing dressings to surgeries…'

'However, I knew that you were still alive', Doctor Shimray pulled up a chair close to the priest, sat down and looked at Ma-Pu. 'Who is she?' he asked.

'She traveled with us. Miss Ma-Pu or Mary, an Anglo-Burmese' the priest replied. 'Our entire group reached this camp last night. We trekked from Mandalay and have a lot more people with us.'

'Good, good! Please sit', the doctor indicated that Ma-Pu sit in an adjacent chair. 'So, Father…please tell me about your journey.'

'Wait…before that, you tell me how you knew for certain that I was alive?' the priest asked.

'Oh…that! Listen, I was then returning from Indaw. When we heard that Indaw would be bombed, we packed up our provisions and materials from the hospital and in the evening left from Mogaung from Indaw by jeep. There were just a few miles left to Mogaung. Suddenly, we came across a jeep that had crashed into a tree on the roadside. The headlights were still on and the horn was still blaring. There were three military men in the front seat. The driver had died before we reached. The steering wheel was pressed to his chest while his hands were still on the wheel. There were two women, an infant and two men in the back... one of these men was a military man. Although his broken bones were sticking out from the calf of his leg, the soldier was still alive. The other man was sick. However, he was already dead from a concussion in his head when we arrived. The two ladies were also severely injured in their heads. Both of them were unconscious. The baby, however, was miraculously unhurt. It's all God's will!' Doctor Shimray touched the cross on his chest and fell silent. He took out a packet of cigarettes from the pocket of his overcoat and offered one to Father Berry. 'American cigarettes...very strong, but with a good flavor. Take one.'

Thunderstruck, Father Berry stared at Shimray. As soon as the doctor fell silent, he started as if from a trance, 'Hmm! What? What happened?' his gaze fell on the packet of cigarettes. 'I don't smoke, thank you. What happened after you witnessed that incident?'

'I faced a lot of trouble by getting involved in that incident. There was no certainty for us...what could we do with the rest? On the other hand, I was a doctor. At the very least, I could not abandon the living ones to their fates. I had a few emergency first-aid supplies in the jeep. I applied some primary dressings and bandages to the two women and the soldier and somehow dragged them along with the infant to my jeep. Sister Cathy was with me at that time...our Sister Catherine. I am sure you remember her?'

The doctor closed his eyes and spoke as if he were narrating an ancient story. 'She is no more.'

'I remember her' Father Berry said. 'That very friendly, slightly plump sister…Cathy! Why, what happened to her?'

'We stopped for a night at Kamaing. She succumbed to cholera there. She passed away within four hours' Shimray said with a sigh. 'She was a very noble soul who has now merged with God', the doctor stared at the distance with a blank gaze.

'Very sad!' Father Berry said. 'Tell me what happened after that?'

'Yeah…after that…', the doctor suddenly woke up, as if he were breaking a spell he had been entranced by. 'There was hardly any space in our vehicle. Sister Cathy herself sat on top of the luggage and cleared some space for the people. She made the mother and the infant sit on her lap. Somehow, we reached Tongni only to hear that bombing had ensued in Mogaung in the meanwhile. The allies were already making preparations to withdraw to Kamaing from there. Therefore, we followed the route towards Kamaing via Farken from Tongni. There was however no hospital in Kamaing. People had started escaping from there as well. Somehow, we managed to tend to the injured people at the military base there. Sister Cathy died that same night. Bombing began in the latter half of the night. Dragging the sick ones with us, we reached Shaduzup in the morning.

Stilwell sahab's army cantonment was based there. We admitted the sick people to the hospital there...Oh, I forgot to tell you! When we were still in Kamaing, we got a prescription signed by you in the army man's pocket. Of course, there was no date or address there. Just looking at the prescription, I assumed that the medicines must be for the younger woman. At least, I got to know that you were still alive and conducting your practice.'

'Practice! Ha!' a mocking smile appeared on Father Berry's lips, as if this were the self-deprecating laughter of a man who pitied himself. 'Okay—please continue. What happened to the injured travellers?'

'What else could have happened? We left the soldier at Shaduzup. Maybe they had to amputate his leg later. I got orders to proceed to Mogaung. Therefore, I reached Mogaung via Walaw-bum by jeep, taking the two women, the infant and an orderly with me. After resting there for two days, they sent me here. I have been treating the sick here for the last fifteen days.'

'What about the two women and the infant?'

'The two women went mad after they attained consciousness in Kamaing...they had sustained severe head injuries. I placed the infant in the maternity ward here. Most probably he is still here. We will know if we ask around.' Doctor Shimray rose, approached Thanu and felt his brow. 'Seems like the fever has reduced a bit. But it would be advisable not to take him back to the camp today. Observation is necessary. If he stays here, treatment will be easier and the risk of infection will be much lesser. However, I need to have a relative or someone else watch over him—we have a severe shortage of nursing staff here.'

'If you don't mind, doctor, it will be very good if you can help us find the two women and the baby. I will be very grateful if you heed this request of mine', Father Berry said. 'I hope I am not inconveniencing you unnecessarily.'

'No issues, Father, I will try my level best. Doing something for you, in fact for anyone else, is a privilege for me. But not today', the doctor held the priest's hands in his own and said. 'I should get back to work now. A long search lies ahead of us. I will send people and make inquiries tomorrow…Haven't you noticed, a long line of patients has already gathered in this short span of time.' The doctor looked at the priest again as he was preparing to leave. 'By the way, who is going to stay with the boy tonight?'

'I will', Ma-Pu interjected.

'Please give him medicine in a timely fashion', the doctor said. 'You won't be able to sleep tonight. You will have to check his temperature every hour.'

'I was a nurse earlier…I mean, a family nurse', Ma-Pu said, a trifle embarrassed. 'I can do it. You will just have to show me what I need to do.'

'Well, well...that's very good news', a smile formed on the doctor's face. 'Father Berry', he turned towards the priest and said , 'I am sure you are experiencing great discomfort in the camp. If you don't mind, you can stay in my tent. Although everything is pretty much the same, you'll get better access to water. It's also a little cleaner.' He smiled again.

'Thank you, doctor, thank you very much. I have a lot of people with me in the camp. They were fellow travellers on a long and difficult road. I am sorry...but it is impossible for me to abandon them and accept your extraordinarily generous offer' Father Berry said. 'And to be honest, I haven't faced great difficulties in the camp.'

'As you wish', the doctor arose and shook Father Berry's hand. 'Good night!'

'Good night!' Father Berry said, looking at both the doctor and Ma-Pu, and slowly walked back to the camp.

XXI

Shimray dispatched people to all the nearby hospitals and shelters the next day. Despite searching the entire day, they could not learn anything about the whereabouts of Lacchmi or Budhu's mother. Father Berry too thoroughly searched everywhere, but didn't find anything. The two women were insane when they were admitted to the hospital and their names, identities or addresses were not on record either. Therefore, searching for them in the camps and the hospitals proved to be an extremely difficult affair. Father Berry himself went to the section where they kept the mentally ill and searched for them. He carefully examined each and every woman with an unknown name. All efforts proved to be futile. However, he learned something from the overseer of this section. Quite a number of people, both male and female, had escaped from this wing. There was a paucity of space, an unending stream of people kept flowing in, and it was impossible to take care of each and every patient. In fact, there weren't a lot of guards in this wing either. It was probable that the women were among those who had bolted and it would be difficult to find them if that were the case. It was impossible for anyone to keep track of a person's whereabouts in this massive sea of humanity. Exhausted after conducting his search for an entire day, Father Berry returned to Shimray's room in the evening.

'What news? Any luck?' the doctor asked, lighting his cigarette.

'The news isn't good. No luck. I didn't learn anything', Father Berry said. 'How is the boy doing?'

'He is better…improving', the doctor looked at the priest with a narrowed gaze. 'That nurse of yours—I mean Mary…she is an angel. You cannot even imagine how she took care of the boy. I have seen a lot of nurses, Father… Anyway, the boy should be certainly fine in a few days. Because he is so feeble, it may possibly take a day or two more than that. I will, however, keep your nurse with me here. I don't have a lot of people to help me here.'

'Keep her here. Where else will she go?' Father Berry said.

'Why, won't she leave with the other refugees?'

'Where will she go? She has left everything behind in

Burma. Moreover, she cannot return to Burma anymore...I mean, she has no desire to go back. She has no one in India. She will probably be grateful to you if you give her work and allow her to stay here.'

'Good, good! Very good!' the doctor said, taking a long drag on his cigarette.

'If you don't mind, can I tell you something else?' the priest said. 'Please give me some work and allow me to stay here. I don't wish to return home till the war is over.'

'I was silently contemplating this. I just didn't have the courage to ask you', the doctor said. 'There will be no better opportunity to serve suffering humanity.'

'That's why I mentioned this. My entire life lies ahead of me if I want go back home and relax and recover. But I want to leave after this destructive battle.'

'Good! Good! Your mind hasn't wavered a bit even after you have faced so many sorrows and privations, Father Berry', the doctor said. 'I will be eternally indebted to you if you agree to assist me in this great, noble mission. There are a number of doctors here, but none of your like to help me perform my responsibilities.'

'However, what about my mission for today?'

'It will definitely be successful. We will find them if we look for them even more carefully', the doctor said. 'Wait, where are the husbands of these two women?'

'The old woman is a widow and has a son. The other

one has a husband. Both the son and the husband are with us.'

'Oh, before I forget again', Shimray took out a key from his pocket, opened a cupboard, and took out a box from inside. 'This was with the people in the jeep. There are many valuable objects here: bars of gold, jade stones, rubies and lots of silver. I don't know whom they belong to though. If you could…'

Father Berry recognised Ballabh's box. 'This box belonged to the dead person', he said. 'He was a businessman. The others are poor farmers. They have nothing of value with them.'

'I didn't have space in the jeep. We couldn't pick up anything else. However, I was unwilling to leave this box behind. These valuable objects may be of some use in the future', the doctor said. 'Now you can take responsibility for this box. Since its owner is dead, you can use it for the activities of the church.'

There were a few gold bars and some packets in the box that the doctor had prised open; a lot of silver as well. Father Berry sighed and closed the lid of the box. 'I don't have a place to stay for now', he said. 'Let these valuables remain with you. We will see what can be done with them later.' He began walking towards the room where Thanu was sleeping.

Although Thanu's fever had receded, he was still very

weak. He momentarily opened his eyes, looked at the priest and fell asleep again. Ma-Pu was sitting nearby. She rose up and greeted the priest with an endearing smile as soon as he entered.

'I have some good news for you', the priest told Ma-Pu. 'Dr Shimray has praised you a lot. He was very impressed with your work. He wants to retain you as a nurse here. I am sure you won't disagree.'

'What will happen to the rest?' Ma-Pu asked. 'These lakhs and lakhs of people who don't have families or homesteads and keep streaming in—what will happen to them?'

'You will assuage their pain and misery. There is no duty greater than that. If you join the procession, you will only swell the ranks of the refugees. You are also mistaken if you think you will be able to help everyone in this world through your sacrifices' the priest said. 'Our personal significance in this vast sea of humanity is minuscule. Therefore, we should move ahead continuing to perform our small duties.' He looked outside. It was then raining steadily outside.

'What do you mean?' Ma-Pu opened her eyes wide and looked at the priest.

'I mean that this is a great opportunity to serve suffering humanity. We keep on doing what we can with our limited abilities' the priest said. 'Do you see those drops of rain falling outside? These drops merge together and create currents in the river that eventually smash hills and mountains. Similarly, our minuscule activities can also merge together and eventually contribute towards the welfare of this massive ocean of humanity.'

'Will you stay here, Father?'

'I have determined to stay here too. I will return once the war is over. If I return at this hour, I will never have peace. My conscience will always prick me.'

'I have no place to go to', Ma-Pu said. 'I was thinking that once I reach India, I will join a Buddhist *vihara* as a nun and spend the rest of my days in that manner.' She lowered her head.

'A Buddhist vihara?' Father Berry was stunned when he heard these words from the Anglo-Burmese girl. 'I thought you would join the Catholic Church.'

'I am not Christian. Although I was educated in a missionary school and have spent my childhood and youth among Christians, I am a heathen…a Buddhist. I heard that my parents were Buddhists, although I haven't had opportunity to be exposed to Buddhist teachings as yet. That's why…'

'Okay, okay! You will have a lot of time to contemplate those aspects later. Now is the time for performing our duties. Can you just meditate in a quiet, isolated Buddhist vihara after witnessing these poignant scenes afflicting suffering humanity?'

'I was thinking about that...', Ma-Pu said.

Shimray entered the room. His face brightened when he checked Thanu's brow and pulse. Looking at the priest, he said. 'The patient is better; no reason to worry.'

'These are joyful tidings', the priest touched the cross on his neck and said. 'The father of the boy has been unconscious since yesterday. All that remains is to locate the woman by hook or by crook. I will begin what you requested after that.'

'I conduct fifty-sixty surgeries a day. On top of that, there are the other patients. Every joint of my fingers is aching', the doctor said. 'I need your help desperately at this time. My assistant, John Grinthlee too has been sick since yesterday; it's as if my right hand has been severed', the doctor laughed ruefully and halted for a few seconds. 'I have designated several people to find information about the missing women. Most probably we will get to know something in a day or two. They are now insane and don't recognise themselves. We have to search for them through guesswork and estimation.'

'I know both of them', the priest said. 'I think it will be useful if I search for them...'

It was a difficult task indeed to find two nameless women who had escaped from the wing meant to sequester the mad from amongst this vast sea of people. The following day, Father Berry was exhausted after roaming around the whole day asking numerous known and unknown people of their whereabouts. As he returned to the camp in the evening dejected by his failure, Ramgobinda suddenly ran towards him from somewhere and embraced him in front of the doorway. 'Where is my Lacchmi? Where is my Thanu?' Unsophisticated, direct questions articulated in a simple, child-like manner—no answers for them, however!

'They are fine. Both of them are fine. The doctors are taking care of them in the hospital' the priest replied.

'I want to go to the hospital too. I am sick as well... don't you see?' Ramgobinda clasped the priest's flowing clothes tightly and haunched on his knees on the floor. His matted hair was looking very unkempt, tears were flowing freely from his eyes. 'Where is the hospital?' he looked at the sky and screamed.

'He regained consciousness in the evening and has been shouting and screaming since then. He constantly wants to run outside.' Chinti emerged from the shelter and whispered in the priest's ear. 'I think he has lost his wits. We may have to shackle him if the need arises.'

Sitting on his haunches at the priest's knee, Ramgobinda was looking at the distance with a blank, poignant gaze. Suddenly he stood up and exclaimed, 'There's my Thanu! Tha-nu!' Shouting thus, he bolted towards the door. Father Berry and Chinti ran after him.

That kitten! Mini! Most probably it was crouching near

the doorway stalking a mouse or something. Before she could realise what happened, Ramgobinda flung himself wildly on her and clasping her to his bosom plastered her with kisses.

'Look, I found him!', Ramgobinda held up the kitten and exclaimed to the priest. 'He came back from the hospital. How can he stay there without me? My Thanu has returned!' He clasped the squirming, terrified kitten even more tightly to his chest. 'I don't need anything else now', he screamed. 'Lacchmi—stay in the hospital. Don't come here. If you do, my Thanu will leave.' Letting the kitten go suddenly, he fell on the grass and began wailing loudly.

After dinner, Nitu, Kalu and Gurcharan approached the priest who was sitting near the fire. They sat down near him. The kitten had curled up into a ball and was sleeping on some straw strewn on the opposite side of the fire.

'How is Thanu?' Nitu asked.

'He is better. The fever has receded, but he is still very weak.'

'On the other hand, I think Ramgobinda has gone insane', Nitu said quietly, stressing each word slowly. 'Budhu is probably going the same way. Did you hear anything about the two women?'

'I was unsuccessful today as well', the priest replied.

'I wonder how long we will be in this place. We should go back to our places of origin…the sooner we leave, the better', Nitu said, warming his hands in the fire.

'You are correct', the priest said, looking at the fire.

'By the way, what do you plan to do now?'

'We need to stay here for a few more days', the priest said. He assumed that Nitu would ask him this question, and had prepared his response a long time ago. 'Now that we are in a safe place, the people who want to leave can leave.'

'Ma-Pu?' Chinti asked.

'Most probably Ma-Pu will be employed as a nurse in the hospital here. The girl has no other place to go either', the priest replied. 'However, I cannot say for certain. I haven't asked her.'

'Budhu, too, is in no condition to leave. Therefore, I too will stay here for about a week or ten days and leave when the circumstances permit it', Chinti said, looking at Nitu.

'Budhu will go to his own place, you will go to yours. He has already gone mad, I think. He will recover when it is time for him to recover. What do you have to do with that?' Nitu gazed curiously at Chinti and tried to divine his intentions. 'Or have you gone mad as well?'

'You leave. Leave for your own places of origin', Chinti replied. 'I will halt here for a few days and leave when I feel like it.'

'Just you see!' Nitu addressed Gurcharan. 'Just look at how he is talking now?'

'That's fine, it's his wish', Gurcharan turned towards the priest. 'We were planning to leave tomorrow.'

The priest did not reply and kept staring at the fire.

Suddenly Ramgobinda made his entry from somewhere. 'I don't have anyone, I have lost everything. Ha! Ha!' he articulated these terrible words very loudly and then stood still entranced by the blazing fire. Looking at him warily from the corner of her eyes, the kitten slowly arose from its slumbering position and quietly slunk out.

'This person has appeared again', saying so, Nitu arose from his position and bade farewell to the priest. 'Okay, we will leave now.'

'Where are you going?' Ramgobinda came in front of Nitu with a jump and stretching out his hands, tried to bar his way. Nitu, Kalu and Gurcharan exited the room without throwing a glance in his direction.

'They have left too! Everyone has left! There is no one now', Ramgobinda said, looking at the direction from where Nitu and the others departed. Tears were welling in his eyes.

'There is no saying what trouble he may cause tonight. Keep a close watch on him. If you can, sleep close to him', Father Berry told Chinti and lay down on the cloth lying on the ground. Chinti accompanied Ramgobinda into the other room.

Chinti suddenly woke up at midnight, hearing some screams and loud noises. There was an illumination like daylight on all sides. There was a fire raging somewhere. He ran out hurriedly and noticed that fire had enveloped two huts on the other side of the row. There was bedlam on all sides. Groups of people who had lost their bearings where running helter-skelter like madmen. Suddenly, his mind went back to the scene of the bombing at Mogaung. Two military fire engines arrived blaring their sirens and began to spray water on the huts through their hoses. In the meantime, the inhabitants of the two huts had run outside.

'Fire! Fire! What fun! Burn, burn till everything is ashes', Ramgobinda was roaming around dancing and flailing and clapping his hands wildly amidst the chaotic crowd running busily hither and thither. 'Everything will be finished now. No one will have anything!' Whooping with joy, he told Chinti whom he noticed emerging from their hut.

'What happened? How did these dwellings catch fire?' Chinti asked.

'I put them on fire. What's the point of letting this go on? Lacchmi is gone…Thanu is gone…everything should be destroyed.'

'You madman!' Chinti said and grabbing hold of Ramgobinda forced him back into the room.

After the fire had been doused in an hour or so, Father Berry entered the room and sat near Chinti. A lot of people were still sitting outside in the open and on the grass at that time. A few military ambulances arrived on the scene and ferried the half-burnt and singed people to the hospital.

'It was sheer luck that no one died.' The priest lowered his head and looking at the dozing figure of Ramgobinda said, 'I had a premonition that he would do something drastic when he went out with a few half-burnt logs from the fire. Although I ran after him, I couldn't catch up. The incident had occurred before that. We should send him to the wing for the insane early in the morning.'

Ramgobinda was admitted to the wing for the insane first thing in the morning.

XXII

Scores of sick, half-dead refugees were transported via push-trolleys and then put on the train to Margherita. Although arrangements were made by the authorities for the refugees to be sent to their places of origin by train after being treated at Margherita's Central Hospital for a few days, many were not in a condition to move. Many refugees were transported by military vehicles from Nampong to Tipong; others, unable to find a vehicle, came walking.

After admitting Ramgobinda to the Nampong hospital, Father Berry searched for some clues about the two missing women among the thousands of refugees clamoring to travel to Tipong from the military base at Nampong. The priest felt very tired walking to the military camp some distance away on that unpaved, rough road in the scorching heat. He sat on one of the small pillars on the side of the road leading down to the plain area in Nampong camp and surveyed the teeming mass of humanity gathered below. Scattered groups of people were moving frenetically in every direction; everyone was occupied with something. His gaze suddenly rested on a peculiar scene playing out in the background of that chaotic melee.

In the glittering rays of the burning sun, a black kitten was playfully gamboling with an old woman with matted hair and wearing shredded rags. She was sitting on a rock with her back turned towards the sun. Since he didn't have a good view of the woman from a distance, the priest began descending the road. Once he got closer, he recognised the kitten—Mini! However, he was flabbergasted by the appearance of the woman—this couldn't be Lacchmi! There were innumerable open welts and wounds on the face of that old woman with protruding cheekbones. 'This cannot be Budhu's mother either'—the priest thought, and with lots of trepidation in his mind glanced at the woman's face again. The woman too stared at him with an empty, meaningless gaze and began scratching her entangled clumps of hair.

However, it was that same face, those same eyes! It wasn't an impossible fact—that woman could very well be Lacchmi. The kitten was playing with her fearlessly. Why would she do that if she weren't known to her? She must surely have recognised her mistress. Animals never forget the humans they are intimate with. The priest's gaze rested on the ring on one of the fingers of that woman tousling her unkempt hair. He recognised that distinctive ring. Gathering courage after seeing this, the priest called out loudly, 'Lacchmi!'

However, there was no discernible change in the woman's face. The forests and hills surrounding the two people re-echoed the priest's call, but the woman kept staring at the hills on the horizon with an unchanging expression as if she were a lifeless doll, as if she hadn't heard anything.

'Lacchmi!', the priest called out her name loudly once again close to her ear. This time, the woman made a slight movement and looked around on all sides like a dumb animal attempting to fathom the source of that noise.

'Lacchmi!', the priest shouted again. 'Ramgobinda is looking for you. Thanu is waiting for you…Ramgobinda… Thanu…'

This time, the woman began scanning the priest from head to toe. 'Hi! Hi! Hi!', the woman began giggling like a madwoman and stood up suddenly. It was scarcely imaginable that a person's laughter could be so frightening and repulsive.

'Tha-nu!', suddenly the woman let loose a sky-piercing screech, all the while gazing at nothingness and collapsed on the ground with a thud.

'What happened? What is going on?' a military officer overseeing the activities of the refugees suddenly appeared on the scene and questioned the priest. He was observing the unfolding scene from the beginning, standing at a distance.

'Nothing has happened. This woman…' Father Berry pointed at the woman lying with her head on the rock and suddenly stopped speaking. Fresh blood was streaming from the unconscious Lacchmi's temple and was flowing in a stream by the side of her ear.

'She is a madwoman and has been here for quite a few days', the officer said. 'Do you know her?'

'Yes! She traveled with us. Her husband and son are in the Nampong hospital. The husband too has gone insane', the priest said.

'Very good!' the officer looked at the woman. 'She needs first aid immediately. There is a post nearby.'

Both of them lifted the woman and carried her to the nearby first-aid post. 'The injury doesn't appear serious' the doctor at the post said. 'For the moment, let me apply some dressings. I don't have the equipment here to check her condition thoroughly.'

'I have a request…' the priest looked at the officer. 'I am a doctor too. It is essential that we thoroughly check-up this woman's condition. It may be a hemorrhage or a concussion. If we don't treat her in time, she may die. It is very important that she remains alive. The life and death of three other people are dependent on her.'

'Please let me know the nature of your request.'

'This woman has to be transported by any means possible to Dr Shimray's hospital in Nampong. He is a very experienced surgeon. He is treating this woman's husband and son. I will take her there right now if you can kindly arrange an ambulance for us.'

'It will be difficult to get an ambulance here so quickly' the officer said. 'Let me ask if I can arrange for a jeep or a van.'

'That will be fine as well. I just need some conveyance quickly. Every minute is a precious commodity at this time', the priest said as the officer went out.

'Do you think her injury could be fatal?', the doctor at the post asked the priest.

'Maybe or maybe not—there is no certainty. But we shouldn't take any risk. Moreover, the way she fell unconscious…'

'The flow of blood has stopped', the doctor gave a satisfied smile.

The officer returned with a military van. 'You can travel in this vehicle' he said. 'I am on duty. I can't go with you.'

Thanking the officer profusely, Father Berry boarded the vehicle with the woman and in a little while reached Shimray's hospital.

The doctor wasn't in his room. Ma-Pu and Thanu were playing in the verandah outside. The priest got down from the vehicle and urgently gestured at Ma-Pu. 'Please help me a little', he said, and the two of them carefully lifted Lacchmi from the vehicle and lay her down on a bed in the patient's wing.

'Where is the doctor?' the priest asked.

'He is on his round and will be here shortly', Ma-Pu said. 'Who is she?'

'Lacchmi', the priest pointed at the unrecognisable figure draped in bandages. 'She has lost her sanity. She hit her head on a rock and fell unconscious just a while ago.'

'This is your mother', Ma-Pu lifted Thanu up and showed him the unconscious figure.

'No!' Thanu shook his head vehemently. Besides the bandages on her head, several bits of shiny plaster glittered on the woman's face. 'She cannot be my mother, my mother is good.' He seemed to have made up his mind when he asked, 'Where did my mother go? Where is Mini?'

Ma-Pu and the priest both looked at each other.

'They are here, everyone's here', Ma-Pu fondled Thanu's head. 'So, this isn't your mother?'

'Um…hmm!' Thanu again shook his head. 'My mother is no longer here. She left long ago.'

He slid down from Ma-Pu's grasp and clasping her at

the knees asked her with great eagerness, 'Would you like to be my mother?'

'Yes, my love! If your mother doesn't return, I will be your mother', Ma-Pu tousled Thanu's hair and looked at the priest with tears welling in her eyes.

'Good morning! Good morning!' Shimray entered the room very busily and hanging his flowing apron on the wall asked, 'So, what news?'

'The news is here, waiting for you', the priest said, pointing towards Lacchmi.

'Who is this?' Shimray approached the woman and asked. 'Oh, that same woman! Where did you find her?' He turned around and looked at the priest.

'Who are you talking about?'

'That same woman from the accident! The one you were looking for.'

'Are you sure? Do you have any doubts?' the priest asked.

'Why should I have any doubts? I treated her myself and admitted her to the hospital. It's the same person. However, how did she come to be in such a condition?' the doctor asked.

'From what I gathered, she was wandering around close to the military base camp after her escape from the wing for the insane. Today she fell on a rock, hurt herself badly and became unconscious', the priest said. 'I want you to check if she is in a serious or a critical condition.'

'There is no swelling. In all probability, the injury is a minor one' the doctor said, looking at Lacchmi and checking her brow. After that he checked her pulse, temperature and breathing and said, 'There is no cause for fear. Everything is normal. How long has it been since the incident?'

'About two hours or so', the priest said.

'Oh…that person you admitted in the morning…he has gone totally insane', the doctor took a syringe and reached for a bottle from his cupboard. 'Due to shock… we will have to treat him intensively for a few days.'

'This woman is that person's wife' the priest said.

'It will take time…' the doctor said worriedly.

'Maybe the chances for recovery will increase if both of them are together?' the priest said and looked at Thanu.

'This is your mother', Ma-Pu once again pointed towards Lacchmi and addressed Thanu. Thanu looked at his mother for a moment and then embraced Ma-Pu tightly.

'Please keep the boy with you until both of them have recovered completely', the doctor addressed Ma-Pu. 'Father Berry is there as well…Now, Father…', the doctor extended his hand towards the priest for a handshake. 'Please participate in my mission from now on. Let Ma-Pu accept her responsibilities as a nurse. Around a thousand refugees streamed in last night. It is virtually impossible for me to operate alone. Who knows how many more will keep streaming in?'

'Who knows?' Father Berry said, turning his melancholic gaze towards the sharp peaks of the green hills on the afternoon horizon. 'Who knows how many destitute people will move from one location to another in the pathways of history and the bosom of time? Who knows how many dreams of unfortunate humanity will be shattered brutally by the storms of progress? Who knows, doctor, who knows?'

XXIII

Ma-Pu was contemplating something deeply, sitting in the moonlight. The priest's words repeatedly rang in her ears.

People come and go—that is the rule. This constant flow of movement sprouting forth among people despite the centrality of numerous conflicts is difficult to prevent, ceaseless. The bonds of love and attachment take shape within this procession of numerous arrivals and farewells; in a few days, their traces too are lost in the flow of time. There are no signs left of the arrivals and the departures. The friendships forged by the destruction of all differences based on nationality or community sometime assume a harmonious hue. Sometimes attachments become stable and permanent, but are eventually weakened by the depredations of time. They are transient, tumultuous.

However, such transience has its own singular value. The call of one's blood makes the blood of the other rise, the experience of one heeds the call of the other when two hungry souls are attracted to each other. One day, maybe even that ardour cools down. But does it mean that such moments have no value? Complete gratification within the limits set by life...is that a minor thing? But, how unbearable were these attachments and deprivations!

This endless journey of displaced, homeless people; this fathomless, uninterrupted movement! A flock arrives just like the refugees in the camp; a flock leaves once again. Once again, a new page is written in the annals of that ancient journey. Their road comes to an end, but the journey does not cease. This motion is the nerve center of limitless creation; this endless movement (jangamata)! Its taste is always new.

Ma-Pu's train of thought was interrupted by the wails of a twenty-two day old baby sleeping in a crib in the hospital. The infant, found a few days ago among other camp new-borns, was bawling loudly. His birth occurred amidst all this movement. His journey began from the time he was born. The baby had tided through the crest of a great war in the first twenty days of his existence. Such a journey was probably unheard of in the world.

Chinti opened the bamboo door and stepped inside hesitantly. He looked at Ma-Pu for a moment before stepping inside, lifted the baby from the crib, came outside to the verandah, and sat on a murha near Ma-Pu. Ma-Pu threw a delighted yet questioning gaze in his direction. 'You?' she asked. She seemed surprised.

'I came back' Chinti lowered his head and looked at the infant. 'I bade farewell to the rest at Lekhapani railway station and returned.'

'But why? Didn't you tell me yesterday that you'd be leaving', Ma-Pu asked.

'I didn't like the thought of it', Chinti replied briefly without elaborating. Both of them fell silent for a while.

'Do you like it here?' Ma-Pu asked.

'I don't know. I don't like it anywhere', Chinti said, gazing at the glittering stars in the distance. 'Something has happened to me in the last few days.'

Ma-Pu gazed directly into Chinti's eyes. In the dim starlight, she noticed tears of agony welling up in Chinti's simple, uncomplicated eyes. Maybe this was the agony of not getting something, maybe the agony of losing something after holding it close. It did not take too long for Ma-Pu to figure out the cause of his dejection.

'I don't understand anything', she said very calmly. However, her voice quivered a bit.

'I understand nothing either', once again, Chinti lowered his head and halted. The baby had begun crying again as if he had nothing else to do but cry!

A thousand storms had begun raging inside Ma-Pu's mind, raised by this uneducated, rural young man who was sitting with his head bowed close to her in the bright, intimate moonlight. He was by her side almost all the while in the past few days. Occasionally he would exchange one or two words with her. However, today in this friendless, almost theatrical situation, she suddenly experienced an outpouring of love for this young man cradling the infant in his lap with his head bowed.

'What has happened to you?' Ma-Pu moistened her lips and swallowed her spittle. Her throat had suddenly gone dry.

'No…nothing has happened.'

'Then why didn't you leave?' Ma-Pu acted as if she were confused. She knew, but she still acted.

'Would you like it if I leave?' Chinti looked directly into Ma-Pu's eyes and said. 'Tell me the truth.' Ma-Pu was pleased hearing the note of certainty in his voice. This young man, whom she didn't know at all earlier, was her companion in a treacherous journey that had concluded just a few days ago. This simple, uncomplicated young man!

'Does it really matter whether I like it or not?' she replied. 'Everyone goes their own way.'

'I don't know my own way…' Chinti said in a trembling voice. He stood up suddenly, took the infant inside and placed him in the crib and returned to the verandah. 'Do you want to know why I didn't leave? For you…only for you! I can't live for a single day if I am away from your side.' Without looking at Ma-Pu even once, Chinti opened the door and left. The celebrated ancient paeans of love withered in shame and merged with the moonlight unable to withstand the force of that single passionate declaration.

Ma-Pu was deeply touched by the force of Chinti's last words. Her entire being trembled to its very roots. A strange sensation enveloped her that shattered and transcended each and every difference engendered by tribe or community, education or illiteracy. An ungovernable passion for the young man wrapped itself like folds around her body. What an ecstatic attachment! The beauty of the humble plea of a simple soul! How entrancing was the spare, simple beauty of this language!

Time, eavesdropping on the music of the moon, the silence and the songs of the cicadas, seemed to have come to a stop. Noticing Father Berry entering through the doorway at that time, Ma-Pu got up from her position and went towards him.

The infant was crying again. Most probably he had been crying all this while, but Ma-Pu heard his agitated wails only at this point. She asked Father Berry to sit with a wordless gesture and went inside to get the baby.

'Where is Thanu?' the priest asked.

'He's with the doctor. The infant has been wailing a lot…so he said that he would keep Thanu with him for a few days', Ma-Pu said. 'I don't have any helpers or servants here. Maybe he thought that it would be inconvenient for me.'

Both of them fell silent for a while. A bevy of thoughts occupied their minds. The sky, nature, the moonlight—everything was silent. There was no sound anywhere other than the occasional whimper of the infant.

'Do you see that hill in the distance?' in a low voice the priest broke the silence and looked at the horizon. 'An orgy of destruction and death is going on, on the other side. However, there is so much peace and tranquility here. So much difference, so many things change in just the span of a few miles! Those terrifying hills look so beautiful from here…but so many people succumbed to their embrace.'

'The journey of those who died has ended. However, those of us who live will keep going on…isn't that so?' Ma-Pu queried.

'Endless, constant movements after a momentary pause…that is the law of life', the priest closed his eyes. 'There is no difference in life without movement and death, Mary. We are exiled, homeless people. We will perpetually travel across this ancient world in groups in new environments, in new guises. This is the ancient instinct of humankind. Although old or new pathways will cease to exist, the mechanisms of this circle of life will keep moving. We are just tiny, helpless beings.'

'But what about our peace? What of the fulfilment of our hopes and desires?'

'In our duty, Mary, in our duty. Continue performing your responsibilities smilingly. You will see that life will be suffused with peace. These wars and battles are all irrelevant and temporary. Peace too is momentary, to be truthful. I wrote a poem when I was in Mandalay at the start of this war—do you want to listen to it?'

Ma-Pu nodded her head. Father Berry recited the poem with total concentration:

This war is ensuing between your god
And my god; when it ends
Your god will lose and become equal with my god.
Then both gods will merge and become one
And eternal peace will reign on this earth.

'But what of our desires and our weaknesses?' Ma-Pu asked. 'What of those small, tiny things which seem to be mere warts on the awe-inspiring background of nature? Don't these have any value? Are moments of joy and sorrow, pleasure and pain just meaningless?'

'Absolutely not! Those moments are like individual

gems in the necklace of this ephemeral existence.' The priest began contemplating something and looking at Ma-Pu asked, 'But why are you asking such questions today?'

'Chinti was here', Ma-Pu was anxiously waiting for this question from the priest for a while. 'He didn't leave with the others.'

'So?' the priest looked with a puzzled expression at Ma-Pu. 'Why, I haven't left either, you too…'

'I am facing a great dilemma, Father. I don't know what to do.'

'Why? Nursing! Didn't the doctor say that a while ago', the priest looked at the star-studded sky. 'It is God's ardent desire that you serve suffering humanity with all the strength and dedication you can muster.'

'I have already determined to do that', Ma-Pu was embarrassed and lowered her head. 'That wasn't what I meant…I mean…I consider you like my father…'

'My sweet girl…' Father Berry said. Suddenly, he felt as if he was struck by a bolt of lightning. He was young once as well. The waves of love had coursed through his body a long time ago. Maybe Chinti had, much like him in an earlier era, swallowed his spittle, gathered courage, and in a trembling voice declared his love for the girl today. Probably he voiced the same words that a young Berry had communicated to his beloved forty years ago in an open, grassy knoll in the shadow of the Curfew Tower in Windsor Castle. Probably he uttered the same words that transformed the greenery in front of him into a carnival of riotous colours. Maybe those words were the ancient truth of creation. In a different guise, in a different language, those same words circled around and wafted their way into Ma-Pu's ears.

Father Berry smiled mischievously. 'That too is the writ of the law of the world', saying so, he rose to leave. 'If the two of you agree, my best wishes and blessings are always with you.'

Ma-Pu felt relieved. Holding the door open for Father Berry, she suddenly asked, 'Where did the other priest go, Father?'

'He went his own way', Father Berry sighed and said. 'His road is different. Actually he is a convict who escaped from prison. He will find his own way.'

Father Berry left. Meanwhile, the infant had fallen asleep after wailing for a long while. Ma-Pu placed him on the crib, adjusted the mosquito net and gazed at him for a while.

The infant was smiling in his sleep. The pure, simple smile of a small child in the future began glittering before Ma-Pu's eyes. This smile was the herald of a new age—the unsullied smile of an innocent child who had no inkling of the privations faced by exiled, homeless people. It was the smile of enduring peace and safety. The drops of dew on the green grass of the infant's forest glittered in the soft light of the morning and was still unsullied by the footsteps of displaced people. Maybe that would usher the dawn of an age of new hope.

An engineer by profession, Debendranath Acharya (1937-1981) was an Assamese litterateur and scholar. His novel *Jangam* posthumously received the Sahitya Akademi Award in 1984. He also wrote three other noteworthy historical novels: *Onyo Jug, Onyo Purux* (1970), *Kaalpurux* (1976) and *Raktarag* (1982). He died at the young age of 44 as MD of the public sector undertaking Assam Gas Co. The entire literary repertoire of his published as well as unpublished works were complied in 2011 under the title 'Rachana Samagrah' and published by Jyoti Prokaxon, Guwahati. The complete work was edited by Mahasweta Acharya, Debendranath's wife.

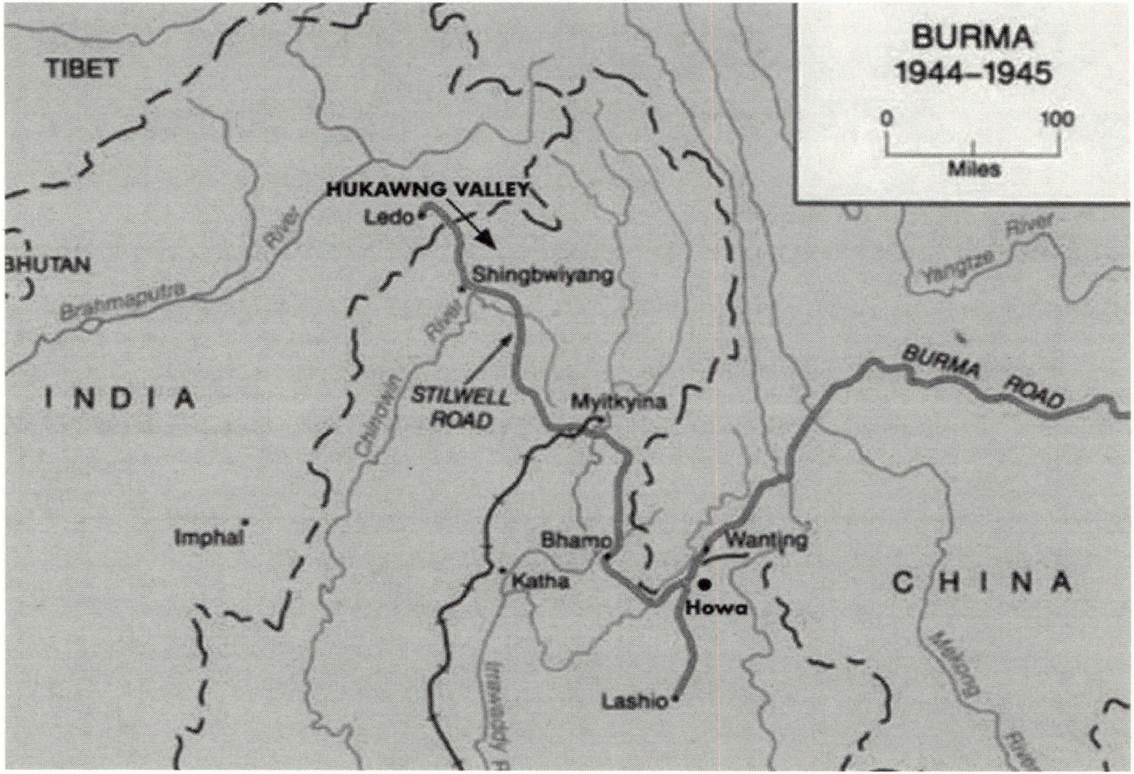
BURMA
1944–1945
0
100
Miles
TIBET
BHUTAN
Brahmaputra
River
HUKAWNG VALLEY
Ledo
Shingbwiyang
River
Chindwin
STILWELL
ROAD
INDIA
Myitkyina
Imphal
Bhamo
Katha
Wanting
Howa
Lashio
BURMA ROAD
Yangtze
River
CHINA
Mekong
River

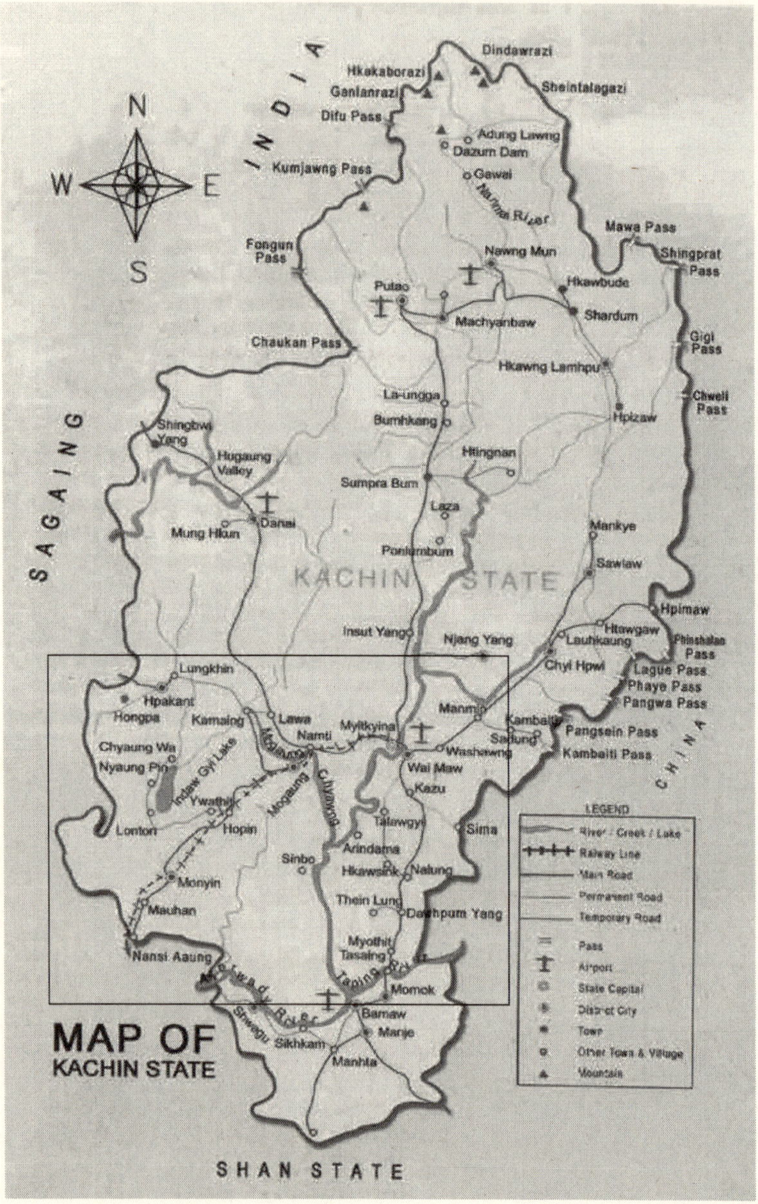

MAP OF
KACHIN STATE

The maps used here are of WWII period, all taken from Creative Commons open source. They have been used only to show the geographical terrain the refugees crossed.

Glossary

Aasol—the long end of the sari

Baba Hukawng—Old Man Hukwang who guards the mountain and the valley and the passes

Bamuni-bhokola—a kind of fish

Bhatou phool, Kopou, Kolmous, Bogori—all flowers

Bidi—country cigarette, locally rolled

Bota—a basket for betel leaf

Changghars—elevated huts

Char—mud flat along river banks

Dao—a curved knife

Dhuti—an apparel wrapped around the waste

Gamocha—towel cloth

Gaonburah—village chieftain

Hooluk bandor—these are hoolock gibbons, primate of three species, found in South Asian forests.

Japi—hat

Kala azar—a fever

Keteki, Xalika, Bulbul, Mynah—kinds of birds

Lungi—wraparound, like a sarong

Machaan—a bamboo platform

Mahajan—money lender

Mahakaal—fate

Mahamuni—Buddha

Maru—an honorific title

Meji—a platform

Mlechchas-untouchables/foreigners

Murha -a cane stool to sit on

Nabis-gold measure

Padmasana—the lotus posture

Phagun- eleventh month in the Assamese calendar

Phoot, Sindoor—vermilion used by Indian women on their foreheads

Pirha—a flat wood to sit on

Pitha, pithaguri—rice flour

Pura—land measure

Riha—carpet/carpet measure

Saku—rice drink

Tathagata—Buddha

Thanaka—a mud pack to protect the skin

Toko, Tal, Ous, Bel, Paniphal, Sal, dhekia —all trees/plants

Uroni—an apparal to cover head

Vihara—a monastery

Xer-seer—a measure

Zindabad—victory call